Bedtime Tales, Sexy Daydreams, and Paranormal Delights

An erotic short story collection by
Michelle Houston

MICHELLE HOUSTON

Dedicated to those who encouraged me, who supported me, and who kicked me in the rear when I doubted myself. You know who you are.

FOREWORD:

More than a decade ago, when I first started my publication journey, a lot of electronic publishers wouldn't even touch short erotic stories. The only real way to get a short story published was to either submit to a print anthology call (which I did numerous times) or put together a bunch of short stories into a collection. Even with a collection, finding a publisher could be rough.

In 2003, Bedtime Tales was accepted, and published by Renaissance E-Books. In 2004, it was followed by the Naughty Whispers collection, and then in 2005 the third volume – Sensual Intimacies – came out. Each of these collections featured a mixture of genres, but all the stories were short and hot erotic tales. They were purposefully written to be light on plot and heavy on sexy action. Even the blurb was written to make that clear: *"Looking for erotica to enjoy when you don't have time, or the inclination, to read a full novel? Do you enjoy getting to the good stuff without all of the 100 page build up? Short, sweet, to the point and packed with sex and emotion, BEDTIME TALES is erotica to read with a lover; passionate prose to satisfy your desires when alone; and tempting morsels of desire to tease your mind, as well as your body, with."*

A decade later, my writing style has slowly evolved, and I am writing longer and longer stories, weaving more plot into each. Yet I still cherish these early stories, since from them I learned a lot about writing, publishing, promotion, and the highs and lows of sharing my work with others.

In late 2010, I had made the decision to start self-publishing, and it was with some of the longer erotic gems that I tested the waters, releasing solo ebooks. I chose to focus on those stories that were also available in print anthologies.

That still left my earlier shorter works, those that range anywhere from one-to-five pages. In the end, I decided to go back to my writing roots and join them together into a collection. I pulled the contemporary couple stories from all three volumes of Bedtime Tales and brought them together in the ebook - Whispers Between Loves: The Bedtime Tales Lovers Tell. The paranormal stories were combined in the ebook - Paranormal Delights. Each of these stories is still in much the same state as that first publication in 2002-2005. Some may be rough in places, others more smoothed out. All of them however show a glimpse at the evolution of my writing style.

As a lover of both ebooks and print, I wanted to find some way that those who enjoy the feel of a paper book in their hands could also enjoy my writings, and so I pooled over 40 short stories together in this collection … and in a nod to both its roots and its current evolution, titled it … Bedtime Tales, Sexy Daydreams, and Paranormal Delights.

I hope you enjoy!

~ Michelle

TABLE OF CONTENTS:

Part 1: Bedtime Tales and Sexy Daydreams
(contemporary erotic stories)

Part 2: Paranormal Delights
(paranormal erotic stories)

About the Author

CLAIMING THE TWILIGHT

Nicholas was exhausted and felt it to the bone. He slouched in front of the time clock, fumbled with his card, and then swiped it through the machine. Done, he crammed it into its designated slot, along with the others belonging to his fellow third shifters. Working the mill wasn't his idea of a dream job, but it paid the bills.

"Night Nick." Ben hollered.

With a halfhearted wave, Nick bid his line-partner goodnight. From 11:00 p.m. to 8:00 a.m., they worked side-by-side and fed boards down a belt. After eight hours of Ben's company, he was always glad to head home and lay down next to his sleeping wife.

The thirty-minute ride home was passed as always, music cranked up as he joined the morning rush crowd. Everyone in a hurry to get to their jobs, not realizing they were in a rut of wishing their lives away. They didn't stop to admire the beauty all around them, to appreciate that which made life truly worth living.

Singing off key, Nicholas drank in the beauty of the passing countryside as he drove. Gently slopping hills bore freshly budded trees and the hint of spring. It never failed to amaze him, the steady flow of it all-nature evolving, constant harmonious change.

Such reflections always brought to mind his wife. Over the years, she had gained a few pounds, developed a few wrinkles and laugh lines, but she was and always would be, the love of his life.

Despite a few bad times, they still had the sexual spark they had enjoyed as teenagers. Just thinking about her naked, in his arms, was enough to make the crotch of his jeans become tight.

The radio played a slow, sad song and Nick turned it off.

Stepping down a bit harder on the gas, he decided he had a reason besides sleep to hurry home. Despite being dog-tired, he was feeling a bit frisky. He only hoped that Heather had gotten to bed early.

He finished the rest of the ride in silence, images of his wife's thighs wrapped around his hips, while his sawdust covered cheeks nuzzled at her breasts. He could almost taste the satiny bead of her hard nipple on his tongue, the silky moist flesh of her pussy parting, enveloping his cock.

Without conscious thought, he turned into his driveway and parked next to the house. Once inside, he tossed the keys on the hall table and kicked off his work boots.

Silently, he padded silently down the hall, to the master bedroom. After arriving home from work in the early hours of the morning, Nicholas always paused in the bedroom doorway to gaze upon the peaceful form of his sleeping wife. Like ships in the night, they often passed each other - one sleeping when the other was awake. But on the mornings Nicholas was lucky enough to get out of work on time, he made sure to let Heather know how much he loved her, and still desired her, even after years of marriage. He stopped to savor the sight of his petite wife splayed over their queen-sized bed. It always astounded him how she managed to take up so much room, for such a tiny woman.

Heather murmured in her sleep and shifted, the top sheet slipping a bit, baring her creamy shoulders. Nicholas' cock hardened further. With hurried movements, he shed his clothes and crossed the room to the master bathroom for a quick shower.

Minutes later, with his hair still wet, but the gritty feel of sawdust gone, he climbed carefully into bed and cuddled against Heather.

"I love you," he whispered as he leaned down and pressed a kiss to her forehead.His lips a butterfly caress against her skin, he moved his way down her cheek to her bare shoulder, his stubble barely brushing her sensitive skin. Pulling the sheet down a bit further, he gazed at her pert breasts, and was tempted to feast upon them, even as his wife slept.

"Time to wake up, Sleepyhead."

Heather murmured and rolled onto her back.

"Your husband's home and horny," he stated, pulling the covers completely off his wife's petite form.

"Damn," she murmured, "have to tell my boyfriend of get out then."

Her eyes still closed, Heather twined her arms around Nicholas' neck and pulled his head down to hers. Her fingers twirled in the curl of hair at the nape of his neck. Kissing her lips softly, Nicholas then pulled away and teased path of tiny kisses down her body.

With gentle nibbles, Nicholas paused occasionally to inhaled the scent of her soft skin, enjoying the sweet fragrance that was all her own.

Arriving at her pussy, Nicholas lightly traced his tongue over her pouty lips, enjoying the shiver of her body. The smooth feel of her inner thighs against his skin was a welcome balm to his dry skin, the silky slide of flesh preferable to the harsh spray of sawdust off his saw.

He slipped a finger into her moist heat, thrust it deep and pulled back, thrusting again. "Are you wet for me baby?" he asked, desire threading through every word. "Do you want me to fuck you until you scream?"

"Yes." Heather gasped as she arched into Nicholas's touch, her hips lifting off the bed. He loved the way she responded to his touch, so open and uninhibited. Nothing faked, nothing held back.

"Do you want to feel my cock stretching you? Do you want me to spank you?" Anticipation filled him with each word he spoke. "Fuck you while I tan your ass? Hold you down, and tease the hell out of you?"

"Yes. Yes. Yes!" Her voice rose with each answer.

"You're so fucking wet, I love it. I get so hot just inhaling your scent." He knew by the tightening of her core around his fingers that he was driving her wild with his words. Her juices flooded her pussy, coating his fingers in her cream.

"Tell me what you want." He pulled his fingers from her pussy and trailed them up her body to her parted lips. Heather sucked his fingers, moaning as she savored her passion.

Pulling his fingers away, Nicholas cocked an eyebrow and waited.

"Fuck me. Spank me. Now!"

He moved between her parted legs, and settled his cock at the opening of her pussy. With a slight shift, he slipped the head of his cock in her, slid in an inch, then another.

Thrusting hard, Nicholas drove his cock all the way into her quivering flesh, watching as her eyes closed. Her body trembled beneath him.

"Tell me." He demanded, grinding his hips against her.

Nicholas gripped her waist, holding her still for his thrusts. "Tell me how you want me to fuck you. How you want me to spank your little, white ass until it's rosy."

"Yes." Heather exclaimed, both in answer to his statements and to the continuation of his motions. "Spank me. Tan my ass baby. Damn you Nicholas, FUCK me!"

Nicholas pulled out of her pussy and moved back. Shifting his grip from her waist to her hips, he flipped Heather over in one smooth movement. They had done this before. Many mornings he had woke Heather up, already tied to the bed, or positioned on her stomach, a pillow under her hips. He had fed his need to dominate, and she had learned to crave it.

His hand landed against her ass, a hearty smack. Heather whimpered and backed into a kneeling position. Arching her back, she offered her ass to her husband, silently begging for more.

Gripping her hips tightly, impaling her pussy from behind, Nicholas slid in deeper. Reaching around her hips, his fingers danced over her clit in small circles, causing her hands to wad the sheet in her fists.

"Yes baby, fuck me."

"Tell me again."

Nicholas pulled out of her pussy long enough to smack her ass then thrust in hard. "Tell me, or I stop."

"I love it when you fuck me and make me talk dirty. I feel so naughty and sexy. God baby, fuck me."

Arching back against him, Heather gasped as he pounded into her, reasserting his claim on her body. He knew from their after sex talks that she enjoyed the long, leisurely love making they some times shared, but she craved Nicholas fucking her like a demon.

His palm rained smack after smack against her ass with each withdrawal.

His balls slapped against her ass, Nicholas groaned as she tightened around him, her sweet little pussy squeezing him.

"Come for me baby. Milk my cock with your hot little cunt." Heather gasped and slid down to lay on her stomach. Nick reveled in every tremor of her lush body.

Nicholas smacked her ass harder. "Come, damn you."

Quivering, her breaths coming in quick gasps, Heather arched into his hand as he smacked her ass again, leaving a nice rosy tint to her soft creamy skin. Nick paused a moment to admire the beauty of his mark upon her, before raining firm blows against her ass-cheek.

Screaming out his name, Heather collapsed on the bed, her pussy clenching him tight. The sight of her reddened flesh, the soft moans as she rode the waves of her orgasm, was enough to push him over the edge. One last slap to her petite ass, and Nicholas pulled out, shooting his come onto her cheeks, one rosy with his lust, the other perfectly white.

"I love you baby," he whispered as he collapsed beside her, pulling her into the haven of his strong arms.

"I love you too." Shifting slightly, Heather groaned. "But I'm still going to need a warm bath later. Going to join me?"

Sliding a hand down her body, he dipped it into her pussy. Raising it to his lips, he sucked the mixture of their juices, the taste exquisite as always. "Only if I get to lick you clean first."

SENSUAL BONDS

Lily leaned against the doorway and watched Jareth sleep. His velvety lips compressed into a smile that never failed to melt her heart. It was no wonder that after all these years he still made her pulse race. True, he was no prince, and could be quite bullheaded at times, but still, he was always considerate of her feelings and her needs, especially in bed.

Twisting the silken rope in her hands, she allowed herself one last moment of debate before approaching the bed. Carefully, she tied his wrists together and attached them to the rails of the headboard. A smile curved her lips at how easy it was. Jareth had a cute habit of sleeping with his arms over his head, almost as if he dreamed nightly of being tied up.

After twisting the other end into a sturdy knot, Lily sat back to admire her handy work in the fading light. Her husband lay sprawled out before her, a masculine buffet waiting for her to nibble at. Already she could imagine him beneath her, his hips rise and falling as he attempted to set the pace.

Climbing off the bed, she stood beside him and slowly pulled the sheet down. Barely, an inch at a time, it took her a while to pull the silken material from his flesh. Her breathing quickened as each inch of his tantalizing flesh was revealed to her hungry gaze.

As his cock came into view, Lily trembled. His cock lay limp against his leg, but she knew it wouldn't lay passive long. Climbing back onto the bed, she gently caressed the head, slipping her hand down the length and raising it carefully. Parting her lips, Lily gently sucked her husband's cock-head into her mouth, savoring the taste of his salty flesh. For this one moment, he was hers, completely within her control. Even limp, his cock was perfection.

* * *

Jareth murmured in his sleep, a wonderful dream pulling at his consciousness. His body screamed for him to wake up, that something was happening, but his mind was savoring the sensations of a petite nymph sucking at his cock.

Arching his hips slightly, he moved to pull his arms down to his sides, to capture his tormentor and coax her to continue her sensual assault. He pulled again as his wrists caught on something. Mumbling in a mixture of desire and frustration, his eyes flickered open as his cock hardened in Lily's mouth.

* * *

"Mmmm," she purred around his cock, her eyes focused on his sleep clouded lids. She saw the exact moment awareness fluttered through his mind. His lips parted, allowing a soft gasp to whisper past. Sluggishly, he arched his hips, offering his cock to her.

Giggling slightly, she returned her attention to his cock. Working slowly up and down, she coaxed him to full hardness while Jareth watched, a look of desire rapidly replacing his normal morning sleepy daze.

As his salty essence leaked down her throat, Lily grinned and let his cock slip from her between her lips. With a wet pop, it sprang free and bobbed for a moment, before settling against his thigh, hard and inviting. The urge to straddle his hips, thrust his cock into her wet pussy and ride him until they were both screaming with orgasm was strong, but the need to be in charge was stronger. So often her husband was the typical alpha male - take charge, lead the way, me Tarzan you Jane. Moments like this were so rare; she had learned to savor them.

* * *

Jareth shifted slightly, twisting his wrists, trying to subtly pull free. His cock throbbed with the need to be deep inside his wife's moist pussy. He knew by now she was dripping wet, he could faintly smell the dainty fragrance of her desire. Years ago, he had told her she tasted finer than ambrosia possibly could and he still believed it. There was tartness, a fire that had crept into her pussy over the years, adding to the succulence of her flesh.

At this moment, he wanted nothing more than to pull free from his bonds, flip Lily onto her back, and sink into her welcoming warmth. To feel her breasts press again his chest, to tangle her nipples with his.

As Lily kneeled next to him, Jareth closed his eyes and inhaled deeply. The musky scent of her arousal filled his senses. He knew he wouldn't be able to take much of her sensual torture.

* * *

"I know what you're thinking," she drawled, her voice deepened by passion. Flicking his right nipple ring softly, she smiled as he groaned. "I know that you want me, that you are dying to taste my pussy, to savor its sweet nectar.

"And soon lover, you will. I'll straddle your face and ride your talented tongue to orgasm, as you devour my quivering flesh." She paused to lick and nibble on his left nipple, stretching it gently by its ring.

17

"But not just yet. First, I want to savor your essence, to have it flooding my mouth."

Pinching his nipple gently, Lily leaned down but paused a moment before slipping his cock-head past her lips. She loved the feel of his cock in her mouth, but rarely was able to savor it. Normally, Jareth was the one leading, determined to make her scream with passion.

* * *

As her soft-spoken words whispered through the night, Jareth's eyes flew open. He knew she meant every word, and the wait, the delicious torment was worth it. He knew what would happen once she had what she wanted.

* * *

Lily tightened her lips and sucked his cock in deeply. Her taste buds tingled in pleasure as the salty taste of him seeped from his slit. Bobbing slowly, she sank down to his base; his pubic hairs tickled her nose as she pulled back, then she dropped down again. Her whole body began to tighten in need. Shifting, she straddled his chest, her wet pussy brushing against his chest hair.

She knew her ass was exposed to him, knew he would fixate on it as his orgasm flooded him, but she didn't care. She wanted the taste of him in her mouth, the feel of his velvety flesh, hard and throbbing, in her mouth.

Pushing her hips back further, she flexed her ass checks, her puckered ring tightening and relaxing, shifting the plug she had worked in while he had slept.

* * *

Jareth stared at the tantalizing flesh before him. His eyes almost crossed when he saw the base of the plug in her ass. Oh yes, he had plans for her tender ass once he was let loose, and it seemed so did she. Sleep would not come quickly to either of them now.

Gritting his teeth, he fought the urge to come. He wanted nothing more than to flood his wife's mouth with his essence, but he held off. Thinking of baseball pitchers, of boxers in the ring, he struggled against her enthusiasm.

As Lily pulled away, her saliva dripping down the length of his cock, he watched her ass quiver. She was tired of playing, just as he knew she would be.

Carefully she climbed off of the bed and stood. Every shift caused the plug to slid with delicious friction. Making sure Jareth could see clearly what she was doing, she bent over and slipped her hands between her legs and pulled the miniature cock free. She was ready for him, and they both knew it.

"One last thing baby, and then you can fuck me," she whispered as she coated two fingers with lubricant and spread them over her ass-ring and dipped inside. Carefully pulling them free, she stood and turned back to face her husband. In the fading light, he looked so handsome, his skin glistening with sweat, his cock hard and ready.

Gripping his throbbing flesh tenderly, she quickly coated him, making sure to lubricate his flesh well, then she climbed onto the bed.

"I want you so bad baby," she whispered as she straddled him. Lowering herself slowly, she sheathed his cock in her tight ass.

Biting the inside of his mouth, Jareth willed himself to remain still until she took him to the hilt. His eyes closed for a moment as her ass-ring expanded around him, only to sharply contract.

Groaning, he opened his eyes again, watching as she fingered her clit and slowly impaled herself on his cock. It was such a delicious torment, and the night was just beginning.

* * *

Lily whimpered slightly as her ass expanded, fitting around his cock like a velvet glove. She loved the fullness of him in her ass. There was something so wildly untamed about him claiming the forbidden territory of her body that impaling herself on his cock always held a thrill.

She loved the way his eyes followed her fingers every motion, the slight wiggle of his hips as she pulled herself up, before thrusting back down. Dipping two fingers into her dampness, she thrust hard and fast for a few moments, coating her finger with her juices. When they were nice and wet, she pulled them free and offered them to Jareth, moaning as he sucked every last drop.

Her pussy craved renewed contact. Her clit was a throbbing ball of nerves begging to be fingered, to be licked and stroked until she was a quivering mass of flesh, ecstasy rippling through her veins. And she knew before the night was over, it would all happen, Jareth would see to it. Until then, her fingers would satisfy her pussy's needs.

There would be time enough for all her passions to be fulfilled, all her needs met. For now, she was enjoying thrusting up and down on his cock, watching him watching her, listening to the breathless groans that escaped his clenched jaws.

There was a power to it, a delicious tingle of euphoria.

* * *

Jareth wasn't sure how much more he could take. Lily's ass tightened more and more with every whispered moan that passed her lips. The smell of her arousal filled his lungs, delicate and passionate.

Her fingers were moved over her clit, faster and faster, teasing the little nubbin of flesh, pulling and twisting and rubbing hard. Clenching his hands tightly around the bonds that held him, Jareth rode the waves of arousal, watching as each crest brought his wife higher and higher, delighting as his own orgasm approached.

He knew that Lily wouldn't last much longer; her eyes were already closing, her breathing sharp and shallow.

She was close, so deliciously, utterly delightfully close. She was clenching him so tightly, wringing every last drop of pre-come from him.

As her head tipped back, her throat muscles worked overtime trying to contain her scream of pleasure, she tightened on him, her ass-ring a vise-grip around his throbbing flesh.

* * *

Wild with need, she rubbed her fingers over her clit, her juices coating and oozing down her flesh. Screaming softly she climaxed, two fingers deep within her quivering pussy, Jareth's cock impaling her ass. She jerked and arched, twisted and rode her passion to its crest as Jareth came within her, shooting hot jets of sperm against the inner walls of her ass.

Collapsing against his chest, she whimpered softly as his cock slid from her, leaving a wet trail of passion within her. Shifting slightly, she enjoyed the feel of her husband's sweat coated chest, his arms trembling above his head.

"I love you baby," she whispered as she reached above them and untied his hands. Exhausted, she settled beside him, focusing on calming her breathing and enjoying the quivering of her flesh. Tiny aftershocks throbbed through pussy as she settled against her love.

* * *

Jareth kissed Lily's sweat dampened forehead and wrapped his arms around her, holding her close.

"You know the night is just beginning," he whispered, anxiously awaiting her slight nod.

Her hair brushed his chest as she agreed, and Jareth felt his cock beginning to stir again.

NATURE'S BLACKOUT

Camille sighed as the power flickered again. Quickly shutting down her computer, she started looking forward to a quiet night at home with her husband. She barely had time to pull a box of candles out of her kitchen cabinet when the lights flickered one more time, then went black. Beeps sounded throughout the house as appliances shut off.

Outside, the wind and rain pounded the house, a symphony of nature's finest elements.

"Honey?" Jason called out, moments before exclaiming "Ow! Damn it to hell."

"You okay baby?" she replied.

"Just fucking peachy. Stubbed my toe on the coffee table." Her husband's voice sounded closer with each word, until moments later, he appeared at the open office door.

"It could be worse. We could be out in that." A streak of lightning racing across the night sky accented her point. For a moment, the sky was lit up almost like daylight.

"Yeah," Jason muttered. Hobbling over to the futon that served as the guest bed, he flopped down. Camilla couldn't help but admire the way the candlelight flickered over his body. It never failed to amaze her just how beautiful he was. "So how was your day?"

Camilla smiled. "It was fine. I got next to nothing accomplished, with the power coming and going all day, but at least it's been quiet."

"Hopefully things will settle down a bit more tomorrow. Although, there is a seventy-five percent chance of more rain and flash flooding tomorrow."

"Yeah. So how was your day, sweetie?" Completely relaxed, he folded his hands behind his head.

Carefully, Camilla crossed the room and kneeled on the futon next to her sprawled out husband. The silk of her nightgown tightened against her sweat moistened bare skin as she shifted. Without much to do, she had spent most of her day planning for when Jason got home. "Long."

"Your back bothering you again?" Camilla asked.

Jason stretched, his fingertips brushing against Camilla's hip. "Not really. Just a bit of tightness here and there. Although, I wouldn't turn down a back rub."

"I guessed that. So, strip already."

With a soft groan, Jason stood and stretched again. A few pops sounded in his back as he arched backwards. "Mmmm, much better."

Straightening, he grabbed the hem of his T-shirt, and pulled it up and over his head. Bared to the waist, he lifted a foot and pulled off a shoe, then repeated the process with the other shoe. As his hands moved to the front of his jeans, Camilla scooted forward.

"Let me," she drawled, her voice husky. Her slender hands gripped his hips and pulled him closer, her face mere inches away from her husband's crotch. "I've been waiting all day for this."

Licking her lips, she unzipped his jeans and slid them down his hips.

Jason stepped free from the denim, his body fully bared to his wife's gaze. Closing his eyes, he let Camilla look her fill. She could feel his jump slightly at the soft touch of her lips against his cock-head. But as the wet heat of her mouth enveloped his cock, she felt him relax.

Sucking gently, Camilla teased Jason, knowing she wasn't near through with him yet. When he lifted his hands, and tangled them in the strands of her ebony hair, she pulled back. Pressing a quick kiss on his cock-head, she moved away. "Ready for that massage?"

Jason's eyelids fluttered up, his blue eyes, glazed. "Huh? Massage?"

Camilla patted the mattress next to her hip. "Lay down here, on your stomach."

"You're kidding right? Tell me you're fucking joking."

Camilla shrugged.

With a soft sigh, Jason flopped down onto the mattress, his bare skin glistening in the candlelight.

Camilla swung her leg over his hips and shifted, so that she straddled him, her crotch rubbing against his bare ass. Pressing the pads of her thumbs to the top of his spine, she began a slow and steady massage. Working her way down his back, she leaned forward, her hair brushing his shoulders and upper back.

As her hands reached the small of his back, Camilla pressed a soft kiss between Jason's shoulder blades. She then worked her fingers back up his spine.Beneath her, Jason shifted, arching into her touch. She could feel the muscles loosening under her gentle touch.

Reaching his neck, she gently worked the muscles of Jason's shoulders, before shifting to the side.

"Time to roll over." A quick swat to his ass had Jason moving to accommodate.

"Yes, Mistress," he retorted, a droll tone to his voice.

Placing her hands on his chest, Camilla swung a leg over his hips, and straddled him again. This time, her bare pussy pressed against his erection, the tip nudging against her clit-hood. She squirmed a bit, giggling as Jason groaned. Gripping the edges of her nightgown, she pulled it up and over her head, tossing it across the room.

"You're killing me here babe." His gaze drifted down her bare body, his point very clear.

Putting a finger on his lips, she said. "Shhh. I need to finish your massage."

Tentatively at first, her hands smoothed over his chest, teasing his sensitive skin. Twisting her fingers in his chest hair, she gently pulled.

Against her pussy lips, Jason's cock twitched. Camilla bit back a moan as sparks of pleasure raced through her clit.

Uncurling her fingers, she slowly massaged Jason's chest, pausing to occasionally pinch his nipples. With each moment that passed, Jason grew more and more restless, his body shifting beneath hers.

Lifting her hands from his chest, Camilla cupped her breasts and lightly pinched her nipples. Gasping softly, she shifted her hips, until Jason's cock-head slipped past her lips into the waiting warmth of her core.

"I want you," she whispered. "Fuck me baby."

Jason's nostrils flared. His calloused hands settled on her hips and pulled her tighter against him. Lifting his hips, he thrust his cock-head deeper with in her pussy. Arching, he plunged higher, driving his cock within her welcoming warmth. Groin to groin, they fit together perfectly.

With a soft moan, Camilla pinched her nipples again. Love shining in her eyes, she met and held Jason's gaze as their lovemaking grew more intense.

Slowly at first, then faster, as they settled into a rhythm, Camilla rocked and ground her pelvis against Jason's. Clenching her muscles tight, she milked his cock as she worked them both closer to orgasm. His hands gripped her hips tightly, guiding her.The metal frame of the futon creaked as their passionate coupling picked up speed.

Sliding her hands down her stomach, Camilla manipulated her clit, pinching and rolling the throbbing nub between her fingers. She could feel the faint threads of her orgasm weaving within her.

Sweat dripped down her back as she ground down against Jason, her sweet essence coating their merged flesh. Lifting her body up, she paused, and then drove down against him. Her eyes fluttered closed as tiny tremors of pleasure raced throughout her body. Beneath her, Jason's movements became less steady and more desperate.

Lifting again, she pinched her clit tightly, and then dropped down again. Camilla trembled as she climaxed. Clenching tightly, she held him deep as she shuddered above him. Jason's hold on her hips tightened.

Arching, he ground his body tightly against her. He groaned as his body tightened and he flooded her with his passion

Her body limp, Camilla collapsed against him, her breasts pressed against the faint sprinkling of curls on his chest.

Slicked with sweat, Jason lay beneath her, his breathing harsh and fast. Camilla slid to the side, her smaller body curled against Jason's toned one.

Across the room, the candles flickered, casting a muted golden light. Camilla watched the play of shadows on the wall, as Jason's fingers smoothed her hair from her sweaty forehead.

"I love you," he whispered, then pressed a soft kiss to her temple. Outside, the storm raged. Neither lover cared as they held each other close, and savored their time together.

In the morning, each would have to go to work, and deal with any number of problems. But as they basked in each other's arms, all that mattered was them.

INTO EACH DAY

Gabriella cuddled against Randy's chest as they listened to the gentle tap tap tap of rain on their tent. Looking out the opened doorway, they watched the trees softly sway to the breeze, their leaves rustling.

Placing a soft kiss against her lover's chest, Gabriella yawned and stretched, her body slightly stiff from a night on an air mattress. "So I guess I have to go out in that to pee huh?"

Chuckling, Randy stretched, his body shifting under Gabriella, his hip brushing against his lover's crotch. "Yep."

Sitting up, Gabriella became aware of every ache of her body from the long day of hiking, and the night of sleeping outdoors without his creature comforts. "Why did I agree to this again?"

Reaching up, Randy pulled Gabriella back down to him, their lips meeting in a tender kiss of love. "Because you love me, and know that I love to camp and hike. Because last vacation, I spent wandering through museums with you, looking at painting by artists that have been dead for centuries. Maybe, just because I asked you to. Now come on, let's go answer nature's call and cuddle some more and listen to the rain."

Several minutes later, Gabriella was standing at the doorway of the bathroom house, looking at their tent in the distance. With a sigh, she watched as the rain continued to drizzle. Feeling Randy pressed behind her, she tried her best to liven up. "Ready love?" she asked.

"Yeah. I already have an idea of what we could do to pass the time as we wait for the rain to stop." Nibbling his way down Gabriella's neck, he soon had her shivering. "Now I'm ready." Grinding his hips against

Gabriella's ass, he proved the truth of his statement. He was ready to go, if his hard cock was an indication.

Holding hands, the two lovers raced across the campgrounds to the tent. Opening the flap, they tried not to drip water all over everything.

Shivering, Gabriella started to strip, her eyes focused on Randy, who was removing his own clothes. Looking at the bronzed skin of her lover, she had to admit that his love of nature paid off. His muscles rippled under his taunt skin with every movement. Shivering in desire, rather than cold, Gabriella moved against the damp skin of her lover, cuddling in his arms, their naked bodies rubbing together. Cool skin rapidly heated as they kissed, their tongues mating as their bodied longed to.

Sliding together onto the downy warmth of the sleeping bags, Gabriella rolled on top of Randy, grinding her pussy against his cock. Undulating against her lover, she felt her clit ring catch on her lover's hair. Whimpering, she pulled slowly away, her pussy throbbing for attention.

"Sweet Jesus," Gabriella moaned, her pussy begging for attention, "I love it when that happens." Randy had to agree, the way Gabriella trembled in his arms when her piercing got caught on hair was exhilarating, knowing that a slender piece of metal pulled at his lover's tiny clit.

Rolling Gabriella onto her back, Randy grinned at the disheveled state of his lover. Her makeup had since been sweated or wiped away, her hair was mussed, and she had never looked sexier. Seeing her so out of her element, made Randy's heart race. Knowing that she was away from her state of the art apartment out of love made it all the more intoxicating.

"I love you," he whispered. Leaning down, he joined their lips again, savoring the dewy heat of his lover's mouth. Growling deep in his chest, Randy ground his hips against Gabriella, his cock rubbing against his lover's stomach.

"I want you." Arching her hips, Gabriella echoed her lover's sentiment.

"Then take me."

Lifting Gabriella's feet to his shoulders, Randy grasped gently caressed his lover's pussy, parting her lips and thrusting deep. Sweet, tangy juices soon coated his hands.

Pulling back, he quickly moved to his bag and pulled out a tube of lubricant. Squirting lube onto his hands, he caressed his own cock, enjoying the sensation, but wanting to feel Gabriella's tight ass more.

Moving the lube to Gabriella's tight ass ring, he squirted it directly inside of her and worked it around, loosing her with his fingers. Gabriella played wit her clit, tugging and pulling on her ring while her lover lubed her ass good. She loved it when he took her that way, working his cock in and out of her ass.

Caressing his own cock, Randy spread a little more lubricant onto his throbbing length, then guided it to Gabriella's' waiting ass. Pressing against his lover's anus ring, he felt it pop as he slid in, a groan escaping his lips.

Gabriella's echoed his moan as she felt her ass expand to take her lover's cock. Clenching tightly, she gripped her lover's hardness with her ass.

"Oh baby, fuck me," she whimpered out, relaxing and clenching as Randy thrust in and out of his lover's hole.

Pumping his hips faster, he worked his cock in faster and faster, watching as his lover's played with herself. Gabriella's hands masturbated her pussy and clit as she enjoyed the sensations of her ass being impaled by her lover's cock.

Inside the tent the gentle tap tap tap of the rain was drowned out by the grunts and moans of passion, the whimpers and gasps of mutual pleasure. Neither remembered, nor cared that it was raining. They were locked in their passionate dance, a duel of the flesh.

Feeling her pussy tighten, Gabriella arched her back, driving the cock deeper into her ass as she flicked her clit to orgasm. Feeling the warm liquid against her fingers, she whimpered in ecstasy.

Clenching her ass tight, she felt the first spurt of her lover's essence in her ass as Randy came. The second landed on her ass, the third on her stomach as Randy moved up her body to collapse on top of her. The peak of her orgasm over, Gabriella tried to put into words how Randy made her feel, but like so many times before, had to settle for "I love you, I love how you make me feel."

Cuddling her close, Randy had to agree. He loved how Gabriella made him feel.

Listening to the sound of the rain, the two lovers held each other, silently sharing their love for each other. They drifted off to sleep to awaken several hours to a sunny day, not a cloud in the sky.

Smiling at each other, they ventured out for a day of hiking and love making under the bright sunny sky, the smell of rain still clinging to the air around them.

THE SYMPHONY OF SPRING

Daniel watched Jessica pull up in their truck. Stabling their prize stallion, he headed out to help her with the groceries.

"Hi, honey," he said, giving her a quick kiss.

"Hi, babe. How was your day?"

"Mine was fine. How was yours?"

"Not too great."

Daniel leaned against the door frame, the last bag brought in, and watched her move about the kitchen – the way she wiggled her hips just a little when she walked, how her hair shifted over her shoulder, caressing her smooth, pale skin.

With a sigh, Jessica put away the last of the groceries and sat down to rest. Daniel moved behind her and began to lightly massage her shoulders, and with a moan, Jessica arched into his touch.

"Sweetheart," he whispered in her ear, a shiver racing down her spine, "how about a ride to the pond and a picnic for dinner?"

Jessica sighed. It sounded like a heavenly idea.

"OK, let me get the picnic ready while you saddle Fancy and Storm."

Daniel smiled and leaned down to press a quick kiss against her lips.

"Meet me outside in ten minutes."

He headed out to the barn, whistling as he went.

* * *

Jessica carried their lunch outside, watching Daniel lead their horse from the corral. Every step he took pulled his jeans tight around his legs.

She loved to watch him walk, and she was so absorbed by the sight that it took her a moment to notice he led only one horse.

"Ready?"

"Yes," she said, handing him the basket, "but where's Fancy?"

He turned and strapped the basket to his saddle, giving Jessica a chance to admire his butt. Even after two years she still felt like a newlywed, and she couldn't get enough of her husband, or his body.

"I decided to let her rest today," he said over his shoulder. "She had a hard workout from this big guy today."

Daniel caught her staring and moved to her, scooping her up in his arms.

"Daniel, what are you doing?" she sputtered.

"Helping my lady to her horse, of course."

Placing her gently in the saddle, he mounted behind her. Every inch of Jessica's back tingled where he settled against her. Grasping the reins, Daniel guided Storm to a light trot, and Jessica soon found herself swaying to the horse's rhythm with Daniel.

Neither spoke, silently enjoying the ride to the pond. Every shift of the horse reminded them that only a layer of clothing separated their bare flesh.

By the time they arrived at their pond, Jessica was having second thoughts about a picnic and many thoughts about tearing the clothing from her husband's body and ravaging him.

Daniel guided Storm to a stop, dismounted, and led him to a tree, tossing the reins over a low branch. He held his arms up for Jessica, and she slid into his arms, twisting herself about him.

His hands went to her behind as they kissed, their tongues mating as they knew their bodies soon would.

"Let's get you cooled off," he whispered and headed toward the pond.

"You wouldn't dare," she gasped, as he stepped to the water's edge.

Daniel gently set her on her feet and began unbuttoning her shirt.

"No baby, I wouldn't toss you in, but I think we both need to cool off a bit."

Her shirt removed, he started to remove his own.

"Mmmm, let me," she purred, her hands sliding over his bare flesh, lightly caressing his nipples.

She loved to touch Daniel, the hard muscle beneath his velvety skin. Twirling her fingers in the light sprinkling of hair on his chest, she smiled and leaned in to lightly graze on one of his nipples.

Daniel took a step back and shed the rest of his clothes, Jessica's eyes following every movement as he bared himself to her view. She always found it nothing short of a miracle, the way he was so hard and muscular and big, but his touch was always so gentle.

Jessica quickly removed her clothes, once he was naked, and stepped into his arms. Her head fit perfectly beneath his chin as they enjoyed the feelings of their naked bodies against each another.

Picking her up, Daniel stepped into the water and held her tight. The natural springs that fed the pond kept the water warm, and soon he found the ledge he favored, sitting with Jessica still cuddled against him.

Water settled about their bodies and Jessica felt herself relax. It was heavenly to be in Daniel's arms enveloped by the warm water, listening to the birds sing their sweet songs of love.

She was growing drowsy and she pulled away, moving off his lap to splash him playfully. Daniel grinned and moved after her. They spent a while playing and splashing, kissing and caressing before Jessica's hunger pulled her from the pond.

Daniel followed, pulling on his jeans as he spread a blanket on the ground. His body was already humming with desire, as was evident to Jessica by the straining of his denim.

With a grin, she dried off and tossed the towel aside, sitting naked on the blanket.

"Going to join me?" she teased.

Daniel smiled, sitting next to her and as he began pulling their lunch from the basket. They ate in silence, admiring the view, and occasionally Daniel would reach out a hand and trail his fingers down Jessica's stomach, or across her breasts. By the time they finished their meal, Jessica was ready to pounce on him and make love, but Daniel had other ideas.

He packed away the rest of their lunch and their towels, turning to say, "Going to get up so I can pack the blanket?"

Jessica stood and watched him roll their blanket and tuck away her clothes, then move to Storm and grasp the reins. Leading the horse to his wife, he whistled.

Jessica grinned and awaited help into the saddle, but Daniel mounted first.

Puzzled, she waited.

"Come here, love. Put your foot in the other way and I'll help you up facing me."

It took some doing, but finally Jessica was settled in his lap, facing him, her body bare but for his open shirt.

Daniel guided Storm with one hand and occupied his other with teasing Jessica to distraction. The friction of the horse's movements slid her already sensitive pussy against Daniel's denimed crotch. His hand teased her nipples and clit until she was moaning and arching into his touch. Guiding the horse to a faster trot, Daniel smiled at her moans.

Her body settled into a smooth rhythm against his, until finally she orgasmed, passion overwhelming her. Daniel pulled her against his chest, and ran his hand up and down her back, soothing her.

They arrived at the barn and Daniel guided Storm into his stall. Carefully, he shifted Jessica against the saddle horn and dismounted. Holding up his arms, he helped her down.

Jessica rubbed her body against his, distracting Daniel from his responsibility.

"Baby, I have to unsaddle Storm."

She leaned against the side of the stall and watched him work, her hands trailing over her body. From the corner of his eye, Daniel watched her every move, growing hotter by the second. Finally, Storm was unsaddled and his tack put up, and Daniel pulled Jessica into his arms and lifted her against him. Her legs wrapped around his back, her lips wildly sucking and kissing his neck and chest.

"God, baby," he whispered, closing the stall door and latching it shut.

"Daniel, make love to me, here, now. I need you inside me."

He moved to the empty stall and set Jessica down, unable to resist a quick kiss of her breasts. As quickly as he could, he grabbed their blanket from Storm's saddlebag and spread it on the hay-covered floor.

Jessica lay down and spread her legs, waiting for her husband to join her, and as he removed his jeans, she slid a hand down her body and lightly played with her sensitive flesh.

Daniel groaned at the sight, tossing his jeans aside and kneeling between her thighs.

"God, baby, you make me so hot," he whispered, leaning down to lick her fingers clean of her juices. Tenderly, he caressed her waiting body, making certain she was ready for him. Even after two years, he still remembered her pain on their first night, and he was never again going to cause her this discomfort.

Jessica twisted beneath him, arching her hips against his hand. Daniel smiled, moving to cover her body with his. Restless, she twisted under his weight and moved her hands to encircle his hard cock. Impatiently she guided him into her waiting warmth, and moaned as his head slid between her lips.

"Yes," she whispered, arching against him. Her legs wrapped around his waist, tightening when he moved to pull away.

Groaning, Daniel thrust against her, the muscles of his ass flexing with every movement. Jessica's ankles rested on his tight cheeks as he slid into her over and over. Her hands fisted in his hair and he pulled his mouth to hers, his tongue mimicking the movements of his body over hers, thrust and retreat, again and again. Jessica's body tingled as she crested, her moans filling the air. The sweet smell of their sweat soon mingled with the smells of the barn.

Perspiration beaded on Daniel's forehead as he claimed her body again and again, eager to satisfy her. Jessica arched again and whimpered, "I want you to come, baby. Make me come, then come with me. Please, baby."

Her body shuddered as her third orgasm began. With a groan, Daniel increased his pace, feeling her body clenching him tight. Thrusting one last time, he collapsed atop of her, feeling the rush of his hot seed.

"Mmmmm," Jessica moaned against his shoulder, her body satisfied, her mind growing heavy.

"I love you," he murmured, rolling to his side, pulling her tight.

"I love you too, baby," she whispered back.

They cuddled on their bed of straw and cloth, touching and loving, until Daniel wrapped Jessica in their blanket and carried her inside to their bed. There they lay, finally claimed by sleep as the crickets began their symphony of the night.

SUMMER STORMS AND HEART'S AFLAME

"So you're back in town now, huh?"

Marci looked up from the horse she was brushing and glanced back down. She had known this day was coming, but she had kind of hoped it would wait at least until she had had a chance to settle in.

Jacob Lassitar glared at her bowed head and hopped the fence. "Too good to speak to me now?"

"Jacob, please," she replied.

"Jacob, please what? Jacob, go away? Jacob, what? I want to know why you're back. After all this time, why the hell did you have to come back again?"

Marci sighed and set the brush on the fence. Grabbing the harness, she began leading the mare from the corral to her stall. It was getting harder and harder to hold back the tears that were stinging her eyes, and she wasn't about to let them fall in front of Jacob.

Jacob quickly caught up and placed his hand on her arm. "I want an answer, Marci. You're not going to pretend I don't exist."

"Look, Jacob, it's been a long time. I'm back to stay now, so we will have to deal with each other. Let's try to do so like adults."

"You're not going to get off so easily. I want to know why you had to come back after ten years. You stayed away that long, why come back at all?"

"You wouldn't understand."

Marci sighed and looked at the ground. Obviously Jacob was as hardheaded and stubborn as ever. Which only made her heart ache more for what she had done, for what she had tossed away.

"I wouldn't understand? What I don't understand could fill books, Marci. I don't understand why you left.

I asked you to marry me, we made love, Christ you gave me your virginity, and then I woke up the next morning and you had left. No note, no explanation, you were just gone. Your dad wouldn't tell me a damn thing." He paused to run his hand through his slightly shaggy hair, before slapping his hat back on his head.

"Him not telling me a damn thing, I don't understand. So why don't we add one more thing: Why the hell are you back?"

"Jacob, look, I'm not ready to talk about it right now. Could we just let it go, please? For now, at least."

"Fine Marci. I've spent ten years waiting for an answer, wondering what the hell I had done to run you off. I guess a couple more days won't really matter. I'll let it go -- for now. But you will give me an answer, I think I deserve at least that much."

Jacob turned on his heel and stalked off. He stepped through the gate and slammed it shut. Marci flinched at the sound, then led the horse back into her stall.

* * *

Day after day Marci checked and rechecked her father's account logs. Everything was in perfect order, just as she suspected. She didn't recheck the math to make sure it was right, she did it for something to do, something to take her mind off the man outside working with the horses.

From the study, she had a perfect view of Jacob, where he couldn't see she was watching. Every day, she watched the strong planes of his back flex as he worked to tame the horses he loved so much.

Their mutual love of horses had been what drew her to him in the first place. Shy by nature, she had always had trouble relating to boys at school, but ever since

Jacob had started working on her father's ranch, she had found herself opening up to him.

She could tell him anything.   At least, almost anything.

With a soft sigh of regret, she turned away from the window and focus her attention back on the ledgers, anything to take her mind off of the one thing she could never get him to understand, despite all her attempts.

That night, she lay in her lonely bed and thought of him until finally, her mind exhausted, she fell into a troubled sleep.   Just like she had every night since she had come home.

For two weeks she managed to avoid the man she had loved ten years earlier, the man she never stopped loving.   Then, fate laughed at her.

She was out riding Bridget, her father's prize mare, when the storm hit.   Unlike storms in the city, this was a sudden, violent downpour.   Within minutes, she was soaked to the skin and shivering from the cold.   She knew she wouldn't make it back to the ranch, so she headed to the old hunting cabin.

She took care of the mare first, stabling her in the shed and brushing her dry.   She knew Bridget would stay put -- she liked being dry just as much as any human.

Heading to the cabin, she jumped as lightning illuminated the sky.   She coughed at the dust she stirred up as she stepped inside, wood still stacked beside the fireplace.   Soon Marci had a fire blazing and had shaken out the bed linen.   Stripping off her clothes, she wrapped herself in the musty-smelling sheet and settled in front of the fire.

With nothing else to do, she found herself thinking about that last spring she had spent on the ranch. The weeks leading up to her high school graduate had been hectic, with calving season heading into full swing, and her budding romance with Jacob taking up what free time they both had.

So many nights they would lay out on a blanket in the back yard and look up at the stars, holding hands and sharing kisses. She had been aware, despite her very limited experience with men, that Jacob had been holding himself back. Given their age difference, she knew a lot of it had to do with waiting for her to be ready.

Despite the love she had felt for him, the timing had never seemed right to go any further, until the night she graduated. The night everything in her life started to unravel.

* * *

Jacob listened to his boss' raving and worrying, then without a word turned on his heel and headed out the door. Within minutes he had his horse saddled and was leading him out of the corral. He was met at the gate.

"Where in tar'nation do you think you're going, boy?"

Jacob pulled his slicker tight against his body and glanced at his boss from beneath his Stetson.

"I'm going after her, sir. Someone has to."

"Jacob, you and I both know Marci was raised on this land. She knows where to head. She'll be holed up in the old hunting cabin waiting out the storm."

"And what if she isn't? What if her horse spooked and threw her? What if she can't get to the cabin? It's been ten years Brad, she could have forgotten the way."

"Son, Bridget is a good mare. She doesn't spook easily. If, and I stress if, she did toss Marci, there's no telling where she might be, and in this storm, you could go in circles before finding her. I'm worried about her too damn it, she my baby girl, but I have to trust her good senses."

"Brad, I have to try. She and I have some unfinished business, and this is as good a time as any to finish it. I'm going to find her, and if she is at the cabin, I'll wait there with her 'til morning. If she's not, I'll come back and we can start a search party. As for her good senses, I'm going to have to agree to disagree with you there."

Brad sighed. He had known Jacob most of his life, helped his momma raise him after his no-good father took off and left her to take care of herself and her teenaged son. It had been Jacob looking for a job to help make ends meet that had introduced them.

Jacob was as hardheaded, as stubborn as any mule. Once he made up his mind, Brad would have to shoot him to stop him from going. He had always hoped for Marci to realize what was standing right in front of her, and for a while there, it had looked like she had.

Maybe Jacob was right; maybe them getting stormed in together would be good for clearing the air. The boy certainly deserved to know why Marci had left.

"Go then, but by God, be careful. If she is at the cabin, stay put. Head back in the morning after the storm is over. And Jacob ... take it easy on her. She had her reasons. Damn good ones, at least they seemed that way at the time. If you insist on knowing, then actually listen to what she has to say."

Brad stopped and waited for Jacob to acknowledge his words. The howl of the wind and rain were the only sounds. Finally Jacob nodded and mounted his horse.

From the porch, Jacob's mom watched her son and Brad talking, then saw her boy ride away. Her tears flowed freely, mingling with the blowing rain.

When he reached the steps, Brad laid a hand on her arm.

"Come inside where it's warm," he said. Martha nodded, but didn't move.

"Brad," she whispered.

"I know, honey. But they have to find their own way. This day has been ten years in coming. It's time for them both to have some closure. They need it."

Martha nodded again and turned to go inside. Brad wrapped his arm around her waist and his hand settled on her hip. Together they climbed the stairs leading to their room, a room they had shared since she had followed her teenage son out to the ranch, and fell in love with the widower running it.

* * *

Jacob called himself many kinds of a fool for being out in a storm like this, for a woman who had broken his heart. He had thought himself over her, but having Marci back on the ranch had shown that the wounds had only scabbed over. They had never healed.

Certainly he had had his share of female interest over the years, but nothing had ever compared to the spring nights laying next to Marci sweet form, holding her against his body as they kissed and petted. Despite the almost innocent quality of their caresses, they were more arousing that the practiced seduction he had previously sampled in his wild youth.

Knowing that he had been the one to awaken Marci's passion, to slowly teach her about her body and his, had been addictive. To only have had one night of being deep within her; one night of her passionate cries ringing in his ears as he had thrust deeper and deeper into her heart, feeling the liquid warmth of her pussy surrounding him – it wasn't enough. He suspected it never would be.

Unlike his father, he was coming to realize he was a one-woman man, and Marci had claimed him years ago.

After what seemed like hours in the saddle, he finally reached the cabin, its windows lit with an orange glow. He dismounted and led his horse into the shed, taking the time to brush him down before heading to the cabin where he knew a showdown awaited.

He prepared himself for any type of greeting Marci would give him. At least, he thought he was ready for anything, until he saw Marci on the hardwood floor in front of the dying fire. She was curled up in a ball, her naked body shivering in her sleep.

"Damn fool woman," he muttered as he crossed the room and knelt down next to her. The sight of her pale skin lit up by the firelight caused a shudder of awareness to course through his body. He ignored it, focusing instead on stoking the fire and heating the cabin. Marci moaned and he glanced at her long enough to see her eyes open, then turned back to his task.

"What are you doing here, Jacob?"

Jacob tossed another log on the fire and turned to her.

"I need to get out of these wet clothes. Toss me one of those sheets and close your eyes. I wouldn't want to offend your modesty."

Marci glared at him as she stood and grabbed one of the sheets on which she had been laying and wrapped it around her body. Tossing the other one to him, she sat back down in front of the fire.

"I want an answer, Jacob."

He locked his gaze on hers as he unbuttoned his shirt. He could feel his lips curling in a facsimile of a smile, but couldn't stop it. He was tired, damn tired of waiting and wondering and torturing himself with questions to which he had no chance of getting answers.

The worst was the fear that the night that held the most beautiful memories of his life might be one that meant something else to Marci. Had he hurt her without knowing it? He knew he was rough, and dominate by nature, but he had thought he had been careful to ease her into things. Had he not done enough?

That lingering fear caused his tone to come out a little more bitter than he had planned. "Yeah? I'm sure you do. There are a lot of answers I want. So I guess we're even."

Jacob's shirt hit the floor and his hands went to the buttons of his jeans.

Marci closed her eyes and turned away for him. Behind her, she heard him chuckle, then the sound of his boots and jeans hitting the floor.

"I'm here for answers, Marci. In this storm, you can't escape, and we're not leaving until I know why you ran away, even if I have to tie you up and keep you here until we are both starving."

Marci turned back to him, her eyes wide in shock.

"You wouldn't dare."

"Try me, sweetheart. I'm not the cow-eyed boy I was back then. I'm a hard, bitter man. So why don't you make my week and try me."

Seeing the truth in his face, she closed her eyes and groaned.

Jacob pulled the sheet tighter around himself and settled himself on the floor with his back to the wall, next to the fireplace. Crossing his legs at the ankles, he focused his gaze on the blonde across from him. She was still a very beautiful woman. Ten years had taken her from a young woman with so much potential, to a truly beautiful woman.

"Jacob, I never met to hurt you," she said softly.

Jacob grunted, and continued studying her form.

"Try another answer, Marci, we both know that one doesn't fly. You tore ass out of town after spending half of the night kissing every inch of my body. You never meant to hurt me? I asked you to marry me and you left. How in the hell do you think that would not hurt me?"

Marci folded her hands together and glanced at her hands.

"I loved you so much. I was just..."

She stopped. Even after all these years, she still couldn't get over her stupidity.

"You want the truth, Jacob? Here it is. I was scared. I had just graduated high school. I was offered a full scholarship, and I loved you so much. But I wanted more than that. I wanted a chance to make something of myself, something more than being a wife and mother."

She looked up at him then, meeting his gaze. Forcing herself to rip away the last scab on her own wounds, she continued.

"But you couldn't accept that. Whenever we talked of me going away to college, you always said I could stay here and go to the state university branch in town. But I wanted so much more. I wanted a chance to see more than this town. You were ready to settle down, but I was still a child. After all that you had been through in your life, moving from place to place every other month, following your drunken father from job to job. By the time you got here, you were ready to settle down. I'd lived in this town all my life. I wanted more."

She fell silent. Tears streaked down her face and angrily she brushed them away. Time after time she had defended herself in her mind, but always there was a feeling of guilt.

"Why didn't you tell me that?"

Marci snorted.

"I had tried Jacob, so many times. But both you and my father were pushing me to settle down, to start a life here. You and my father had my life all planned out, when I didn't have a clue what I wanted. You had already been to college and graduated. I was barely out of high school. I had no clue what I wanted, and I felt so alone. I had to leave, I had to find what I wanted out of life."

"Then why did you come back?"

Jacob was trying to understand, but after ten years of wondering what he had done wrong, why she had run, he now knew. Ten years of cursing her, of blaming her for his broken heart, now he found that he was as much to blame as she was, if not more so. Thankfully though, the blame he bore wasn't because he had physically hurt her, as he had feared. Although, knowing he had caused his fragile love to think he wasn't listening to her hurt just as bad.

"Because," she whispered, her voice choked with tears.

Jacob waited, knowing she had more to say.

"Because I found that after graduating, after making it in at a prestigious accounting firm, I was lonely. My job didn't make me happy, my home was empty and no other man could take your place. I dated a few, but I could never get past the first kiss. They were just shadows of the man you are. So I came back home. After all these years, it was time. I knew you might already be married, I knew you would definitely still hate me, but I had to come back."

"So you didn't find what you were looking for?"

Marci sighed, the words she needed to say on the tip of her tongue. Swallowing, she said them, feeling her heart in her throat, waiting for him to laugh at her.

"No. I couldn't. What I was looking for was here. It took years of loneliness, of crying myself to sleep at night, to figure that out. Years of existing, but not truly living. What I was looking for was you. I just had to go away to find that out. By the time I did, pride kept me away."

"Pride? Ten damn years wasted, over pride?"

"And fear Jacob. Fear that you would reject me, would walk away and leave me lonely with no hope. That I would come back, and you wouldn't want me in your life anymore. At least there I had hope. That maybe one day, you would come for me. That we would be together again."

Jacob groaned. Marci raised her eyes and met his gaze. Love shined in his eyes, but she could hardly believe it. Was it possible? After all these years, after all the pain and loneliness, after how she had hurt him, could he still love her?

"I almost did come after you several times. Each time, it was not knowing why you ran that held me back. It tore me apart thinking that I had hurt you, that you ran away because I was too rough when we made love."

Marci let the tears fall at his ragged tone. Hearing the worry and pain in his voice was her undoing. She knew she had been immature, but at eighteen she wasn't strong enough to stand up for what she thought she needed. So she had run away. Never, in all the years since, had she thought Jacob would blame himself for her actions.

"No, that night was the most precious of my life. I can close my eyes right now and still remember every kiss, every touch, every whispered word we exchanged."

With a soft groan, Jacob stood and headed over to her. Dropping to his knees, he wrapped a hand in her damp hair and pulled her to him. Pressing his lips to hers, he let her feel the pain in his heart, and the love.

"I still love you, Jacob," she whispered against his lips, then deepened the kiss. "I never stopped. I just needed time to grow up."

As their tongues mated, a growl rose in Jacob's chest. Pushing her back onto the floor, he separated the edges of her sheet and pressed his body along the length of hers. His hands caressed her, feeling the differences ten years had made. Her chest had filled out and her stomach had softened slightly. She no longer had the toned flesh of her youth, but rather the softness of the woman she had become.

"You're grown up now. Have you had enough time?"

"Yes! I know what I want Jacob, what I have always wanted." Her hands caressed his back and neck before fisting in his hair, holding his lips to hers as she poured all her heartache and need for him into her kiss, trying to show him without words what she needed. Jacob pulled back and winced as she pulled his hair.

"Marci, baby, let go. Wrap your arms around me."

Marci moved her hands up and down his body, stroke softly along the sun-roughened skin of his shoulders and back. Jacob kissed her jaw, then moved down along the sleek column of her neck to her shoulder blade, and down to her breasts. He teased the tender flesh with his lips and teeth before taking one of her nipples into his mouth. He nibbled and sucked the hardened bud, delighted when she moaned and arched against him.

Her hips shifted beneath his, her pussy leaving a wet trail against his leg. A sense of déjà vu almost overwhelmed him, as he remembered that night ten year before.It had been such sensual torture awakening Marci's body, pausing to test and sample along the way, to make sure she was with him at every step.

Thinking back on it, he wasn't sure how he had ever feared he had hurt her, other than it feeding from his own insecurities. He had always worried he wasn't good enough for someone so precious, so perfect.

It had taken her running away, and ten years of time passing, for him to realize that the pedestal he had put her on placed a lot of pressure on her, as well as unrealistic expectations. There was no way she ever could have met them all. Now, having her back in his arms, he knew they had a lot of catching up to do, ten years worth of memories and events to share. But all that mattered for the moment was the feel of her in his arms. He had ached to hold her, to feel her flesh against his again, and now that it was happening, he wasn't about to push her away for further conversation.

Moving a hand down between them, he parted her nether-lips and slid a finger inside her. Feeling her stretch, Jacob remembered how she had felt that first time, so long ago. How she had slowly opened for him, her body relaxing and allowing his invasion deep inside. He eased a second finger to join the first, slowly scissoring them apart as his lips teasing her other nipple.

"Jacob," Marci gasped, her tone deepening with desire. Her voice had lost some of its girlish breathless quality over the years, had deepened into a woman's sexy tones.

Jacob smiled and continued his tender assault. He knew just how she felt, the urgency, but after ten years of waiting, he wanted it to last as long as it could.

Sliding down further, he removed his fingers and licked them, before flicking her navel with the wet heat of his tongue. Marci shifted restlessly under him, her body restless, waiting, hoping for his next move.

Moving lower still, he parted her pussy lips with his wet fingers and slid his tongue between them. Coating it with her juices, he savored her taste for a moment before flicking the tip of his tongue against her clit. Marci arched against him, moaning. Her legs tightened, and as Jacob flicked her clit again, shockwaves raced through her body. Jacob smiled and laid his head on her inner thigh, waiting for her body to stop trembling.

As soon as she stilled, he started his tender assault again, this time continuing even as she twisted and undulated beneath him. Her juices flowed freely, and he savored them as he stroked her higher and higher, until her legs tightened around his head as she climaxed. Flicking his tongue against her clit, he worked her through her orgasm, drawing it out as long as he could until his own body started demanding his attention.

He shifted back to kneel between her legs, his hands stroking along the length of his erection as he waited for her to come back to herself.

Marci's eyelids flickered up, and reality slowly returned to her languid gaze as she trailed it down his body. "Make love to me," she whispered, her attention caught on the sight of him stroking his own cock.

"Marry me," he responded.

Marci's heart swelled with love. After ten years, the words she most wanted to hear filled her mind.

"Yes." Euphoria swept through her body, and she could only hope he wouldn't change his mind come morning. That he wouldn't feel they needed to get to know each other again first. Looking into his love-filled gaze, she knew everything she needed to know.

Jacob smiled again and moved back up her body. Pressing his lips to hers, she had a moment to adjust to the taste of herself on his mouth before he slid his cock inside her, thrusting in just to briefest amount. For a tiny moment, she felt a spark of pain, and then the thrill of his body joined to hers started to twirl inside of her.

"Are you okay?" Jacob asked, his voice tight. Dots of sweat coated his brow as he held himself still inside of her.

Marci nodded and realized she must have whimpered.

Pulling back, Jacob asked again, needing to see the answer in her eyes.

"Yes," she whispered, "but I'd be better if you would stop looking at me and start making love to me."

Jacob smiled. "My pleasure."

Leaning back down, he nipped at her neck as he thrust his hips against hers. Marci moaned as she arched, driving him deeper. Time seemed to fade away, and in that moment, the years they had spent apart didn't matter. Their bodies knew each other.

As he started thrusting against her, Marci slid her hands to his ass, gripping the firm cheeks. Her fingertips pressed into the calluses that had formed from years spent in the saddle, caressing the hard surfaces even as she pulled his tighter into her body.

Jacob's hands grasped her legs and pulled them up to his hips, and coaxed her to wrap them around his waist. Marci gasped as he slid his hands down her ribcage, briefly tickling the sensitive skin as he worked his way up her back to clasp hold of her shoulders. With the leverage, he pulled her down and into each of his thrusts, driving his cock deeper and deeper into her body, until she wasn't certain where he ended and she began.

Together, they settled into a steady rhythm of thrusting and arching that soon had them moaning and sweating.

"Come for me," Jacob whispered into Marci's ear. "Let me feel you warm and wet and tight around me. Squeeze me deep inside like you never want to let me go again."

At his words, Marci felt her heart tighten even as her pussy clamped down on his erection. He thrust once more and sent her spiraling into orgasm. She grabbed his shoulders and tightened her legs around his waist as waves of pleasure crashed through her body.

After ten years of abstinence, the clenching of her inner muscles drove Jacob wild. With a groan, he poured his hot seed into her body and collapsed on top of her. Marci gently rubbed his back as his breathing slowly returned to normal.

"I think I'm dead," he groaned as he moved himself off her and pulled her tight.

"And I love you too," Marci replied.

Playfully swatting her ass, he grinned at her.

"I've waited ten years to touch you again, to make love to you, to tell you how much I still love you, and to hear you tell me you love me. After all that time, all I get is a sarcastic 'I love you'?"

Marci giggled and buried her head against his chest. Flicking his nipple with her tongue, she giggled again at his shudder.

"I said I still love you Jacob, and I do. I always have. I just needed to grow up some."

"This time, when I wake up will you be here?" he whispered, as once again old insecurities flooded him.

"Definitely. Even without the storm outside, I would be here. I want to wake up next to you every morning for the rest of my life, and fall asleep in your arms every night."

"Lady, you have got yourself a deal. Now about that sleeping part, I hope you don't plan on much tonight."

Giggling again, Marci ducked her head again and teased his nipple.

"I wouldn't dream of it."

"I would. I have. But honey, you've got all of my dreams beat."

As the storm raged outside, another tore through that little cabin. A storm of passion found, and love remembered.

PARADISE VALLEY

Amanda shifted on the lounger, trying to get comfortable. As the sun beat down on her golden tanned skin, she flopped over onto her stomach and sighed. She stretched like a cat, reached behind her, and unclasped her bikini top. Breathing a sign of contentment, she snuggled down into the cushion of the lounger and let the sun heat her skin.

Several minutes passed, and she fell into a light doze. A cool fall breeze helped to dispel the stifling heat.

All around her, the sounds of lawnmowers continued to keep her on the edge of wakefulness. Frustrated, she flopped over onto her back, and tried to relax and enjoy her sun bathing.

Ever since her husband's promotion, which moved them from their house in the country to the suburbs, she hadn't been able to enjoy sun bathing. Her neighbors delicate sensibilities had to be considered - ergo, she couldn't sunbathe nude. As it was, she was pushing it being topless.

She also couldn't swim nude, and make love with Mark in the rain, or under the stars, or any number of other things they had once enjoyed.

A shadow blocked out a portion of the sun, and Amanda's eyes fluttered open. "Mark?"

"Yeah sweetie, it's me." The lounger creaked as he sat next to her hip. Amanda slid over slightly to give him more room.

"You're home early."

"I decided to take a half day. I finished all the pressing tasks this morning, and pushed everything else off for tomorrow. It's too nice a day to stay cooped up inside the office. "

"Ummm," Amanda couldn't agree more.

Mark leaned down and nipped at her nipple, gently sucking the tip into his mouth. Arching slightly, Amanda offered him her breast.

He pulled back, and gently cupped her breasts in his hands. "I've missed this."

"Me too."

"But we really should go inside."

Amanda sighed and moved away from his hands. "I think I'll stay out here for a while longer."

"Amanda?" He leaned down and kissed the side of her neck, his touch coaxing and arousing.

"Why don't you go put your shorts on, and we can cuddle in the hammock for a while?"

Mark pulled back, a question obvious in his gaze. Amanda smiled softly. "I'm enjoying the sunshine on my skin. Mrs. Lowenstine left about a half hour ago on her weekly grocery trip. She shouldn't be back for another hour or more. You're welcome to join me."

Mark nodded and stood. His long legged stride ate up the distance to the door, and Amanda trailed her gaze down his back to his ass, watching the flex of his muscles under his slacks. She trembled at the delicious shiver the imagery invoked.

While he was inside changing, Amanda moved from the lounger to the hammock. They had debated for weeks over just the perfect placement when they first moved in. Now, with the first stirrings of fall, the trees were still lush and green, and the hedges they had planted in late spring had filled in, affording them a small modicum of privacy. Their next-door neighbor, the widow Lowenstine was the only one who could see into their little retreat.

Amanda carefully tied her wrap around her waist and slid her bikini bottoms off. Tying her top back in place, she was decently covered to anyone looking.

Climbing carefully into the hammock, she gave it a gentle push and laid back, settling against the smooth ropes. She had just closed her eyes and relaxed into the soothing rhythm when a shadow loomed over her, blocking out the sun.

"Want some company?"

Amanda opened her eyes and nodded. Carefully, she moved over, and turned on her side, making room for Mark to curl up behind her. As soon as he was settled, he pressed his lips against her neck, nuzzling the tender flesh with faint stubble.

"I love you baby," he whispered against her neck. Cupping a breast in his right hand, he slid his left between her body and the hammock, gripping her thigh and holding her steady as he shifted behind her, rubbing his groin against her ass. Amanda moaned as he tweaked her nipple.

Reaching back, she unbuttoned the front of his lounge pants and slipped his cock free. The warmth of arousal spread through her veins as she raised her wrap, baring her ass, while keeping her front covered.

"In the mood to be naughty I see." Mark nipped at her earlobe.

In response, Amanda squeezed his cock, knowing it would drive him wild. "Always. Hurry up and fuck me."

She released his cock and wiggled her ass against him, just in case he needed further coaxing. He slid his hand down along her leg to her inner thigh, brushing a finger along her moist slit.

He continued to tease, even when Amanda shifted and draped her leg over his, opening herself to his touch, to his cock. Dipping his finger deep, he twirled it around into her, his watchband rubbing against her mons.

"Mark," she pleaded, arching into his touch. Her movements sent the hammock swinging, almost tumbling them into the grass.

"Relax, baby," he whispered against her shoulder, then paused to lovingly nip the skin. "Just listen to the birds and the water in the fountain, let me take care of you."

Amanda almost wept in relief as he pulled his finger free and slid his cock along the cleft of her ass. But no sooner had he nudged his cock-head past the lips of her pussy, he stopped. The hand he had gripping her hips held her firmly, pulling her back against his crotch. With his other hand wrapped around her, he gently caressed her clit, while holding her completely still.

Slowly, what seemed to her to be a millimeter at a time, he slid within her, his cock sliding slowly along her slick walls, until he was buried to his balls. Rocking his hips, he started the hammock swaying his motions slow and steady.

Amanda gasped in pleasure as each motion alternately pulled her away and pressed her back against him.Cupping her breasts in her hands, she alternately pinched and rolled the nipples, sending tiny rivulets of pleasure throughout her body.

Focusing her breathing, she followed Mark's rhythm, until they seemed to become one. Inhale, sway forward and back, exhale, sway forward and back. Again. And again.

Calm, yet aroused. Content, while needing more.

She wiggled against Mark, evoking a soft moan from him. Clenching her inner muscles tight, she fought to keep her breathing steady. She could feel intense pressure building within her, tightness in her breasts, tingling deep in her core.

"Mark," she whispered, her insides tightened into a tiny ball and exploded, sending sparks rushing through her veins. The sweet euphoria lasted but a few moments, but it heralded the climax to come.

Mark's grip on her hips tightened, holding her steady even as he picked up the pace. The hammock jerked, threatening to dump them both to the ground.

Her breathing no longer even, Amanda ground back against him, clenching his cock with each of his thrusts. Soft moans blended with the background noise, drowned out by the neighbors' lawnmower.

"Yes, oh yes," she gasped, needing more, craving more. Mark gave it to her, pounding into her slick, heated flesh as fast as the swaying hammock would allow, driving her closer to sexual fulfillment.

Amanda whimpered as she came, the rush of sensation painfully sweet. Behind her, Mark continued to thrust until with a jerk, he flooded her pussy.

His grip on her relaxed, and Amanda shifted slightly, calming the erratic movements of the hammock, until it fell still.Mark's breathing was harsh in her ear. "Damn, I missed that," he panted, as he struggled to gain control of his lungs once more.

Amanda carefully rolled over, so that she lay facing her husband, her legs tucked between his. Her touch gentle, she tucked his limp cock back into his pants and buttoned him back up. Lying there, in his arms, she enjoyed the sensation of the breeze against her skin, the feel of Mark's arms around her.

An hour later, the sound of a car pulling in the driveway next to them startled them from their light doze. Amanda yawned and stretched contentedly; while Mark pulled her wrap down to cover her ass-cheeks. Not yet ready to leave their little haven, Mark started the hammock swaying gently again and cuddled Amanda close. She closed her eyes and listened to the steady thump-thump of his heart, breathing in a slow rhythm to match his, in perfect harmony.

CASTLES IN THE SAND

Suzanne trailed her fingers through the sand in a lazy motion, as she watched the surfers rushing to and from the waves. The temperature was perfect for relaxing on the beach and enjoying life, unlike what she would have to return to the next day. The weather report had given New York record lows for the next several days. Despite a noon flight, she was in no hurry to return home. All that awaited was a lonely apartment she shared with a steadily dying plant, which no amount of water, fresh soil, or TLC had been able to cure, a dead end job and a love life, which resembled the Sahara.

Several times during her vacation, she had been tempted to have a fling with a sun-kissed beach dweller, one of the many smooth-talking men she had bumped into at the hotel bar, or even the friendly bellboy at her hotel who filled out his uniform in a such a delightful way, especially below the belt. But always cautious and levelheaded, she had denied her urges and focused on the consequences of casual sex.

Sighing softly, Suzanne couldn't help but wonder if she would spend the rest of her life alone. Maybe she'd get lucky and the right man would come along, and she'd give in to her hormones for once. Closing her eyes to the sight of men she wouldn't allow herself to have, she drifted of sleep, lightly dozing - dreaming of what could be.

* * *

A trail of cold water trickled down her golden skin, startling her awake. Stifling a soft scream, Suzanne sat up suddenly. A figure stood over her, his features shadowed by the sun at his back.

"You looked so peaceful laying there, I hate to wake you, but there's a volleyball game starting up and they're worried about possibly injuring you."

The stranger shifted, squatting next to her. Suddenly, Suzanne could see his face, and his mostly bare body. Clad in only a pair of white shorts, he was easily 175 pounds of tanned, toned, and mostly naked male.

Licking her lips, Suzanne swallowed, trying to moisten her suddenly dry throat. "Um, no problem. I need to get out of the sun anyways."

"Need a hand?"

Suzanne studied the hand he held out, the tanned skin, the light dusting of golden hair, leading up his arm from his wrist. It perfectly matched the v of hair that started at his nipples and lead teasingly past the waistband of his shorts.

Drawing her gaze from the temping arrow of blond hair, she lifted her hand and shifted her weight, letting him pull her up.

Standing next to him, she felt almost comfortable. He didn't tower over her like most men. Although, given her slight frame, that wasn't saying much. In shoes, she'd guess he stood no taller than five foot eight. Barefooted, he lost at least an inch.

"Thank you," she whispered, her throat still dry.

Bending down, she grabbed her blanket while the stranger picked up her tote and handed it to her. As their hands brushed, she felt a zing of awareness.

"My pleasure."

After one last quick perusal, she turned and walked away, already wondering if she'd spend another sleepless night wondering what if. He had definitely seemed worth breaking her no casual sex rule over.

* * *

Flopping onto her back, Suzanne finally admitted defeat and climbed out of bed. The clock mocked her, blinking its red 1:00 am at her.

Changing from her silk nightgown to a comfortable skirt and a red tank top, she strapped on her sandals, pocketed her room key, and headed out of her bungalow. Sultry island music wrapped itself around her, mingling with the warm ocean breeze. Lifting her arms to the air, she swayed with the music as she headed down the path to the outdoor bar, the lure of one last umbrella drink, one last sensual dance with a stranger, too strong to resist.

The bartender nodded his head at her as she settled on the next to last barstool. It took him several moments to work his way down to her, and Suzanne patiently waited, letting the sultry beat flow through her, bringing a fire to her veins.

"You're usual Q?"

Suzanne smiled at the whimsical nickname the bartender had given her on her first night on the island, after trying out Suzie Q and being rewarded by her grimace. "Yeah."

"One sex on the beach coming up. What do you women see in that drink anyway?"

Suzanne just laughed and tossed money on the counter, enough for her drink and a sizable tip.

As the bartender walked away, a whiff of a familiar scent tickled her nose. Turning slightly, she caught the gaze of the blonde from the beach as he settled himself onto the stool next to her.

"I didn't get a chance earlier to ask your name."

"Suzanne."

He held out his hand. "I'm Etienne."

Suzanne slid her hand in his, trembling slightly at the heady rush of sensation it evoked. Earlier, standing above her, his body covered in only a pair of form fitting shorts he was delicious. But now, hair still damp from a shower, smelling of shampoo and that exotic scent that was all his own, dressed in a simple light blue button-up shirt that he had left unbuttoned and white pants, he was nothing short of temptation. A temptation she had sworn to resist. Yet with the passion of the music surrounding her, and the pull of it being her last night in paradise, she was ready to give in.

The bartender set her drink down in front of her and discreetly moved away. Suzanne picked it up and took a drink, then asked, "Would you like to go for a walk on the beach?" Uncertain just how to make a pass at him, she settled for a simple excuse for them to leave the crowded bar and be alone, if he was willing. Etienne's blue eyes darkened to a warm, deep indigo.

"Yes." He held out his hand, and she hesitantly clasped it, leaving her mostly full glass sitting on the bar. Leisurely, they strolled down the boardwalk to the beach, pausing to kick off their shoes, before walking in silence down the moonlit strip of milky, white sand.

Suzanne wanted to say something, anything, to let him know what she was feeling, the heady dose of desire that curled within her belly, but she didn't know how. Years of busting her ass working, and neglecting her social life to achieve the career she had dreamed of, had left her woefully inept with men.

Knowing she would never see Etienne again, she settled for action instead of words. Stopping suddenly, she threw her arms around his neck and kissed him, pouring all the passion within her into it.

Instead of pushing her away, Etienne clasped her hips in his hands and pulled her close, responding with equal intensity, until Suzanne couldn't tell who was leading, and who followed. It was a sensual blur of desire.

She wasn't even aware of them dropping to the ground, until the cool sand brushed against the back of her neck. With a soft gasp, she pulled back, uncertainty warring with need.

"Do you want to stop?" Etienne's voice was so husky she trembled in reaction.

"No. I'm just not sure if this is the best place to be doing this."

Suzanne ran her fingers through his thick mane of hair as she debated if it was worth the risk, or if they should head back to one of their rooms.

"Do you want to head back?"

Damn caution and inhibitions. She was in paradise, with a gorgeous, willing man, and she wasn't about to let the moment slip past her. She shook her head, the most minute of movements. "No."

Her fingers tightened their grip in his hair, pulling his head back down to hers. Etienne's lips pressed against her, his tongue delving into her mouth. Suzanne shifted against him, coaxing him to settle on top of her. His hips pressed her down into the sand, the coolness a jarring contrast against the heat of his body.

Suddenly restless, she shifted beneath him, her hips rocking slightly, grinding her groin against his. Etienne responded in kind, slowly thrusting his linen-clad crotch against the flimsy cotton of her skirt. It would have taken her back to those fumbling backseat grind sessions in high school; except for the tender way, Etienne was caressing her, his fingertips drawing small circles on her outer rib cage and thighs.

She slid her hands from his hair and down his chest to his waistband. Grabbing the edge of his shirt she pushed it off his shoulders. Etienne shifted so he could kneel between her spread legs and she could push the shirt all the way off.

Flashing a grin, he gripped the bottom of her top and raised it, slowly baring her stomach and breasts to his view. Suzanne held her breath, waiting for his next move.

He shifted, leaning down to press soft kisses against her stomach. She giggled at the tickling sensation of his whiskers on her skin. In response, he brushed his cheeks against her ribs, first one, then the other, eliciting startled gasps from her. Suzanne didn't know whether to beg him to stop, to coax him to keep going, in the hopes he'd move further down. In the end, she settled for lying breathless beneath him as he slowly teased her, his fingertips dancing against her flesh, drifting up to brush the underside of her breasts, before sliding back down, barely slipping past the waist of her skirt. His mouth moved to her neck, nipping gently on the column of her throat.

Not one to be outdone, she lifted her hands to his chest, caressing the tiny beads of his nipples, tracing the faint vee of hair to where it disappeared in his jeans. She tipped her head to the side and caught his earlobe between her teeth. Drawing it out slowly, she let go, only to capture it again.

"More," she breathed into his ear. Her fingers captured the button on his jeans and slowly worked it free. The rushing of the waves against the shore drowned the rasp of his zipper out as she slowly slid it down.

Etienne pulled back and nipped at the tender skin of her breasts, before wrapping his lips around her nipple. Suzanne arched into his touch, even as she worked to slide his jeans down his ass. Cupping the firm cheeks in her hands, she squeezed, as threads of molten pleasure wove throughout her veins.

"I want to feel all of you," she gasped, her fingers clenched in the silken material of his boxers.

Etienne moved back and stood. While she watched, he pulled off his jeans and boxers. His cock jutted out proudly from the curly patch of hair at his groin, drawing her hungry gaze.

Unconsciously, her fingers traced small circles over her breasts and stomach.

Etienne dropped to his knees between her spread legs. "You're turn."

Suzanne lifted her hips and slid her skirt down her legs, where Etienne pulled it free. He cupped one foot in his hands, and placed a soft kiss along her arch before letting go.

Her fingers returned of their teasing of her stomach. His gaze followed their path. Self conscious, her fingers stilled.

"Non, Suzanne. Don't stop. Enjoy yourself." His hands dropped to his lap, one cupping his balls, while the other slowly stroked his cock.

"There are few taboos between lovers, and this isn't one of them."

A light breeze drifted over them, cooling Suzanne's skin. In the distance, a seagull squawked. Closing her eyes, she gave herself up to the moment. With one hand, she alternated attention between her breasts, while the other leisurely slid down her body.

Her fingertips traced the cleft between her legs, one finger slipping past her flushed lips, delving into her pussy. Drawing it up, she twirled it over her clit, shivering at the tingle it evoked. The faint hairs on Etienne's legs brushed against her inner thighs as he shifted between them, sliding closer. His hands gently pushed her legs wider apart.

Suzanne felt the warm rush of his breath a moment before his lips pressed against her inner thigh.

"Keep going," he whispered.

Her movements slow and steady, Suzanne manipulated her clit, circling it with her fingertip. She gasped as Etienne thrust his tongue past her nether lips, diving into her core.

Suzanne felt wild and wanton as she arched against him. While still teasing her tiny pearl, she brushed her other hand through his hair, guiding him to where she craved his touch.

Etienne thrust his tongue deep, rubbing it along her slick inner walls. He mimicked the thrusting motions of a cock, but it wasn't enough. Suzanne undulated beneath him, seeking deeper contact, whimpering with each breath.

"I need more." Fisting her hand in his hair, she tugged. She opened her eyes and met Etienne's intense gaze. His eyes had deepened with passion, becoming a vibrant indigo, deep enough she could loose herself within them if she wasn't careful.

"More!" Tired of taking a submissive role in her life, Suzanne was determined to give as much as she received, and to live up her wild fling. She moved her hand from her clit to his cock, gripping it firmly.

Etienne grinned at her as he leaned to the side and reached for his jeans. Moonlight glinted off the foil packet as he tore it open and pulled the condom out. Suzanne's gaze followed his motions as he rolled the latex sheath over his cock and shifted to lie on his back.

Suzanne sat up and swung her leg over his hip, straddling him. She leaned down for a kiss as he guided his way past her pussy lips. As he slid into her core, she arched against him, grinding down.

'Sweet Goddess, it felt good,' she thought, as she rocked against him.

The pounding of the waves against the shore set the rhythm, as his hands settled on her hips and guided her into a steady up and down grind against him. She felt exquisitely alive for the first time in a very long time.

Every muscle in her lower body tingled as Etienne's cock pounded into her, his slender hips arching upward with each down stroke of her body. She closed her eyes and embraced the maelstrom he had unleashed within her.

Whimpering with need, she took control. His hands left her hips to cup her breasts as she quickened her pace, driving them both closer to the euphoria they both sought. Her breasts bounced softly in his hands as she worked his cock in and out of her moistness, tightening her pussy with each of his thrusts.

With one hand braced on his chest, she slid the other between them and rubbing her fingers in tiny circles around her clit, eliciting sparks of pleasure. Within her, a volcano of built up needs and desires exploded. Throwing back her head, she screamed into the breeze, as she came.

Suzanne collapsed against Etienne's chest, gasping softly for breath. His hands slid down her body and cupped her ass as he rolled them together, moving her beneath him. Holding her hips tightly, he thrust into her, over and over. Suzanne wrapped her arms around his neck and rocked her hips with each of his thrusts.

Her body quickly built to another explosion. Thrashing beneath him, she climaxed. She could feel her muscles clench him as he thrust into her one last time before collapsing against her. His raspy breaths mingled with hers.

The sound of the waves grew closer as she held him against her, savoring the afterglow. Cold droplets landed against her arches. The next rush, water brushed slightly against her feet. With the next, her ankles were wet.

She giggled as Etienne burst into laughter. Hurriedly they stood and dressed. She wasn't sure what to expect from him. Would he pull away? Or did he want to spend more time with her?

It was always the 'after' worries that had dissuaded her from flings, which was all her chaotic schedule would allow. Yet he didn't have to say anything to settle her fears. His warm hand clasping hers said it all.

* * *

When Suzanne woke, she opened her eyes to find a hibiscus, fresh from the garden outside her cottage lying on the pillow next to her. A drop of dew still clung to its petals. Next to it was a simple invitation – a card with an email address.

Feeling more carefree than she had in years, she climbed out of bed and moved about the room, gathering her things before pausing next to the bed. Carefully she picked up the card and slid it into her wallet.

A NIGHT OF FRENCH PASSION

"So you really want to learn to speak French huh?" I looked across the table at him, noting the mischievous sparkle to his eyes.

"Yes."

"How badly do you want to learn?"

"Very badly," I purred, almost able to predict what would come next.

"Bad enough to be totally submissive tonight? To let me truly love you as you should be loved."

As a take-charge kind of person, I could never bring myself to be fully submissive, to let him pamper me as he wanted to. I knew he wanted to try it, but I could never seem to work up the nerve to be totally submissive to anyone. It just wasn't in my nature. I wasn't used to anyone taking care of me.

"Yes." I replied, figuring what the hell. I had taken French before in school. What was one night of submission and pampering, to learn a language? He certainly had his work cut out for him, with me as a student. I could give him one night and a fantasy in exchange.

"Oui."

"Pardon?" I asked, lost at what he had said.

"Say, Oui. It means yes. And excuse-moi means pardon me."

"Oh, yeah I remember that. Oui, I want to learn French."

* * *

After arriving home from dinner, I was uncertain what he would expect me to do. As soon as the front door closed, he clasped my shoulders in his hands, his body pressing against my back. Nuzzling against my neck, he pushed my head to the side and nipped my neck. "Cou," he whispered, "the word cou means neck."

"Cou," I repeated, my accent a bit off. He slid his hands down my arms and back up, causing shivers to trickle down my spine. I leaned against him, settling my weight against his body, feeling his heat against my back.

Nibbling his way up my neck, he caressed my body through my dress. His hands, so knowledgeable of my desires, weaved their way down the front of my body, his knuckles brushing against my hardened nipples, his fingertips pressing lightly against my mound through the silken material. Moving his hands to my hair, he gathered it in his strong hands and lifted it atop my head. Nipping the back of my neck as he slid down my zipper, he whispered, "Cheveux. Hair."

Repeating the word, I trembled as his breath whispered across my sensitive neck.

Lifting my hands to my hair, I held it as he gently slid the silken dress off of my shoulders. Caressing the smooth skin, he kissed my left shoulder. "Epaule, Shoulder."

Trembling, I repeated after him. Already the urge to turn in his arms and kiss him was growing. This is his night, I reminded myself, his night to pamper and to play.

Sliding the dress from my body, he came to kneel in front of me. Lifting first one foot, then the other, he removed the pool of silken material, and rose. Gently grasping my hips, he pulled me against his suit-clad body. I felt silly and rather exposed standing in the hallway wearing nothing but my lingerie.

Leaning down he kissed me, and as my body curled to his, I forgot everything else. I loved the way his lips claimed mine, the heat of his tongue sliding past my lips and into my mouth to mate with my tongue.

"Kiss," he whispered nibbling on my lips. "Baiser. To kiss is faire baiser."

Whispering his lips over my cheek, he continued to weave his spell around me, teasing me with the lilt to his voice as his voice deepened with each French translation.

Sweeping me into his arms, he carried me to the bedroom, and by the time he laid me down on the silk sheets, I was ready to admit that I enjoyed the way he was making me feel. Carefully he removed my panties and bra, leaving me in a garter belt and stalking. Standing back, he slowly removed all of his clothes, teasing me with the flesh I longed to explore. Few things gave me more pleasure then to run my hands over his heated flesh, to feel his body trembled with each touch.

Moving to kneel on the bed, he gently parted my black silk clad thighs, and settled his weight between them, his cock resting near, but teasingly far away.

"Breast," he explained, cupping my small breasts in his hands, "Do you know love, that the French believe that a woman's breast should fill a champagne glass, no more, no less. They think that the nipple should be small, and sit centered on the breast. Looking at your breasts mon amour, I very much agree. Perfection." Sucking one of my hardened nipples into his mouth, he bite down and with a gasp, I arched into his touch, craving more. He knew just where to touch to please me.

"Nipple," he murmured, "Mamelon." Working his way down my stomach, he whispered the words for parts of my flesh, from breast to stomach, navel to pussy. Caressing my bare mound, he looked up at me and smiled. My breathing already heavy from his loving I gasped, sure of what he was about to do. Lowering his head, he flicked my clit with his tongue, and then sucked it slowly into his mouth.

With a moan, I thrust my hips against his mouth, desperate for more. Threading my fingers through his hair, I tried to pull him up to me, to convince him to thrust his cock into me.

Grasping my wrists, he pulled away.

"No." Moving over my body, he placed my hands behind my head. "They are to stay there." Locking my fingers, I vaguely wondered how I would manage that.

Moving back down my body, he took his sweet time, trailing kisses over my breasts and stomach and stopping to dip his tongue into my navel.

Arriving back at my quivering pussy, he gently parted the lips, and pressed a kiss to my center. "I think I love this most, mon amour, this part of you. So soft, so fragrant, and only for me. I love knowing that I was your first, your only lover. That your flesh knows my touch so well, that just a kiss to your shoulder causes your sweet pussy to drip its essence, craving to be filled with my cock."

I moaned at his words. Normally he talked a bit sexy to me, but never with the thread of possession to his voice. In that instant, my body knew it was his, intimately, and would always be.

Tonguing my clit, he had me gasping to be made love to, but still he continued his sweet teasing.

"Sweet God, " I gasped, my orgasm so close, yet impossible to reach. I had totally surpassed my normal frustration threshold. By now I would have pulled him up my body, wrapped my long legs around his back and thrust his cock into my aching pussy.

"Please," I begged and corrected to s'il te plait at his instruction. "Jesus, mon amour."

Flicking my clit one last time, he caused my body to tremble, every nerve alive to his touch. Sliding up my body, his hard nipples rubbed against my stomach, then against my breasts as his weight pressed me into the mattress. As always, the sprinkle of hair on his chest teased my sensitive nipples as he covered me in his familiar and loved weight. Bending my knees, I wrapped my legs about his waist, rubbing my pussy against his cock, wetting it with my leaking essence.

"S'il te plait," I begged. Grinning, he pressed a kiss to my lips and gently grasped my hips, lifting me against him. His cock slid in but an inch, just enough to tease my quivering flesh.

"Do you want more?" he asked, his voice whispering through my soul. God, how I love his voice when it's hoarse with restrained passion.

"Yes," I breathed, the sound so faint I wasn't sure he heard me.

"Then say it."

"I want you."

"No mon amour, say, Je veux ton bitte dans moi. Je veux que tu me remplisse."

Whispering the words, I had an idea of what they meant. They were words I couldn't say, not in English. As soon as the last syllable left my lips, he thrust deep inside of me. It felt so incredible, after all of his teasing, to feel his cock where I ached for him. Clenching tight, I felt his cock slip from me, only to return again.

Arching against him, my body begged for his passion, his domination. For once I wanted to be taken, to be claimed, to fully be his.

Pumping his cock into me, he claimed my body and my soul in the way man had for millions of years, through gentle, sensual domination.

I could feel my body blooming under his, my pussy growing wetter than normal, my nipples so hard against his chest. Every sense was truly alive like never before.

As my orgasm built, I couldn't believe how incredible it was. Hearing him whisper sweet French words, words which I had no idea their meaning - hot words, sex words - my mind whirled.

Clenching him tight, I kept my word. I fisted my hands in the sheet under my head as his body pumped into mine, the velvety hardness of his cock caressing every sensitive inch of my pussy.

Waves of pressure built and the stars started to shine behind my eyes.

"Oh god, baby, I'm going to come," I whispered, my voice deep with passion.

"Michele, mon amour," he whispered, "come for me, Baby, come for me."

Moaning his name, I came. His hands held my hips still for his thrusts, I was unable to do anything more than ride the wave of our passion and clench my body tight.

I felt his body tightening over me, his hands gripping my hips. I knew I would have slight bruises, but I didn't care, it felt too good to feel his body moving over mine, into mine. As he climaxes the hot flow of his come filled my pussy, mixing with my juices.

Collapsing on top of me, his lips lightly kissed my neck, his breath a sweet seduction against my skin.

Carefully rolling, he pulled me with him, so that he was lying on his back, my body stretched out over him, his soft cock still cradled against my mound.

His hands caressed my back and my hair, gently running through the auburn strands.

"Thank you," he whispered.

"Mmmm, merci beaucoup, mon amour." I replied.

A SOFTER KIND OF LOVE

Holding his daughter in his arms, Brandon looked down at her sleeping face, the pure angelic aura of her tiny form. Looking up, his eyes met his wife's and a love more powerful that the sun melted into his eyes. Smiling, Naomi reached down and gently removed their daughter from her husband's arms and laid her in her crib.

Feeling Brandon press against her back, she melted against him, as always the feeling of his arms around her a welcome comfort.

"Come on love, let's get you to bed," he whispered, softly guiding Naomi to their bedroom and into their warm bed. Holding her in his arms, he marveled at the changes a few years had brought to his life. First he had found the love of his life and now, a second female, his newborn daughter, had stolen his heart.

Pulling Naomi against his chest, Brandon listened as her breathing eased into the soft rhythms of sleep. Closing his eyes, he drifted off.

* * *

Several hours later, a whimpered cry woke Brandon up. Carefully pulling his arm from under Naomi's head, he climbed from the bed and padded silently down the hall to take care of their daughter. After caring for her, he gently rubbed her back until she fell asleep again, and then with a yawn, headed back into the bedroom.

Lying down, he spooned against Naomi and bit back a moan as she shifted against him in her sleep. Wrapping his arm around her waist, he pulled her against him hoping that her movements would still.

They didn't. Grinding against his groin, her petite ass soon had him rock hard. Knowing he wouldn't get back to sleep until she stopped shifting, Brandon slowly slid his hand down her ribs and stomach to the curve of her pelvis. Gliding his fingers down her smooth skin, he tenderly cupped her pussy. Wetness coated his palm as he gently rubbed it against her lips.

A soft moan whispered through the stillness of the room. Brandon smoothed Naomi's hair from her neck and placed soft kisses on her tender skin as his fingers gently caressed her swollen lips and throbbing clit.

Grinding back against him, Naomi couldn't hold back her gasp as his cock slid between the cheeks of her ass and rubbed against her.

"You're awake, aren't you?" Brandon whispered.

"Yes. I woke up when you left the bed."

Shifting her hips, Naomi caused his cock to brush against her lips, and a shiver to trail down her spine. "Mmmm, I have missed this so much."

Arching into his touch, Naomi purred as his fingers rubbed small circles over her clit, teasing her body into awareness.

Brandon rubbed his cock against the cleft of her ass, the soft skin smooth against the ridges of his flesh. Sliding against her, he allowed the tip of his cock to rub gently against her lips.

Naomi moaned as the tip of his cock slid into her aching pussy, teasing her with its hardness. Pushing back against him, she tilted her hips, his cock sliding in another inch.

"Please," she moaned, needing to feel his cock filling her. After months of pregnancy-forced abstinence, she was about to climb walls without his tender touch.

"Are you sure you're ready?" Brandon could feel the seductive pull of her pussy already dragging him in deeper. Her hair whispered across his chest and shoulders as she nodded.

"God, yes!" Naomi exclaimed softly as he pushed gently against her. Grinding her hips against him, she moaned as his fingers rubbed her clit a bit faster, sending sparks of remembered pleasure through her body.

Pumping his hips softly against her, he slid in and out of her wet heat, groaning as she clenched him, teasing his cock with every stroke.

"Jesus, baby, you feel so good," he whispered against her shoulder. Naomi trembled in his arms as she came softly, her pussy clenching him tightly.

Pumping his hips a bit faster, Brandon felt his balls lightly slap against her ass as he felt her orgasm around him. He held her close, as he worked his fingers over her clit, keeping her in the hazy clouds of sexual euphoria. Moments passed, as her gasping moans filled his ears with their sweet sound.

His balls began to tingle and Brandon knew he would soon come. Kissing her neck and shoulder, he placed little love bites along her flesh as he orgasmed, his groan music to Naomi's ears. Arching back against him, she welcomed the hot jets of his passion into her body.

In the stillness of the night, the two held each other as the haze of passion faded and their bodies grew tired and lethargic in the afterglow of desire.

"I love you so much," Brandon whispered into Naomi's ear as she snuggled back against him, his softened cock nestled in the cleft of her ass.

"I love you too," she responded. Moments later, his soft breathing teased her ears as she surrendered to Morpheus.

A TASTE OF HEAVEN

He checked in by himself. That in its self wasn't enough to intrigue me. The fact that he was tall, dark haired and handsome added to him being alone was. The other clerk, Beth, had to run to the bathroom, so it was my luck to be at the front desk, when he asked for a room. He wasn't picky, which was good, since we only had one room left. Valentine's day seemed to be a busy time for us, of which we all were glad.

"We only have the one room left sir. Room ten, right down the hall."

"That we be fine, and please, call me Seth," he answered softly. I handed him the sign in log and took his credit card and finished the forms.

"Everything is all set." I grabbed the room key and headed around the desk and moved to pick up his bag, but he was quicker.

"I can get it, if you'll just show me which way to go." I nodded and moved ahead of him. Opening the door to his room, I stepped inside and turned to face him. "I'm Dakota. If there is anything you need, just ask."

He smiled, but his eyes were sad. "I'll do that. Thank you Dakota." I smiled again and left. As I walked away, I felt funny, almost as if I shouldn't be leaving, that I was passing up something in my life. Shaking it off, I continued about my work.

* * *

Later, I was rushing about in the kitchen, grabbing plates of food and putting them on my tray. The dinner rush had hit and we all were feeling it hard. Some wished to dine in their room or cabin and other chose to dine in the dining room. Getting all of their orders prepared and to them within a reasonable time was straining us all. After dropping my second plate, I grew rather frustrated.

My boss patted my shoulder and told me to take a break. Sighing I looked at her to apologize. "It's ok Dakota. You're still trying to get the hang of this. The rest of us have already dealt with Christmas and New Year's so we are old hands at it.

"Just go sit down for a little while. Relax, and calm down. It will be ok." Turning to her trusty cook, she helped him fix another plate for the diner whose food was all over the floor. Another waitress was cleaning up the mess as I left.

Sitting down at the one empty table in the dinning room, I sighed. I enjoyed my job and I didn't want to loose it. It was fun work and I got to meet interesting people.

At that moment, Seth entered the room and looked around. He headed towards me, and I got up to let him have the table.

"Please, don't get up. I could use some company." I sat back down and scooted over so he could sit next to me. The curved couch was roomy, but he still ended up pressed against my side. His long legs stretched out under him, his left leg pressed against the length of my right one.

"I can't stay long. I'm on a break."

"You look like it has been a rough day." I nodded and sighed again.

"Sometimes it helps to talk about it."

"Oh, I wouldn't want to bother you." He grinned and placed his hand over mine.

"Sometimes, it helps to hear about other people's days. It helps keep me grounded."

"What do you mean?" I glanced at him, noticing the shadows under his eyes. He looked tired and almost, depressed.

"Life hasn't been all it is dreamed to be the last year. Sometimes, I get so stuck in my own misery, I forget that the world goes on. If you tell me about your day, it will help."

The heat of his hand over mine was nice, and comforting. As I told him about the last hour, I felt almost like it wasn't so bad.

My boss peeked her head out of the kitchen and I looked at Seth again. "I need to get back to work. I'm sorry, but we are really busy, and ..."

"I understand." Standing, I asked him what he wanted for dinner.

"Something simple, a burger and fries or chicken. I'm not real hungry."

"Ok. I'll have it out to you soon."

As I turned to leave, he whispered my name. It was so faint; I almost thought I imagined it. "Dakota, what time do you get off of work?"

"In about an hour. Why?"

"Would you meet me in the game room? I could use some company, if you want to that is." I grinned and assured him I didn't mind.

"I'll be there in about an hour."

* * *

The next hour passed in a blur of motion. I seemed to have regained my footing and a co-worker even stopped me to comment on my grin. Until then, I wasn't aware that I had even been grinning.

After clocking out, I went into the bathroom and changed clothes, then grabbed my bag and headed for the game room.

Opening the door, I immediately noticed Seth leaning over the table to take a shot at the eight ball. I took a moment to admire the lines of his body then closed the door after he sank the ball.

"Hi," he whispered.

"Hi."

"How was the rest of your shift?"

"Good," dragging a chair over to the pool table, I sat down and sighed. It felt so good to rest for a while.

He lined up another shot, and sank the nine ball, ending his game. Pulling out the other chair, he sat down and faced me, his deep blue eyes shrouded with thoughts I could only guess at.

"So ..." I said, not one to like long silences.

He grinned and covered my hand with his again. Giving it a quick squeeze, he pulled away.

"Thank you Dakota."

"For what?" I had an idea what he meant, but I wanted it to be clear.

"For being here. For taking some time, and keeping me company. Hell, just for smiling. It has been so long since I have seen a woman smile at me." His voice dropped as he continued.

"My wife died a year ago. We were coming back from a romantic night on the town. Money was tight, so we weren't able to get away like we wanted, so we settled for dinner, when all I wanted was to give her the stars.

"Another car slid on a patch of ice and slammed into her side of the car. She died on the way to the hospital. I was knocked unconscious, temporarily and woke up to the ambulance staff loading her into their rig. I never got a chance to say goodbye."

Tears slid down my face as he told of his wife's death. His own eyes misted, as he raised a hand to wipe the tears from my checks.

"She wouldn't want you to cry. She loved to make people laugh. She loved to laugh, hell, she just loved; life, children, snowflakes, and kittens, it didn't matter. She was so full of love. It didn't matter than I couldn't provide much for her, all that mattered was that she loved me."

He fell silent, and I wasn't sure what to say. I'm sorry seemed so trite, compared to what he had lost, so I said nothing.

"I'm sorry Dakota. I didn't mean to make you cry."

"It's ok," I whispered back. He slid his hand over mine again and curled his fingers around my palm.

* * *

We sat like that for a while, in silence, just holding hands. It felt peaceful.

"I should let you get home." He finally spoke.

I nodded, but inside, I didn't want to leave. Something about this man drew me to him, and I wanted to comfort him, in any way I could.

"Yes, I could leave or ..."

"Or?"

"Or, you could invite me stay with you. I have tomorrow off and no one will wonder where I am." He smiled gently, some of the shadows leaving his blue eyes.

"I don't want you to do anything you don't want to."

"I won't." Standing up, I leaned down and kissed him. It was just the touching of lips, but it was incredible. He slid a hand in my hair, and wrapped his other arm around my waist. Needing to deepen the kiss, I pressed my tongue against his lips and as he opened them, rubbed it against his.

The door opened and two women came in, giggling to each other. I pulled away from Seth.

"Oh, sorry, we didn't know anyone was in here."

Seth stood and said, "It's ok. We were just leaving." Clasping my hand in his, he led the way to his room. Closing the door behind us, he stepped away.

"Dakota, I didn't intend …"

I moved towards him, wrapped my arms around his waist. "I know. Neither did I, but life gives us so few precious moments. This is one of them for me." Seth leaned down and kissed me. Moving backwards, we tumbled onto the bed, our lips still joined.

Pulling away, he whispered, "I want to make love to you, but I don't know if I should. I came here to celebrate the memory of my wife."

Tears fell from my eyes as I looked at his beautiful face. Raw passion mixed with sadness in the depths of his blue eyes. He was obviously struggling, as was I. I had felt so alone for so long, and with him, I didn't feel that way. I wanted him in my life; even if could only be for one night.

"Would she have wanted you to move on, to find what happiness you could?"

"Yes," he whispered, his words chocked with tears, "her last words to the EMT were for me to love again, to find happiness. She didn't want me to be lonely."

Leaning down, I licked the salty trails of tears on his cheeks, and then lightly kissed his lips. "Is this what you want? I'll stay, and we can just hold each other and talk if that is what you want."

Groaning like a man tortured, he wrapped his arms around me, wrapping one hand in my blond locks of hair. "I want this…" he whispered, then kissed me. Every emotion he was feeling poured into that kiss. I moved my hands to his chest and began unbuttoning his shirt. His hands followed suit and soon we were bare breast to bare chest. The sprinkling of hair on his chest tickled my nipples as I rubbed against him.

"Stand up for a minute." I crawled off of him and stood. Seth scooted to the edge of the bed and sat up. He removed his shoes and stood. My eyes locked on his hands, and watched every motion as he unzipped his slacks and slid them down his toned hips. The man was in a word, gorgeous. Carefully, he leaned down and unbuttoned my jeans. Kissing my stomach, he slid them form my hips and then flicked his tongue against the top of my hip. Moaning, I slid my hand sin his hand and shifted slightly. I wanted him, more than anyone else in my life.

Grabbing the material of my panties in his teeth, he pulled then down my thighs, then slid his hands into the band to move them down my legs. I parted my legs as he removed my panties, giving him space for him to nudge against my inner thighs, and lick against my pussy lips. My hands fisted in this hair. Seth slid off of the bed and pulled back. My legs barely felt like they would hold me.

"Sit on the edge of the bed love," he whispered. With his help, I moved around him and climbed onto the bed. His hand lightly pushed against my chest, pushing me onto my back. His head dipped and I gasped, waiting for his touch. The warmth of his tongue settled against my pussy lips again. Flicking my clit, he soon had me gasping and begging for more. It felt so good.

Sooner than I would have thought possible, I was arching my hips and clenching my inner muscles, enjoying the rush of pleasure that accompanied my orgasm.

Seth flicked my clit one last time and stood. He grasped my hips and helped me to side further back on the bed. Then the hard warmth of his body covered mine. Tan, well toned, his body was a study in contrasts from my pale, soft flesh.

Seth rolled us over and I wound up on top of him. Grinning, I pulled my legs up so that I straddled him and slowly lowered myself onto his pulsing cock. Seth lifted his hips and thrust deeper inside of me. I was filled with the hard warmth of his cock. Rocking my hips, I started a rhythm that soon had up breathing hard and gasping for more. Seth looked so sexy lying under me, his eyes closed.

I twirled my hips as I lowered myself onto him. His eyes opened and locked on mine. Seth stared running his hands over my body, pinching my nipples softly, caressing my hips and stomach; doing every thing he could to drive me crazy.

"Dakota, baby, I'm sorry. It has been so long ... I can't ..."

Moving a hand between us, I started rubbing it against the sensitive nub of my clit. Seth continued to thrust against me, sweat glistening on his skin.

Moaning, I threw back my head and gave way to the passion rising in my body. Seth soon joined me in orgasm, his body tightening under mine.

Collapsing on his chest, I struggled to regain my breath. Seth shifted me to his side, and pulled the covers over us. Cuddling, I felt the dampness of my tears against his chest.

"Shhh, don't cry," he whispered.

"I'm trying not to, but ..."

"I know." He held me against him and we drifted off to sleep, wrapped in each other's arms.

* * *

He extended his stay, and we enjoyed a week of each other's company. When knew it couldn't last, but neither of us was in a hurry for it to be over.

I was scheduled for only short shifts, so we were able to enjoy many of the comforts of being away form the city. Long hikes offered plenty of chances to make love. And we did, calling out of ecstasy into the wind.

The night before Seth was to leave, we stayed together, cuddling in his bed, neither of us saying much, just holding on tight until finally we drifted off to sleep.

The next morning, I woke to find Seth awake, his blue eyes filled with tears. "I have to go," he whispered, his voice once again chocked with emotion. I could feel my heart breaking, but I knew it had to be.

"Dakota, I ..."

I placed a finger over his lips and shushed him. "Just kiss me goodbye and close your eyes. Don't open them until you hear the door close." Leaning down, I kissed him, the sweetest, most tender kiss of my life. Pulling away, I saw his eyes were closed. As quickly as I could, I gathered my clothes and dressed. As I closed the door behind me, I let the tears fall freely. Something inside of me cried out for me to ask him to stay, but I couldn't. As I walked away from the door, I felt a sense of loss. I knew it would be a long time before it faded into a distant memory.

A TEASE AND A TASTE

There was something so incredible about watching him slowly stroke his cock. The way the purplish head disappeared into his strong fist, then peeked over the top, winking at me.

His eyes closed and his head tipped back, the strong cords of his neck standing out with every breath he took. It was incredible, the way his body was perfect in the early morning light, the arch of his feet as he leaned back in his chair, the curve of his hip blending into his ass.

It was torture watching him, but so delicious a torment. I wanted him so much, but I wanted to watch every second of his pleasure. The slightest part of his lips as he gasped for air. The tiny jerks of his hips, driving his cock into his fisted hand. The way he cupped his balls, massaging the firm sac in his hand as he stroked faster and harder.

His groans filled the stillness of the room.

I wanted him, needed him. But it was too soon.

Over and over his cockhead winked at me, precome glistening in the morning light. The urge to taste him, to feel his come sliding down my throat, was strong, but I waited … breathless for him to tell me to. Hands fisted at my sides, I waited.

"Oh fuck, lover, I'm gonna come."

At last. I watched as his hands quaked, sliding up and down his hard cock almost in a blur of motion. His hips rocked in the chair, its leather surface creaking at the force of his motions.

"Now, baby. Now," he gasped. Pulling his hands away, he sat still, his hands clenched, and beads of sweat dripping from his forehead.

It took all my will power to pull my fingers from their dance over my sobbing clit, to stop the gentle thrusting into my dripping pussy. Legs trembling, I moved to his side and waited.

Carefully, he stood and pushed me forward into the chair. Kneeling, I grasped the back and arched forward, offering myself to him.

Grasping his cock, he guided it carefully to my weeping pussy and slid forward, impaling me on his cock. The tightness of my pussy swallowed him and for a moment I was dizzy with the intensity of his thrust.

Smacking my ass, he growled, "Relax, damn it. I want to make this last."

Slowly, he began to thrust in and out, teasing me with his cock.

Sliding my hands down my body, I started playing with my aching clit again, almost faint with need.

"Oh yes," I muttered.

Pumping his hips harder, he slid all of his length into my pussy, the velvety flesh hard and deep within me.

Rocking my hips, I worked myself with him, matching his rhythm. I wanted badly to see where out flesh joined. It always amazed me how perfect it was, the contrast of pinks and purples where our flesh joined.

"Harder," I gasped, demanding more.

Grinding his hips against the soft flesh of my ass, he worked his cock in and out of my pussy, his groans once again filling the room. The rhythm of our bodies had the chair creaking beneath our weight and motion. Smacking my ass slightly, he gasped as I suddenly clenched tight, the feeling more intense than before.

"YES! Smack my ass, baby. It feels so fucking incredible."

As he slapped my ass again, I bit back a moan.

Soon flowing into a rhythm, he thrust hard against me, then pulled out a bit, smacking his hand over my reddening flesh as he slid in. The dual sensation was intoxicating. I never wanted it to end, but I knew that soon it would.

Pumping harder into me, he worked us both into a state of blind lust. We didn't care about anything but fucking each other into mindless oblivion.

I could feel him gripping the firm leather of the armrests. Slick with his sweat and precome, I could only image how it felt, wet and warm, against his hands.

Arching forward against his thrusts, I rocked back with each withdrawal, forcing him to take me harder and harder, pumping as fast and hard as he could. I knew I was going to be sore, but I didn't care. I wanted him. I needed to fill his pussy with my come.

His hand landed again. The sound of flesh meeting flesh was barely muted by our moans. *Smack. Thrust. Smack. Thrust.* It was a steady rhythm, older than time, but still intense.

I felt my pussy clench, and knew it was almost over. He was drawing it out as long as he could, but I knew it was almost over, for us both. He thrust hand and I saw stars. Thrusting deep, he ground his hips against my ass as I came.

Groaning in my ear, he pulled back, then slammed hard against me, trembling against me. Grinding my hips against him, I felt the moment he came. His whole body tightened against mine, then suddenly went limp. I could feel warm jets of come filling me, leaking down our flesh, coating us both with the sticky essence of our passion.

Collapsing against my back, he lay there for a few moments, gasping for breath.

"Damn, baby," he whispered, "that was ... oh god, that was ... incredible."

"Mmmm," I murmured. "You are such a delightful tease."

ASSUME THE POSITION

"You have the right to remain silent."

The click of the cuffs around her wrists made Heather jump. Wiggling her hands, she grimaced in what appeared to be discomfort. The cuffs were tight enough to hold her wrists securely, but loose enough to still be comfortable. Officer Shane Davis smiled at her movements and stepped closer, pressing his hard body against her silk clad form.

"Anything you say and do can be held against you."

Thrilled at having the tall brunette within his power, he shifted against her, rubbing his groin against the softness of her ass.

"Officer, please, I didn't do anything wrong."

"That's what they all say. Just once it would be nice to hear someone accept responsibility for their actions."

Shifting his hips again, he had to bite back a moan of appreciation as the woman before him instinctively responded to his touch; her legs parted slightly, unconsciously forming a cradle for his firm body.

It wasn't in their script for him to go easy on her yet. Forcing himself to play his role to the fullest, despite the temptation of his wife in a silk negligee and handcuffs, he stepped back, temporarily regaining control of his racing libido.

"What am I being charged with?" Heather's voice trembled.

Shane gently grasped her elbow and turned her to face him, then pushed her back against the bed, forcing her to sit down.

"Indecent exposure. Running around with your perky tits barely covered and your ass hanging out of a thong, is by law, indecent, although I must admit off the record," Shane took a deep breath. "- it's also an incredible turn on."

Stepping back to admire his collar, he smiled. "We can come to an agreement though. Maybe time off for good behavior. I get to see and explore what's under that bit of black silk, and you get off. Without going to jail, I mean." His hands fiddled with the zipper of his pants as he waited. "So, what is it going to be? Jail, or me?"

Shane watched as his wife's eyes twinkled. Despite the effort she put into playing the helpless victim, she couldn't contain her delight at their newest game. He knew the crotch of her panties would be was soaked with her juices.

"I can't go to jail officer, I just can't." Her beautiful mouth turned down in a pout even as her eyes sparkled with enjoyment. "If I have your word that after we're through you'll let me go, without charges, then I'll do what ever you want."

Her full lips trembled; lust packed a punch to his gut as Shane anticipated the next step their game would take.

"Prove it then. Drop to your knees."

After a moment's hesitation, Heather stood and slowly dropped to her knees, Shane's hands held her shoulders to steady her. As she settled herself on the plush carpet, his hands moved to his zipper and the sound of the metal teeth scraping together mingled with her small whispery breaths.

Biting back a moan as his hand grasped his cock, Shane slipped it free of his uniform. He watched Heather lick her lips, anticipation lighting up her face. He knew she wanted to wrap her lips around his cock as much, if not more, than he wanted her to. His sweet wife simply loved to give head.

"Suck my cock."

Leaning forward, her lips pressed a soft kiss against his tip, and then parted to slip over his cock. Sliding down the length, she bobbed back and forth, alternating her depth and suction, slowly teasing him.

Fisting his hands in her hair, Shane forced her head still and thrust his hips, driving his cock deep, then pulling back. The sweet sounds of her wet mouth milking him barely masked his own harsh breathing. Over and over, he worked his cock into her mouth, her wet heat as tantalizing as her clenching pussy.

His eyes locked on his wife's soft blues ones, Shane nodded his head moments before he climaxed. His warm come flooded her mouth as she worked to swallow it all. Despite her efforts, small dribbles of his essence leaked from the corner of her mouth, tiny pearls that glistened in the room's soft lighting.

"Damn baby," he muttered, so wrapped up in his enjoyment of her sensual gift he momentarily forgot his role. His watched as her pink tongue peaked out and licked at the remnants of his passion.

"Am I free to go?"

Subtly reminded of his role, Shane reached down, slid his softening cock back into his pants, and zipped up.

"Not yet. First, I think a small punishment is in order, to keep you from repeating your offense. Stand up."

He bent down slightly and again gripped her elbow, assisting her in standing up again. "Lay face down on the bed and hold still. Grip your hands together tight."

With his assistance, his wife was soon prone on their king sized bed, her smooth skin barely covered by the edges of the lace and silk nightgown she wore. Gripping the edge of the lingerie, he flipped it up, exposing the band of her thong and her cream colored cheeks. Hidden between her pert globes was the strap of the g-string.

Shane moved to his dresser and grabbed a wide leather belt from a drawer. Folding it in half, he snapped it and watched as Heather trembled. They had played with spankings before, but he had plans for a new addition. Since he had graduated from the police academy, Heather had hinted about the games they could play with his new equipment. His uniform belt and handcuffs were only a few items she had admitted to fantasizing about.

Lightly, he tapped the belt against his wife's ass and grinned as she wriggled and moaned. Swinging it slightly harder, he smacked her tender ass again, leaving a bright pink stripe to her cheek.

Again, he stroked her gently with the leather, following with a harder stroke. Continuously, he teased her, as she had teased him with her fantasies. Light touches, then hard strokes. Her gasps filled the room, but he kept up his sensual play until she begged him to quit teasing.

Tossing the belt aside, he slid his foot between his wife's legs and parted her thighs. Shifting, he pushed harder, until she was spread out wide for him, her pussy lips parted by the material of her thong. Shane knew that with each lurch and shift of her hips, the thong had wedged tighter and tighter against her throbbing clit, teasing her quivering flesh. Reaching down, he grabbed to band and pulled gently, stripping the thong from her, leaving her in only a wispy bit of silk.

Stepping back, he stared at her in the sprawled position and groaned to himself. He again moved to the dresser, this time to return with a newly purchased nightstick. Tossing the nightstick on the bed, so that it lay next to his wife's head, he bit back a chuckle when her eyes widened.

"Um, Shane ..."

Using his freed hand, he delivered a stinging smack to her tender ass-cheeks. "That's Officer Davis to you. Be a good girl and take your punishment. Just remember, we can put this on the record at any time. Just say the word and it all stops."

She nodded, then fell back into her role. Whimpering softly, Heather closed her eyes. The sides of her face were flushed and small beads of sweat glistened on her shoulders.

Standing behind her, with her tantalizing flesh bared to his gaze, he couldn't help the impulse that guided him to his knees behind her. Sticking out his tongue, he lapped at her glistening lips. Wiggling his tongue against her, he soon had her squirming and gasping, her body on the edge of orgasm. After blowing softly against her pussy lips, he pulled back and stood. He watched for a few minutes as his wife writhed in sexual frustration before he reached down and grabbed their newest toy.

Holding the black rod by the grip, he slowly stroked it against Heather's pussy lips, but found in her position he couldn't drive it deep within her.

"I'm going to release your hands and roll you over. Don't try anything cute." After setting the nightstick aside again, Shane stretched out over his wife's trembling body. He could tell by how she undulated beneath him the extent of her arousal. She was ready to come unhinged at any moment. He hurriedly removed the cuffs from her hands and crawled back. Gripping her thighs, he helped her to flip over, then stretched out over her again and pulled her hands over her head. Cuffing them together again, he pulled back, making sure to grind his hips against her bare pussy.

Heather's head tossed from side to side and her hands fisted in the air above her. Watching her sensuous movements, Shane's cock stirred to life again.

Remembering that this was Heather's fantasy, he forced himself to grip the nightstick again and press it against his wife's slick nether lips. Pushing firmly, but gently, he watched as the first half inch slipped into her core. Applying more pressure, another inch slipped in, then a bit more, until she had six inches of his weapon buried within her. Pulling back slightly, he thrust it in again. Her hips arched off the bed, allowing another inch to sink within her.

As he manipulated his nightstick within his wife's drenched feminine flesh, he couldn't help but grow fully hard again. One handed, he unzipped is pants and freed his cock. Rubbing his hand over his leaking slit, he slid it down his cock and stroked himself in time to the thrusts of his stick. All the while, he drove the black rod into his wife's pussy.

Heather's moans and gasps echoed off the walls as his manipulations drove her closer to the edge. Forgetting their roles, Shane didn't stop her as she brought her hands down to her pussy and started to play with her clit. He loved watching her touch herself; although this time it was made all the more erotic by the silver metal holding her wrists together.

Her fingers a blur of motion, she arched and tightened, a silent scream forming on her lips. Driving the nightstick a bit deeper, he watched as her eyes closed and her head flopped back. Her entire body trembled, as little mewling sounds passed her lips.

Slipping the nightstick free, he tossed it aside. About to orgasm himself, Shane leaned down and grabbed the silver shackles, forcing Heather's arms over her head again. His free hand stopped stroking and guided his cock into her welcoming heat. Thrusting deep, he groaned as she clenched tight around him. Her legs wrapped around his waist, holding him prisoner against her.

Pulling back slightly, Shane thrust deeper, burying himself to the hilt in his wife. Already at the edge of his control, he pounded into her, driving deep then pulling back. Her body clenched him, then released him, only to draw him in deeply again.

Beneath him, Heather sobbed out her passion, her gasping demands growing more urgent. He could feel her climax building again. Determined to join her, Shane flexed his hips and quickened his pace.

Heather's grunts turned into a keening scream as her body convulsed in orgasm beneath him. Her legs tightened, holding him against her as her wet heat clenched around his cock.

His balls tight, Shane tossed back his head and groaned as his orgasm rushed through him. A hot jet of come flooded into his wife's pussy, followed by several others, until she milked the last drop of his climax from his shaft.

Collapsing against her, Shane fought to control his harsh breathing. He vaguely heard a soft clink of metal against metal, then felt Heather's freed hands caressing his back, soothing him. Sweaty and sticky, but without the energy to move, Shane lay there for a few more moments before rolling to the side and pulling his wife's sated body against his.

"God I love you baby," he whispered as his hands caressed her hair, smoothing the tangled tresses from her face.

"Mmmm," she murmured, "I love you too."

Cuddling his wife close, Shane mentally sorted through the fantasies they had already acted out, and those they had yet to fulfill. While each fantasy was wonderful and sexy in its own way, he had a sneaking feeling that seeing his wife impaled on his nightstick, her slender wrists handcuffed together, would always be his favorite.

EARLY TO RISE

Cuddling beside him, Gina watched as Zack's body shifted, restless in his sleep. Running her hand over her lover's hip, Gina pulled him close, feeling his pussy start to quiver again as Zack's ass shifted slightly against her groin. Just an hour before, she had pumped a strap-on hard, into tight virgin territory. Listening to his moans, feeling her lover's ass tighten around her cock had done Gina in. She had loved every minute of it, from the first thrust to the last. Her body trembling in orgasm, she had felt every jiggle of Zack's body as he jerked himself into an orgasm.

Now, feeling her lover shift in his sleep, knowing he was dreaming about sex, Gina found herself trembling again. "I can't believe it, I want him again."

Zack shifted again and Gina groaned, her breath whispered across her lover's ear causing him to moan in his sleep.

Pulling back carefully, she gently rolled Zack onto his back and slid the sheet down his toned body. Studying her lover's cock, Gina quivered, imaging his hard length pounding into her pussy, or even better, her ass. Sliding down in the bed, she kneeled next to Zack and nuzzled at his cock lightly, careful not to wake his lover too soon.

Working Zack's cock in and out of her mouth, Gina felt it go from semi hard to fully rigid against her tongue. It was an incredible sensation, to suck a cock into hardness. Moving slowly, she sucked just hard enough to get Zack going, but not to let him come.

Moaning, Zack shifted on the bed, his eyes flickering open as delightful sensations pulled him to consciousness.

His eyes open, Zack felt for a moment that he was still dreaming as he saw his brown haired lover kneeling at his side, sucking his cock into the velvet heat of her mouth.

Glancing up, Gina saw that Zack was awake and moved back, feeling a twinge of regret as the hard cock slipped past her lips.

"Ohhhh, god lover don't stop," Zack groaned, his cock twitching in lust.

Reaching onto the nightstand, Gina grabbed a condom and the lubrication and teasingly opened the foil package with her teeth. Carefully rolling the condom on Zack's cock, she looked into his eyes, seeing the exact moment he understood what was about to happen.

Squirting a glob of lub in her hand, Gina jerked Zack's cock a few times, just enough to get him moaning and trembling, then stopped again.

"You fucking tease," Zack growled as he sat up.

With a grin, Gina leaned in and kissed her lover, their tongues each vying for dominance. Kissing her way up her lover's cheek, she reached his ear and whispered, "Fuck me. Make my ass yours. It's been too damn long baby."

Sliding the tube into Zack's hand, Gina pulled back and moved to the middle of the bed, and presented her tight ass to her lover. Moving behind her, Zack carefully parted her cheeks and coated his fingers with lubrication. Thrusting them gently into Gina's ass, he trembled, knowing what she was going though at that moment. The electric shock of contact, the faint pull of his anus stretching to the pressure, each new sensation intoxicating and delightful. As much as he enjoyed fucking Gina's ass, he also enjoyed her fucking his.

As his fingers slid in and out of his lover's ass, lubricating her petite ring, he remembered the last time she had strapped on her cock, pinned him to the bed and fucked him mindless. Just thinking about it made him tremble in need.

Making sure his lover was good and coated, as was his cock, Zack shifted to kneel behind his lover and pressed the head of his aching cock against the tight ring. Pushing forward slowly, he felt a pop as his lover's ass ring expended, allowing him entrance.

His first thrust into Gina's ass almost had him passing out. The tightness was intense, not as wet as her sweet pussy, but tighter. Gently he grasped Gina's hips and began to lightly pump into her ass, hearing as much as feeling his balls slap against his lover's tender flesh.

Gina groaned and pushed back against him, driving Zack's cock all the way into her quivering ass. Not so gently, her fingers rubbed over her clit. Sparks of pleasure jolted throughout body.

"Fuck me you tease," she whimpered, working to tighten her ass on the hard cock inside it.

Loving it when she talked dirty, Zack closed his eyes in enjoyment. Pumping his hips faster, Zack worked his cock almost all of the way out, before thrusting it back in, Gina's gasps and whimpers music to his ears.

Balancing was hard, but with Zack's hands steadying her, Gina managed to keep flicking her clit.

"Oh god lover, fuck me, fuck my ass." Feeling so close, Gina worked fingers faster over her clit.

Her body quivering, Gina's pussy exploded in a series of contractions, her sweet juices coating her fingers and inner thighs. Sliding down on to the bed, she ground her pussy against the silk, craving the friction as her orgasm raced through her. Tightening her ass ring as hard as she could, Gina trembled at Zack's gasp of pleasure.

"Fuck, yes!" he exclaimed as he came, his hot come quickly filling the condom.

Pulling out, he removed the latex from his cock in time for the last stream to hit Gina's ass. Collapsing to the side, he lay there gasping as Gina quivered beside him.

"That ... was ... in ... cred ... i ... ble," Gina gasped, her breathing still shallow and harsh. Looking at his lover, Zack managed a weak smile.

"What a way to wake up," he responded, his breath slowly returning to normal.

Cuddling against her lover, Gina ran her hands over her lover's strong chest as her head laid in the natural cradle of his shoulder. "I thought that you might like that."

FULL EXPOSURE

With a glance around the dark courtyard, Natalie stepped out the back door onto the cool tile. Padding quietly from her apartment to the poolside, she looked around again, making sure no one was watching. With only six apartments in the whole complex, each facing the pool, it offered some seclusion, while still risking exposure.

Before she could change her mind, she let the towel fall from her naked form and she dived into the pool. Her smooth strokes cut through the water, and soon she was swimming around the pool, her laps steady and confident.

She forgot about time, lost in the sensation of cool water against heated skin. The heady smell of the chlorine almost appealing.

It wasn't until her arms protested that she swam to the side and stopped, settling on the two-foot wide steps that slowly sloped into the water.

"Nice night for a swim."

Startled, she slipped beneath the surface and came up sputtering in time to hear someone jump into the pool. Natalie watched in growing morbid fascination as with smooth strokes, the intruder moved closer, stopping but a few feet away. Her new neighbor, Avery stood on the ledge next to her. Just great, the guy she had been fantasizing about for months was in the pool with her, while she was naked.

"Normally, I don't indulge in a late night swim, but for some reason tonight, I just couldn't resist."

"Go away."

"Huh uh. I'm rather enjoying myself." With a devilish grin, he moved closer.

Natalie shifted away, worried that he could see her naked body through the water thanks to the underwater lights.

"You're supposed to be working." She had been well and truly caught, yet she couldn't force herself to just climb out of the pool, wrap her towel around herself, and leave. What had seemed like such a good idea had quickly turned embarrassing.

"It's my night off."

"Would you at least turn your back so I can get out?" Natalie backed up further, skirting the edge of the pool, her toes completely leaving the ledge around the pool.

His grin widened. "And why would I need to do that, my little mermaid. Were you doing something naughty?"

"I was just. Well, I wanted to. I figured that. You jerk. Just let me out."

Very nonchalantly, he moved over to the edge of the steps and settled himself. It was then that Natalie noticed the lack of swim trunks coloring the water. Instead, his tan, toned flesh led all the way down to his toes.

She lost her grip on the pool's rim and went under, and came back up sputtering. Moments later, firm hands gripped her shoulders even as she locked her hand over the pool's edge. "You ok?"

Blinking quickly at the faint sting of the chlorine in her eyes, she looked up into worried hazel eyes. "Fine. I'm completely embarrassed. Almost drowned, twice. I'm in a public pool, naked, with an equally naked male neighbor. Everything is just peachy. I'd like to go in now before I do something completely stupid, like make a pass at you, and make an even bigger ass of myself."

With a gasp, she shut her mouth, horrified at what she had just said. Knowing intimately how a deer caught in the car's headlights felt, she waited for him to laugh or push her away. Instead, he surprised her.

"What would be so stupid about making a pass at me?" A shiver raced down her spine as he touched her arm. "I've been trying to come up with a way to approach you for weeks. But you always seemed so untouchable."

"You're touching me now." Touch was too tame a word for what he was doing. Arousing. Teasing. Tempting. All fit much better than touch.

"Yeah, I guess I am."

The distance between them closed, until she was pressed between his very firm and slightly hairy chest, and the cool tile of the pool. She wasn't sure which of them had closed the distance, or who leaned to kiss the other first, but it didn't matter.

The first touch of his lips against hers was electric. She felt the jolt of solid lust all the way to her curled toes, as his tongue swept playfully into her mouth, before retreating, coaxing hers to follow.

Without a second though, she did, slipping her tongue into his mouth, rubbing against his, even as her body pressed into him. His firm hands slid down her arms, moved to her waist, and cupped her ass, lifting her against his body.

Headless of just how much she was tempting fate, she wrapped her legs around his waist. Lost in the sensation of his kiss, she didn't notice they had both let go of the pool edge until then slipped under the surface. Lips locked together, they continued dueling for possession of each other's mouth until the need for oxygen won out and they moved apart and broke the surface.

Heart racing, Natalie drew in several deep breaths as she moved away from Avery. She needed time to process the rapid changes to her life. "I, um, I don't quite know what to say." She hadn't though he was interested in her, and now, finding out that he was, was a heady experience. As was that kiss they had shared.

"Just say yes." His hazel eyes earnest, he closed the distance between them again and pressed his full length against her.

"Yes to what?" Her voice trembled and she hated it.

"Yes to exploring the possibilities. Yes to taking a chance. Yes to some frisky bedroom games, breakfast at my place tomorrow, and maybe even the next morning. Yes to whatever you're willing to go for."

Unable to form a response, Natalie leaned against him and took possession of his mouth again. Letting her body speak for her, she wrapped her legs around his waist again. His hand slid down her back and cupped her ass, holding her tight against him. The cool water swished around them as he turned and pressed Natalie's back against the cool tile. It felt good, even as she briefly wondered at her sanity. Normally levelheaded, she didn't just go with the flow.

The warmth of his chest contrasted deliciously to the cool water dripping down her breasts from her wet hair. Trembling at the duel sensations, she tightened her grip on him and rubbed against his cock.

Pulling back from the kiss, she tried to grasp at reason even as her body was on fire. "You know this is crazy, right?"

"Then we'll be committed tomorrow." Avery nipped at the side of her neck, pressing tiny kisses down along her shoulder.

Natalie raised his head up and resumed their kiss. Pressing down on his shoulders, she silently guided him to slip beneath the surface. As the water closed over their heads, she gripped his cock in her hand and pressed it firmly against her lips. His hold on her hips tightened, and he thrust upward, joining them together as the motion pushed them back above the water's surface.

He pinned against the tile once more, slowly sliding his cock in and out of her pussy, as their tongues continued to duel. Natalie raised her hands to massage her aching breasts. Cupping them, she rubbed them against the wet mat of hair on his chest, tickling her sensitive nipples.

Avery pulled his lips away, moving them over her cheek, and down the column of her throat. "I've wanted to do this for so long, " he said between kisses.

The water swirled around them with every thrust of his hips against hers. His cock slid gently in and out, brushing against her swollen nether lips.

"So have I." Natalie tipped her head back, resting it on the rim of the pool as Avery nipped at the top edges of her breasts. It all felt so delicious, the subtle motions of his body against hers, the cool water around her heated flesh. But all too soon, soft teasing movements weren't enough. Desire swept through her veins, demanding more.

Natalie shifted impatiently against him, her breasts aching, her pussy clenching in need. She wanted, needed more of him. She craved being claimed. After watching him play handball, she had lain awake half the night fantasizing over the ripple of his muscles, the sheer masculine power of his movements. She wanted it now, wanted to feel the unleashed, purely physical power in his form.

Uncertain how to express her desires, she whispered, "more", even as she tightened her legs around his waist. Avery's hand tightened slightly on her hip as his head lifted, his hazel gaze met hers.

"More?"

Natalie moved her hands to his shoulders, nails digging tiny crescents into his skin. "I want it all."

She watched the ripple of muscles in his arm tighten as he strengthened his grip on the pool's edge. His other hand lifted and joined it, bracketing her between him and the tile. "Hold tight."

As swiftly as the water would allow, he moved them over to the steps and laid her back, her upper body resting on the painted cement, bared to the night air, her hips raised and again held in his hands. Standing fully erect, the water barely came to his waist.

Natalie wondered if she would be bruised in the morning, but as he drove his cock in and out of her, she quit caring. Screw the bruises; all that mattered was the utterly luscious feeling of his cock filling her, the sheer masculinity of her lover claiming her.

Her legs tight around his waist, Natalie raised her hands to her own breasts and rolled the nipples between her fingertips. A faint grunt of encouragement reached her ears. Empowered by Avery's approval, she grew bolder and pinched the tight buds, releasing shivers of pleasure throughout her body.

Each tingle found her clit, teasing the blood engorged bit of flesh. Her gaze met his and Natalie dropped a hand down her own body, to where their flesh met, and flicked lightly over her throbbing clit. Gasping at the utterly wicked feelings it aroused, she settled her finger firmly over the nub and manipulated it in time to his thrusts.

Her cries of pleasure mingled with the splash of the water slapping into the tile and against their bare skin. His faint grunts joined hers as he moved faster and harder, his hips grinding against hers.

She slid another finger between them, pinching the sensitive bud of her sexuality between them, and sensation exploded. Clenching her pussy tight, she milked his cock as she climaxed. Avery continued to thrust unsteadily as she rode the waves of her orgasm. Her whole body hummed with satisfaction.

Groaning softly, Avery collapsed against her as he joined her in orgasm. Natalie shifted beneath him, even as she gripped his shoulders, holding him close.

"I take it back," he gasped, "You're not a mermaid, you're a siren, tempting me to my death."

Natalie couldn't help it. She giggled against his shoulder. It felt so good to get something she had wanted for so long, if only she knew where they were going from here. It was definitely a sobering thought.

Avery must have sensed the sudden shift in her mood; he moved back and kneeled on the steps between her legs. His concerned gaze met hers. "Regrets?"

Natalie shook her head, even as she debated how to put her feelings to words. His next words had her nodding in agreement, even as she wondered if he was suffering the same insecurities.

"Wondering what's next?"

"Yeah."

"How about we start with breakfast, and see where it goes from there."

No sooner had Natalie nodded, than he stood again and picked her up in his arms. She wasn't certain how they managed it, but he carried her up the stairs and gently set her on her feet on the cement surrounding the pool. Somehow, they managed to gather their clothing without being seen, and hurried into Avery's apartment.

Natalie didn't have much of a chance to look around the darkened living room, before she was hustled into his bedroom. Avery scooped her up from behind, startling a yelp from her and tossed her onto his waterbed.

"Your sheets!" she gasped, trying to move.

"They'll dry," he answered as he gently flipped her onto her stomach and straddled her. His warm, firm hands settled on her shoulders, massaging the concrete bruised muscles, eliciting a shuddered of pleasure as her body suddenly grew sluggish and tired.

* * *

Natalie woke the next morning, startled at first by the unfamiliar light blue sheets. The light floral scent that permeated her room was missing; instead a musky aroma teased her nose. A heavy weight pressed against her back, hairs tickling her sensitive skin. Twisting slightly, she was treated to the blurry sight of Avery lying naked against her. Blinking wide eyed like an owl, she tried to make sense of what she was seeing, but her caffeine-deprived mind just wouldn't cooperate.

A soft snore dispelled that delusion. As her mind slowly started to working, she remembered vividly the events of the night before. Desire awakened within her as she intimately recalled the feel of Avery pressing against her, his cock buried deep in her core.

Snuggling into Avery's arms, Natalie closed her eyes and allowed the memories to wash over her.

She tried to keep still as she grew restless, her body demanding a repeat of the night before. The deep rumble of Avery's voice brushed softly across her neck, "Hungry?"

Her pussy clenched at the huskiness of his voice. Turning in his arms, she pressed little kisses against his chest. "Yeah. But not for food."

Avery rolled over, pulling her on top of him. "Brunch it is then."

IN THE DARK OF THE NIGHT

Setting the last plate into the dishwasher, Shauna smiled to herself. Now was her favorite time of the evening, when realities of the day faded into whispers in the night. It was her special time with Josh, when he entered her world, sharing the darkness with her. Hearing him enter the room, she tilted her face up, waiting for his kiss.

"I love you," he whispered a moment before his warm lips met hers. Thrusting his tongue past her parted lips, he invaded her mouth, conquering and claiming. Feeling her knees grow weak, Shauna leaned against him, allowing his arms to wrap around her waist, holding her against him.

Purring softly, she wrapped her arms around his neck and gasped softly into his mouth as he picked her up and settled her slight frame against his chest. Trailing his lips from her across her cheek to her ear, he whispered softly, "Ready for bedtime love?"

Nodding softly against his chest, Shauna snuggled against him, trusting herself into his strong arms. Carefully he picked her up, not wanting to scare her with sudden moves.

As Shauna's sightless eyes closed, she cuddled to Josh's chest, confident he would carry her safely to their room, as he had so many nights before.

Feeling the sheets beneath her, Shauna startled for a moment, Josh's soothing whispers against her hair. "I've got you, love. Shhhhh, it's ok." Tightening her arms about his neck, Shauna settled against the bed, pulling him down with her.

"Make love to me," she whispered.

"Mmmm," he murmured as his warm hands started unbuttoning her shirt. "My pleasure love." As her shirt parted, Josh allowed himself a brief glimpse of her creamy flesh before he flipped the lights off. With the curtains closed, the room was perfectly dark, and he entered Shauna's world. A world of touches and whispered movements.

Shifting in the dark, Josh slowly removed Shauna's jeans, his hands worshiping each inch of flesh a moment before his lips paid their homage. Beneath him, Shauna murmured encouraging words, or sometimes just whimpered in desire.

His passion rising, Josh sought to please his lover. Every inch of her fragrant skin, the tiny triangles of pleasure at the backs of her knees, the calloused soles of her feet. Even her pinky toes received his attention before he moved up to her silky inner thighs.

"I love you," he whispered against her right thigh. "I need you," he murmured against her left.

"I want you," he rasped a moment before his tongue slipped past her dewy pussy lips. The tangy scent of her arousal filled his nose as he inhaled deeply, before thrusting his tongue within her, claiming her for his own. Slowly, drawing out every caress, he ignited her passion to a raging inferno, her body releasing a sweet juice to cool the flames.

Savoring her sweet essence, her whimpered cries, Josh worked his tongue within her, his fingers upon her tiny nub of pleasure until she arched against him, screaming with the waves of her orgasm.

Josh gave her sweet nether lips one last kiss before he moved up her body. Nibbling, sucking and licking, he worshiped the rest of her pale flesh, intoxicated by her smell, her taste, the feel of her velvety skin beneath him.

As his lips reached hers, sharing the bounty of her pleasure, his cock slipped within her gates, drawing moans from their bodies. Thrusting and withdrawing, over and over, the tempo of passion beat within them. Their hearts racing, their breathing quickening, Josh and Shauna each sought to please the other within their world of darkness.

His balls tightening, Josh pumped his hips faster, driving his cock harder within her quivering pussy. Words of love, sex words, and passionate murmurings filled the air as Josh took Shauna closer and closer to desire's edge. Tightening her legs around his hips, Shauna wrapped her arms around his shoulders, her fingernails digging into his back.

Moaning, her body tightening around him, Shauna orgasmed, screaming his name in the stillness of the night. Moments later, Josh joined her in ecstasy's grasp, his hot essence flooding within her. Trembling, Josh collapsed on top of Shauna, her slight frame warm and slick with sweat.

Passions spent, Josh shifted to lie beside his lover, his arms holding her close. His hands shaking with the aftermath of intense pleasure, Josh smoothed Shauna's sweat-dampened hair form her face and kissed her gently. Murmuring his love to her, he held her close as she cried softly, the beauty of their love never failing to bring tears to her eyes. At first Josh had been upset by it, but now, years later, he loved her for it. For her gentle soul and ability to see what others ignored. But most of all, he loved her for the way she made him feel, the way she made him want to be a better man.

INSPIRATION

Removing her glasses, Sherry closed her eyes and rubbed the bridge of her nose. Feeling cross-eyed after editing for the last three hours, she leaned back in her chair and zoned into her dream world where she was naked on the bed with her lover.

Gentle hands clasped her shoulders, kneading the tightened flesh. Tipping her head back, she opened her eyes and smiled at Luke.

"Hi, baby."

"Mmmm, hi, lover. You're home from work early."

"Yeah. It was a slow night, so they let some of us go early. How has your work gone?"

Sighing, Sherry closed her eyes again and rolled her shoulders under his hands. "Shitty," she muttered. "I am tired of looking at the same paragraph over and over. I just can't concentrate tonight."

Shifting her ponytail aside, Luke nibbled her neck. "Need some help with your focus?" His breath whispered across her skin, raising goose bumps along her shoulders and neck. Tipping her head to the side, Sherry leaned back into his touch.

"I'd like that," she purred.

Luke slid his hands down her shoulders to cup her breaths through her bra. "It drives me crazy sometimes, while I am trying to work, to know that you are sitting at home, in nothing but a bra and jeans. I want so bad to come home and sit you in my lap at your computer and have you work while my cock thrusts into you."

As her breathing altered, Sherry's mind filled with the vivid image inspired by his words.

"God, yes," she mumbled, an idea coming to life. Carefully standing, her legs already feeling like Jell-O, she turned to Luke and clasped his hand. Guiding him to her chair, she pushing him into the cushioned seat and kneeled before him. Carefully unbuttoning his jeans, she freed his semi hard cock and stroked it to life.

Placing little kisses along his shaft, Sherry enjoyed the soft sound of his moans as his cock reached full hardness.

Sherry carefully stood, her pussy quivering against the denim of her jeans. Sliding her hand down the crotch, her fingers came away damp.

"Getting a bit turned on love?" Luke whispered, calmer now that she was no longer teasing hic cock. Reaching out, he gently unsnapped her jeans, then carefully slid the zipper down. Although her skin was smooth shaven, he still worried about hurting her each time he unzipped her jeans.

As Luke slid the denim down her legs, Sherry reached behind her and unclasped her bra, letting it flutter down her arms and fall to the floor.

Looking at Luke's hard cock bobbing with every shift of his hips, she felt her mouth water and her pussy clench.

His mouth but a breath away from her pussy, Luke leaned forward and slid the jeans from her body and wrapped his arms around her hips. He pulled her against his mouth and lightly licked at the juices trickling down her inner thighs. Inhaling deeply, he saturated his senses with her scent, the light fragrance of her arousal.

He flicked his tongue against the hard bud of her clit, as Luke held her tight against his mouth as she trembled, little gasping moans filling the air.

"Oh god, baby," Sherry whimpered, "please."

Rubbing his tongue harder against her little nub, he soon had her quivering in his arms as she came. Lapping at her lips as her sweet juices flowed from her pussy, he coated his tongue and throat with their essence.

Leaning back, he turned her to face away from him and pulled her onto his lap. Sherry spread her legs wide and straddled him, the fine hairs of his thighs tickling the sensitive skin of her legs.

Grasping his cock, she guided him into her aching pussy, lifting up slightly, them coming down hard, impaling herself on his throbbing flesh.

A gasp escaped her lips as his hardness filled her. Lifting his hips, Luke settled into a soft rocking motion, up and in, back and out.

Sherry gasped "Oh yes, lover," as she trembled in his arms.

Luke's hands were free to run over her body as she leaned back against him, free to pinch her nipples and caress her tender clit. Knowing where to tease, to caress, just the right pressure, he soon had Sherry wiggling in his arms, working herself up and down on his cock as she sought the bliss of orgasm.

He pumped his hips harder as he thrust his cock into her as deep as possible, her moans of pleasure were sweet music to his ears.

"Oh god, baby, oh god, yes," she moaned, as she tightened her pussy to clench him. Sherry softly screamed as she collapsed back against Luke, waves of orgasm washing through her body.

Moving his hands to grip her thighs, Luke pumped into her pussy, feeling her heat spasming around him. A tingling settled in his balls, and with a groan, he orgasmed, shooting hot jets of come into her pussy.

His hands loosened their grip, and Sherry's breathing returned to normal. Lying against him, she basked in their post orgasmic haze.

* * *

My fingers fairly flew over the keys, trying to get the last words from my mind, before I could no longer express them. Gentle fingers pinched my nipples, bringing a gasp from my lips as I typed out for Sherry to orgasm, followed by Luke. Giving them a nice cuddling scene, I collapsed back against his chest, his fingers magic on my flesh. Pinching, and caressing, I was soon nothing more than a babbling idiot, my mind consumed with his touch.

The delicious hardness of his cock rubbed against my g-spot and had me quivering as my orgasm hit. Trembling in his arms, I felt every twitch of his cock, every tickle of his groin hair against my ass, every breath against my shoulder, everything. My whole world was focused on his touch, our bodies joined together, and the delicious sensations flowing through me.

Breathing heavily, I melted against him, my body no longer capable of remaining upright. His hips pumped upward into me, lifting us both from my chair. The creak of the wood sounded softly in the room, drowned out by my lover's harsh breath as he neared orgasm.

Biting the tender flesh of my neck as his nimble fingers manipulated my clit, he had me climaxing again. Pushing hard and fast into my pussy, his cock throbbed, shooting a hot spray of come into my wet heat.

"Oh, love," I gasped, his groan echoing through my quivering body. Clenching him tight, I milked his cock for every drop of his come, tightening then relaxing.

As out bodies relaxed, and our breathing calmed, his arms wrapped around me, holding me.

"I love you," he whispered softly.

"I love you too, babe."

"And I love it when you get writer's block." Giggling softly, I admitted to myself that although most writers hate writer's block, I had come to enjoy it. He was always such a delightful inspiration.

JEANS AND A SMILE

"Come on in." he hollered through the doorway. The apartment was dark, so I was a bit hesitant, knowing that Marshal had just redecorated the apartment yesterday.

"What happened to all of the lights?"

"I turned them off, smartass. Now get in here before you freeze." It was cold out and the apartment was so warm and inviting. I stepped through the doorway, feeling my way around in the dark. The soft, gentle sounds of Enigma filled the air with the vibrant beat.

"Where are you?"

"I'm in my bedroom. Would you just get in here already. Don't worry about watching your step, there isn't anything in your way."

"Now he tells me," I muttered, walking more self-assuredly. I couldn't help but wonder what Marshal was so secretive about. I headed toward his bedroom door and felt for the door. It stood open.

"Take off your clothes and lie down on the bed."

"What the hell? Marshal, you are kidding – right?"

"Well, you did say that you wanted a massage some day right? Well, today is the day. Now strip and lie down on the bed."

"Yes, massah." I joked. My hands went to the buttons of my shirt and quickly undid them, sure that a light would come on soon if I didn't. I sat down on the bed, once I found the confounded thing and removed my shoes and socks. Then I stood again to get rid of my jeans, panties and bra. With a flop I landed on the bed and bounced twice.

"This thing sure is bouncy." His chuckle filed the room.

"I like it that way. You ready?"

"As I can get, I guess." I felt the bed dip as he sat down beside me. His hands found my ankle and moved up form there, trying to find out how I was laying. I lay there on my stomach feeling more self-assured than I should, given the situation.

His jeans rubbed against my legs as he swung his leg over to straddle my hips.

"This may feel a bit cold." That was all the warning I got before he squirted lotion on my back. I felt myself jump a little at the unexpected sensation. Gently his hands began working the kinks out of my shoulders and back. I felt myself growing woozy, lost in a state of half wakefulness, just delighting in the sensations he was causing.

Tenderly his hands worked down my back, then back up. I could feel the tension of the past few months leaving me bit by bit.

"That's it, just relax. Let your cares fade away. Just focus on the music, on my hands, on feeling free and alive," I sighed into the pillow, and did what he asked. After all, how could I not, it felt too damn good not to.

His hands worked down my arms. I shivered as he leaned down, brushing his chest against my back. Heat radiate from him, I felt like I was lying under a hard, warm blanket.

Pulling back, he worked back up my arms and started to rub my neck. I turned my face into the pillow and slowed my breathing. I didn't want to suffocate, but I did want his hands over more of me.

Marshal and I had talked about him giving me a massage before, but it had been so long ago, I thought that my friend had forgotten. To my delight, he hadn't.

His touch still tender, he worked down my back once more then shifted off of me.

"Roll over," he whispered, his voice down a few pitches. I could tell it was affecting him the same way as it was me. It was a form of delicious torture, feeling his strong hands running over me. So much more awaited me though, so with a satisfied sigh, I rolled over.

Again, he straddled my hips, his groin resting just over mine. The rough feel of his jeans brushed against my tender skin, causing goose bumps. One of my favorite fantasies was coming true. One I had kept locked in my thoughts, not telling anyone, least of all the object of said fantasy. After all, it wasn't something that you could just bring up during a normal conversation. It might have sounded a bit odd. Kind of like, hi, how are you, by the way, would you mind giving me a massage while wearing nothing but your jeans and a smile? Nah, better to keep it to myself.

I focused again on his touch as he began circling my breasts with his fingertips. Soothing and yet arousing he rubbed my breasts, then down to my ribs. Stopping to lightly tickle, he caused me to buck under him. We both groaned.

"God, that feels good," he muttered then returned to his task with a new intensity. I could feel my body's involuntary response and only hoped that it wasn't too obvious to him. Maybe he didn't notice my hip slightly shifting or my hands grasping the bed sheets. Just maybe.

"This bothering you?" he asked, his hands again caressing my breasts, this time including the hard buds of my nipples.

"No," I breathed, certain he could tell the change in my voice. I cleared my throat and tried again. "Not at all."

"Hum."

He shifted off of me again and moved to the foot of the bed. Grasping my ankles firmly, he pulled me down slightly, and then he crawled back up onto the bed and moved up by my head. I felt his legs brush my hair as he kneeled just inches from my head. I scooted back upward so that my head lay on the pillow of his legs.

A sigh escaped my lips as he again started working on my arms and shoulders, relaxing my stiff muscles. I stopped caring if he noticed what he was doing to me. It felt too good to care.

My body began to awaken again, this time not in pain, but in pleasure. My friend certainly knew his way around a massage.

"Jesus, Marshal," I whispered, as his hands returned to my breasts. He soothed them with his touch, almost like his presence soothed my emotions. It just felt so good lying there like that with his hands working the cares from my body.

"Now for the legs. Lift your head a bit." I murmured a sound of protest but did as he asked. I didn't really care about my legs, but I was curious to see what else he might do.

Marshal settled down beside my calf and lifted my ankle onto his shoulder. I parted my legs and shifted my hips to get comfortable, then gave my body up to his touch.

He chuckled again, then began working on my calf.

"Feel good?"

"Mmmmm," was all I could manage, but it seemed to be enough for him. He continued his way down my leg, stopping just above where my pelvis and hip meet.

"Want me to stop?" he asked, uncertainty in his voice.

"No."

His hands moved down, working the hip socket. Almost teasingly his knuckles brushed over my sex. I knew he had to feel the heat and wetness, but he kept working on my hip, massaging gently.

Carefully he pulled back when he was done and lowered my ankle to the bed.

"Now the other one." He parted my legs further, then settled between then and pulled my other ankle to his shoulder.

As he worked his way down, I was hard pressed to keep from grabbing him and pulling him down over me. For a year we had flirted and teased each other but nothing ever came of it. As I lay there, feeling pleasantly aroused, I wondered why.

His hands worked to my hipbone again and I quit thinking. As he massaged my hip and pelvis, it dawned on me that his knuckles were no longer accidentally brushing against me. It happened way too often. Too shy to just come out and say anything, I just moaned. It seemed to be all the hint he needed as he lowered my leg back to the bed, but stayed between my spread thighs. His warm hands began caressing my hips, then down lower.

Tenderly he worked the muscles beside my pussy, and then he shocked me. Marshal pulled back a little bit, leaned down and kissed me, right on my pussy lips. I moaned. He chuckled against me, his breath teasing my sensitive flesh.

Warm and velvety his tongue slid up my lips, then down again, parting then to his quest. Seconds later, his quest ended, he found his goal. Flicking against my clit, he teased me to the brink of orgasm, then pulled away. His hands resumed their massage of my pussy, this time focusing on my lips and clit.

I started shifting against him, coaxing his hands to where I wanted them. Tenderly, he rubbed his fingertips over my clit, setting every nerve ending in my body on fire. I wanted him. I wanted to feel one of my best friends inside of me. I began to crave it.

"Marshal ... please." I gasped. Almost immediately I got a response. As soon as he could get himself positioned, his tongue was inside of me, rubbing against my lips, then flicking my clit. I lifted my legs over his shoulders, giving him the best access I could, given how I was lying. His short hair didn't give me much to grasp, so I slid hands over his shoulders and started half massaging, half caressing them.

Fireworks exploded inside of me. Aurora Borealis shone its lights behind my eyes. The world stopped spinning and time stood still. All that mattered was his touch, his gentle sweet hands on my hips, his tongue inside of me.

I moaned again as my orgasm built. Then it exploded. What had come before was nothing compared to the feelings inside of me at that moment. At most, the stars had to have realigned themselves – it was that good, that intense, that perfect.

Marshal pulled back again and settled himself beside me, his hands caressing my stomach, soothing my body. I rolled against him, wanting him to hold me.

"What about you?" I whispered, feeling pleasantly tired.

"There's time enough for that later. Now shhhh, and sleep a bit." His arms wrapped around me, and I fell into a satisfied sleep, wondering what the night ahead would bring.

MAKING TIME

Sheryl rolled over, her body instinctively seeking her husband's warmth. As she encountered empty space, her eyes fluttered open. Flopping on her back, she listened carefully. There, softly muted by the door, were the sounds of water against tile. Michael was already up, and in the shower.

Sheryl sighed and thought about all she needed to get done today. As much as she knew she should get up and get a move on, the steady sound of the shower beckoned her.

Sheryl grinned as she imagined the look on Michael's face as she joined him in the shower. They normally shared a shower at night, not in the morning. He knew she had to hit the floor running in the mornings and did nothing to get in the way.

Debating with herself as she climbed out of bed and sipped on her room, she decided what the hell.

Walking down the hall, she mentally listed off all that needed to be completed for the day and what could be put off for the next day. Satisfied that time could be spared, and even if it couldn't, that she deserved a bit of fun playing hooky, she slowly opened the bathroom door.

Upon entering the bathroom, Sheryl was welcomed by a warm mist in the air. Closing the door, she trapped the heat in the tiny room, but the breeze was enough to capture Michael's attention.

Removing her robe, she quickly hung it on the hook.

"Babe? Whatcha need?"

Parting the curtain, Sheryl stepped under the warm spray of water, her body rubbing against her husband. "Nothing love, just though that I would join you."

Cuddling against his back, Sheryl wrapped her arms around his waist, tracing her fingers up and down the soapy planes of his stomach. Sliding her hands down further, she encircled the softened length of his cock with her hands, stroking gently, knowing he would be sensitive.

"So do you mind sharing your shower with me?" Michael flushed slightly, glad that Sheryl was against his back and couldn't see his face. He definitely liked the idea.

Tightening her grip slightly, Sheryl felt his ass flex against her stomach as her touch agitated his sensitive cock-head.

"You want me to leave? Or are you happy to see me?"

Michael's cock jerked in her hand, giving her an unspoken answer. Rubbing her breasts lightly against his back, she shivered as the hardened peaks tingled with pleasure at the contact.

Loosening her grip, Sheryl started to caress up and down Michael slowly hardening cock, her body humming with need. Moving one hand from his cock to his shoulder, she pushed his arm out of her way and stepped in front to him. Grasping his hand, she moved in between her legs, rubbing her damp pussy against his fingers, then returned to stroking his cock to full length.

Stroking her wet flesh, he imagined dropping to his knees and licking her into an orgasmic frenzy.

"Do you want me to lick you?" he asked as he thrust a finger into her aching pussy. "Or lean you against the tile and fuck you senseless?" Sheryl trembled and leaned against him, her hands momentarily tightening on his cock.

"Yes," she drawled. Resuming her motions, Sheryl could feel her knees growing weak with every thrust of her husband's fingers.

Her legs trembling, Sheryl leaned back against the tile and enjoyed the quivering of her body. Michael's finger's felt so good against the sensitive skin Samantha had touched but minutes before.

"Fuck me Michael," she gasped, "Fuck me here, now, hard."

Moving between her legs, Michael grasped Sheryl's ass and lifted her against him, her long legs wrapping around his hips. Pressing her against the tile wall of the shower, he started to pump his hips slowly, sliding his cock in an inch at a time.

Sheryl's nails racked down his back and she ground against him. "More," she gasped, "Harder. Jesus Michael, don't tease me, fuck me. Make my pussy yours."

The image of his cock sliding into Sheryl's pussy inflamed him. She was so beautiful when aroused. The way her eyes closed and her lips parted on a gasp. The slim column of her throat, the flush to her skin.

Looking at her now, her eyes closed and head leaned back again the shower wall, he fought the urge to come. Pumping faster and harder he drove himself like a wild man into Sheryl's quivering pussy, seeking to satisfy them both.

Gasping moans escaped her lips as Sheryl felt her pussy being pounded by the hard cock of her husband. In so many ways, he was the perfect man for her. Submissive, dominant, willing to share, and willing to claim.

"Yes baby," she gasped as the beginnings of her orgasm welled inside of her. Clenching him tight, Sheryl arched against Michael as she milked his cock with her inner walls as she orgasmed. She craved the feeling of his essence flowing into her, the sticky heat of his come.

The tightness of the pussy, the way she begged to be taken, Michael couldn't stand it any more. Thrusting hard and fast several more times, he orgasmed, his body collapsing against Sheryl, pinning her to the shower wall.

Carefully unwrapping her legs, Sheryl used his body and the wall for support as she slowly stood on shaking legs.

"Let's go back to bed baby."

"But it isn't even noon yet. And what about all you told me yesterday that you had to do today?"

"I know. But sometimes, you have to make time. There's nothing that can't wait, except maybe this." Reaching between them, she grasped his cock, letting her fingers do the rest of the talking.

PASSION'S FLAME BURNS

"Hello?"

"Hi, honey."

Her voice changed, from formal to seductive. "Hey babe, I missed you."

"I missed you too. I'm on my way home, I should be there in about fifteen minutes. Did you make reservations for dinner?"

"Don't worry, I have plans made and set for tonight."

"Good, see you in a few."

* * *

Kira smiled as she sat and waited for her husband to get home. She smoothed down the sides of her lacy outfit, making sure it hadn't gotten wrinkled in her mad dash about the house to get everything ready.

His cab dropped him off in the driveway. Moments later he was striding through the door. Allen's petite wife launched herself at him, wrapping her arms around his neck, pressing her lips against his.

"I..." She kissed his cheek. "Missed you..." She kissed his neck. "So much." Her lips pressed against his again. Allen let his briefcase and his carryon bag thud to the floor. His strong arms wrapped around her back and pulled her tighter against him. Kira molded her body to his. She tipped her head back, and looked him in the eyes.

"I hate it when you take these long trips."

"I know, babe, but I have to – it's part of my job."

"Mmmm, " she murmured as she kissed him again, "well, you're mine for the weekend at least. Come on." She reached behind her, removed his arms and grasped his hand. Walking backward, she led the way. No obstacles obscured her path.

The bedroom door stood open, the room bathed in candlelight. Kira sat on the bed and pulled her love down beside her. The black lacy bra pulled tight for a moment, as did her crotchless panties, but wiggling adjusted them. Allen seemed to notice for the first time what she was wearing, and his eyes almost bugged out.

"Where did you get these?"

"Hum?" She stopped kissing down his neck. "Oh, Sandy took me shopping this week. You like?"

"I love. Very hot."

"Mmm, stop talking and kiss me." Allen smiled against her lips, he loved it when his wife took the lead.

Her hands went to the buttons of his shirt, and soon had it off him. Soon he had kicked off his shoes to join his shirt on the floor. Lifting up, he allowed her hands room to undo his pants.

"Honey, you should know after ten years that I need to stand up to take my pants off."

"Mmmm, just hurry back." Her hands began roaming over her body as soon as his weight left her. Her breasts tingled as she lightly pinched her nipples. Allen's pants tangled around his ankles as he watched his beloved wife caressing herself. Kira smiled and began a teasing show for him, stroking down her stomach and hips to her pussy. Her body tingled from her practiced touch, but it just wasn't enough. As much as she loved touching herself, she always missed his weight on her as she orgasmed from masturbating.

She spread her thighs wider, giving her husband the full effect of the panties. Her hands began to caress her pussy lips, making Allen's mouth go dry. With a twinkle in her eyes, she dipped a finger in her wetness, and then brought it to her mouth. Allen watched, breath held as she licked her finger clean, then began playing with her pussy again. He groaned. Even after ten years together, she still made his head spin.

"God, Kira, it makes me so hot watching you touch yourself. Oh babe, yeah, flick that clit." Allen lay down beside her, naked, his flesh tickled by the lace covering parts of her body. "Oh God, baby, I want you so bad."

Kira's hands stopped playing with her wet flesh and moved to his arms.

"Then have me. Come here, stud." Allen rolled over on top of her, and in one movement slid his cock into her. Kira moaned at his deep thrust, loving the feel of his body joined with hers.

"Oh yeah, honey, fuck me, make me yours." Kira loved talking dirty sometimes, it made her feel wicked, and so wild.

"Yeah baby, suck me in." Allen thrust again, and again. Kira's breasts strained against her bra, the smooth lace rubbing deliciously against her nipples. Their lips met again, and Allen slid his tongue into her mouth. Kira's rubbed against it.

"Harder, Allen. I need it harder." Already he could feel himself ready to come. All week he had imagined himself deep inside of her as he masturbated at night, his hand just no comparison to her wet heat.

They both felt the effects of his movements over her, within her. His cock slid in so deep, driving against her sensitive walls. Kira's body began to rise up to meet his thrusts, grinding their pelvises against each other. His balls slapped lightly against her ass.

"Yes, Allen, oh yes! I'm so close baby, make it happen. Oh love, fuck me!"

Kira could feel the beginnings of an orgasm deep inside her pussy. Already her muscles were spasming around him. Her head tipped back, her eyes closed.

"Oh shit, yeah," Allen mumbled as her body convulsed against his. Her muscles clenched him, then released, and then clenched again. He orgasmed with her, shooting his essence deep within her pussy.

He collapsed on top of her. Kira's hands ran up and down his back, soothing him. "Oh honey, I may hate you going out of town, but God, do I love it when you get back." Allen grinned, as he shifted off of her. Their eyes met, he leaned down and kissed her lips gently, once, twice.

"I love you."

"I love you too, Allen. When do you have to leave again?"

Rolling into his back, Allen pulled her with him, settling her against his side. Running his hands through her mussed hair, he sighed.

"Two days, and I'll be gone for a week."

"Mmm, then I guess we had best make the most of the next two days then."

RYAN

He sat still with a Cheshire cat grin on his face. How could he not, after all – any self respecting, hot blooded heterosexual male would, given the right circumstances. These would definitely be the right circumstances.

The stripper wrapped her shirt around Ryan's neck and leaned over him, shaking her lovely, pert breasts in his face. Ryan's eyes closed briefly. "Probably thanking whatever deity he believes in." I thought.

Star moved on, and Ryan swallowed heavily. I chuckled at his obvious dilemma. Ok, so I'm weird, I like seeing my lover turned on by other women. I must admit, he also likes seeing women turn me on.

"Hey Steph!" I leaned over towards Ryan, to hear him over the loud thump of the music's base. "Thank you for bringing me here."

* * *

Two more lap-dances, and an hour and a half later Ryan began to get edgy. In-tune to him after dating for a year, I knew he was ready to leave. That was fine with me. There was only so much arousal I could take before I had to have some relief. Since I wasn't too fond of the idea of being arrested for public exposure, I figured it would be best to leave. Handing him the keys, I waited while he opened my door, my hand discreetly brushing over his ass, cupping the firm cheeks.

"Hurry up and get me home, baby. I want to fuck," I whispered, nibbling his ear. Clearly, he was torn between the desire to toss me onto the hood, or take me home for less dangerous sex. The urge to not spend the night in jail clearly won.

I paused to pull my panties off while Ryan headed around to his side. The car started with a well-tempered purr, its vibrations working throughout my body. Watching the beautiful women gyrate and grind had affected me almost as much as Ryan, I just was a bit less obvious about it.

As Ryan pulled out into traffic, I settled back in my seat and slipped my heels off. Placing my feet against the dashboard, I shimmied my shirt up to my waist and parted my thighs. Ryan groaned beside me as he pulled to a stop at a red light.

Grinning wickedly, I pinched my nipples through my dress with one hand and ran the other over my smooth shaven lips. After the light turned green, Ryan divided his attention between the road and my actions. I wasn't looking for an accident, but I was interested in teasing Ryan further. I love the reaction I get after his frustration reaches its peak. Savage and passionate, he fucks like a wild man, starved for something only I can provide.

Thrusting a finger in and out of my wet pussy, I giggled as squishing sounds filled the car. I knew Ryan was about half crazed with need.

"Like what you see, baby?"

"Fuck, yes!"

"Mmmm, good." Pulling my finger from between my lips, I offered it to him. Sucking it clean, he pulled into the driveway and slammed the car into park.

Squealing, I pulled my finger back and climbed out of the car, and ran to the house, Ryan close on my heels.

We barely made it in the front door and Ryan was on me. His hands running up and down my back, his lips pressed against mine. I opened my mouth, and felt the warm heat of his tongue against mine. Wrapping my arms around his neck, I braced myself. His hands curved under my ass and lifted me against the wall. In a matter of moments, my skirt was pushed up around my waist, his zipper went down and he was inside of me, filling me in the way only he can. I love the hard feel of him, the way he pushes deep and then freezes on the deep stroke, before pulling back.

I threw back my head and moaned, all thoughts but enjoying the moment gone from my passion clouded mind. Over and over Ryan thrust up against and into me. I closed my eyes, whimpers of pleasure escaping my tender lips. The night's entertainment heightened and increased my arousal to the point of orgasm in only minutes. I screamed, a high-pitched keening sound and slumped against Ryan. Bracing my weight, he thrust twice more and came as well. Our limp bodies slid to the floor, arms and legs entwined.

* * *

"Oh God, Steph, that was..." Words escaped him, as they always do in emotional moments. I nodded against his chest, and he sighed in contentment.

"Ryan?" I whispered.

"Hum?"

"You're squishing me." He chuckled and shifted to my side. I cuddled against him, for the moment, happy to just be held.

The clock chimed and I knew I had to get the big lump on our floor moving. "Come on Ryan, time to get up off of the floor." I stood and grinned down at him, still feeling tingles deep inside my pussy.

"I get first dibs on the shower," I shouted and raced down the hall.

"The hell you do," I head him mutter. I giggled.

* * *

The shower was an experience. I love the feel of warm, crisp water flowing over every inch of my body, washing my cares away. A pair of warm, soapy, masculine hands help as well. Ryan's hands ran all over my body, soaping me up, and then washing me down. I just stood there, my body feeling pleasantly lethargic.

"Babe, have I told you today how much I love you?' I asked, feeling so loved, and so desired at that moment. He leaned down and turned the taps off.

"Yeah," He whispered back. "Have I told you how much I love you?"

"Mmm hum," I nodded. As he slid to his knees and showed me the depths of his love, I couldn't help making plans in the back of my mind for another night out on the town the following weekend. Maybe a night at a club, bumping and grinding on a dance floor would unleash his inner conqueror again.

THE SCENT OF LAVENDER

Breanna leaned back against the tub, letting the light vapors of the lavender bubble bath sooth her frazzled nerves. Teaching kindergarten was always an interesting and rewarding experience, but a tiring one, too. Gavin stood in the doorway watching her slender hands brush bubbles over her soft skin. Little wisps of black hair curled at the nape of her neck, making his lips ache to kiss the moist flesh.

Gavin stifled a moan as he watched Breanna trail a hand over her nipples, coating them in a layer of bubbles. "Need any help?" he asked, his voice hoarse with desire. Breanna opened her green eyes and looked at her lover. Smiling teasingly, she swirled her fingertips over her nipples, causing them to harden. Gavin's hands fisted at his sides, the palms yearning to caress her hardened buds.

The black haired temptress sat up straighter in the tub and turned towards her brown haired love. "Mmmm," she moaned as her fingers played down her breasts to her ribs, her eyes daring Gavin to join her in the tub. "I could use someone to wash my back ... if a certain man was willing to get into a lavender scented bubble bath." Gavin grinned, his hands already unbuttoning his shirt. Within moments he was naked and joining her in the bath. Breanna scooted forward and made room for him.

He slid behind her, watching the water level in their tub reaching dangerous levels. Already a few splashes spilled over the edge of the tub into the tiled floor.

Handing Gavin the soap, Breanna leaned forward and enjoyed his hand running the washcloth over her back, lightly caressing her heat-reddened flesh.

Within minutes the bath turned sensual and Breanna had to bite her lip to hold back her moans. "Baby," she whimpered, "I want you."

Gavin wrapped his arms around her and held her to his chest for a moment, then stood and leaned over her, pulling the drain to let the water out of the tub.

"Dang it," Breanna muttered as she pushed the plug back in.

Gavin climbed out of the tub and stood facing her. "What?"

"I still need to shave. I didn't last night and now..." Groaning she leaned back in the tub, her desire quickly cooling. Gavin grabbed her razor and leaned down her, placing a quick kiss on her pouting lips.

"Hop up and I'll shave you." Breanna stood and settled herself on the bath seat on the edge of the tub. Leaning back, she scooted as far forward as she could.

"Just be careful, ok?"

"What's wrong, babe, don't you trust me?" Gavin's blue eyes sparkled with mischief.

"Yes, but I cut myself enough shaving on my own." Grabbing the shaving cream, she sprayed some in her hand and lathered her pussy and surrounding area, then did her best to relax. Gavin kneeled in the tub, and settled himself between her wide spread thighs.

"Ready?" Lifting the razor, he waited until she nodded, then gently began to slide the blade over her flesh, leaving her smooth to the touch. Breanna watched as he slowly removed her stubble, amazed at how arousing it was. As each minute passed, she could feel herself growing more aroused, until she knew she had to be leaking her sweet juices from between her lips. Leaning back, she closed her eyes and tried not to shift as Gavin's breath whispered across her skin.

Rinsing the washcloth, Gavin wiped the remaining shaving cream from her flesh and leaned in to inhale her scent. Breanna shuddered as his tongue flicked again her lips.

Gavin leaned back and grinned at her frustrated moan. Standing up, he stepped out of the tub and lifted her trembling body in his arms. "Better get you dried off, love," he whispered against her ear as he nibbled the sensitive lobe. Setting Breanna down, he held her close as he toweled her dry. A few flicks of the towel had him dried off as well. Leaning down, he brushed her nipples with his shoulder as he pulled the plug, draining the remaining water from the tub. Breanna moaned and leaned into his body, feeling light-headed with desire.

Gavin slid an arm around her shoulders as he slid the other under her legs and lifted her into his arms again. Cradling her close, he enjoyed the velvety feel of the skin against his; rubbing lightly with every step he took. Leaning back in his arms, Breanna enjoyed the feeling of helplessness that being held in his arms gave her. She enjoyed being pampered by her lover.

Laying her gently on their satin covered bed, Gavin followed her, covering her with his muscular body. Sliding a leg between hers, he nudged her silky thighs apart and settled his weight between them. Breanna pulled his head down to her and pressed her lips against his, nibbling his before teasing him with her tongue. Gavin growled in his throat and slid his tongue against hers, causing Breanna to gasp with delight.

"Gavin," she whimpered, "make love to me ... I need you inside me, please..." Savoring her words, Gavin slid his hands down and grasped her ass, then rolled, pulling her with him so that she wound up on top of him.

Breanna grinned and sat up, sliding her moist flesh against his groin, leaving a trail of her sweet juices on his stomach and pubic bone. His pubic curls teased her clit as she grasped his cock and mounted him. Sliding up and down slowly, she rocked against Gavin, thrusting his cock into her aching wetness, at her pace. Her nimble fingers manipulated her throbbing clit as she undulated herself on Gavin's hardness.

It felt heavenly, the fullness of Gavin inside of her as she rubbed her clit in small light circles. Gavin leaned forward slightly, just enough to bring his lips within reach of her nipples. Closing their warmth about her succulent flesh, he nibbled the coral bud lightly with his teeth, causing Breanna to shiver with delight. Soon she was moaning as she worked herself harder and faster on his cock. Gavin lay back under her, enjoying the sensations her pussy was causing as it squeezed him tight with each motion of her body. He planted his feet on the bed and lightly thrust against her, just enough to drive her wild. Breanna screamed as waves of orgasm flooded her body. Gavin groaned as she collapsed on his chest. Entwining his hand in her hair, he tipped her head back and kissed her, thrusting his tongue in her mouth.

With his other hand he grasped her hips and gently rocked her against his pelvis, as he thrust up against her. Breanna gasped as desire again threaded through her body. Leaning back, she against started to ride him, traces of her orgasm still lingering in her passion-soaked pussy. Small tremors of orgasm caused her pussy to clench, teasing Gavin all the more. Finally, he succumbed to his passion, and orgasmed. Closing his eyes, he arched against her, grinding his groin against her shaven skin.

Breanna gave a whimpered scream as she collapsed against him, threads of orgasm working their way through her body again. Sweat glistened on their flesh, as they lay entwined on the bed, cuddling and enjoying the feel of each other.

Gavin groaned and pulled Breanna close for a kiss. "You get the lavender bubble bath and I'll run the water?" he tempted her. Breanna shifted against him, her body delightfully drained.

"Mmmm. I doubt I could move right now if someone shouted fire. But if you add some strawberries and a light wine to the mix, I might be able to summon the strength." Gavin chuckled and pulled away from her. Lightly swatting her butt, he agreed. "All right, I'll run the tub, put in the bubble bath and get the strawberries and wine." Breanna grinned and rolled over.

Spreading her legs, she dipped a finger in their combined juices and lifted it to her lips. Flicking her tongue against her fingertip, she shivered at the taste salty taste of his come mixed with her sweet essence. Gavin felt his cock stirring at the sensuality of her actions.

"Keep doing that and we'll never make it to the bathtub."

Breanna grinned and dipped her finger into her pussy again.

"Would that be so bad? You don't like my lavender bubble bath anyway."

S IS FOR SEX, SWINGING AND SO LONG

Russ mashed out his cigarette in disgust. Watching his ex-wife flirt her scantly clad ass off was enough to give him a serious case of indigestion, without the bitter taste of a stale cigarette.

He knew he should have tossed the damned invitation in the trash the day it arrived, but he'd succeeded in convincing himself that she wouldn't dare show up at the swinger's ball, not without the man who introduced her to the life. If she'd even been invited to the party of the year.

Yet another fuck up on his part.

Just like all of the others. First, it was his fault that she cheated, then his fault for taking her back, which only encouraged her to cheat again. But it was when he introduced her to swinging, and to the rich man she left him for that topped it all off. He had hoped that by offering a condoned variety of cocks, she wouldn't feel the need to stray outside of the swinging parties. Another mistake.

Yep, it was fucked up all right. And it looked like it was only going to get worse. She'd spotted him.

Suddenly, his sight was blocked. Reaching up, his fingers encircled slender wrists and pulled the hand away.

"It's okay, Russ. It's Tina, remember me?"

As her hands pulled away, Russ turned to look at the tall redhead. She was something else. Always one to do her own thing, his ex-girlfriend from college was sporting six earrings in each ear, a leather collar around her neck and not much else.

"Tina! It's been a long time. What are you doing here?"

"You know Mistress Diana hosts this party every year. This year, I was one o her pets, and I was selected to co-host on my last day with her. I was just mingling, when I saw you standing there, looking so much like I remember you. Bitter, alone, and perfectly content to be that way."

Russ couldn't help but laugh at himself. She still seemed to be one to cut through to the truth.

"So, you're into BDSM huh? I still remember all those time you wanted me to tie you up and spank you."

"As I recall it, darlin', you weren't objecting too much to anything I wanted either."

Across the room, Russ' ex-wife was glaring at him, moving slowly towards him. But for once, he didn't care. She could fuck half the room, and given that she was cock hungry and it was a swinger's party, that seemed very likely to happen, and he wouldn't care. Just seeing Tina again reminded him of something he had forgotten long ago. No one should ever be allowed to rip you apart twice.

Tina had taught him that. Years ago.

"How's life treating you?" Russ asked.

Tina gasped in answer.

Before Russ could question her odd response, he felt a leather-clad hand slid over his bare shoulder. "I see you've found a friend, my little slut. You aren't planning to sneak away and fuck him are you?"

"No, Mistress Diana," Tina said, as she slid to her knees, her back a perfect straight line.

As Mistress Diana came into view, Russ felt his eyes widen. Despite seeing her numerous times before from a distance, he couldn't help his reaction. She was exquisite, a well-proportioned china doll. Every step was measured, performed with a perfected ease.

Turning to face him, she moved against Tina's side and sat down-using the redhead's back as a bench seat. Tina's arms barely trembled with the effort. All around them, the room had settled into a hush, as everyone watched the lady of the hour.

"I see Tina has chosen well. I was going to direct her your way Russell, but she has come to know me so well, she knew just what mood I'm in. "

"You know who I am?"

Despite her ladylike bearing, the petite thing snorted softly. Russ couldn't believe it. "Do I know you? Darling, who the hell do you think sends out the invitations? Not just anyone can get into one of my parties."

"Sorry, Mistress."

"Although, I am curious as to how THAT came to get an invitation." Her pointed gaze settled on Russ' ex, who visibly cringed. "Must have slunk in with someone who has a thing for cheap accessories." Faint twitters filled the room as Mistress' victim fled.

"Don't you think?" Mistress asked.

"Indeed." Her jade gaze turned back to him, making Russ wonder at his own audacity.

"I see you came dressed as ordered, a Roman General fresh from battle." Imperiously, she beckoned him closer, and without thought, he stepped forward. Something in her confident matter drew him, as no woman had before. "I shall be your Goddess, above you, able to bend you to my will. Agreed?"

He nodded. Uncertain what he was letting himself in for; but he couldn't help the curiosity that drove him to find out.

"Then kneel before your Goddess, slave." Holding his fake scabbard and sword steady, Russ dropped to one knee.The cold marble floor was uncomfortable against his bare skin. He felt some small bits of sympathy for Tina, despite her breaking his heart years before.

Mistress Diana parted her leather-clad thighs, revealing a sliver of flesh not covered by tanned animal skin. Tight black curls covered her sex, neatly trimmed and glistening in the ballroom's light. "Tongue fuck me."

Aware of his audience, Russ hesitantly shifted forward. He extended his tongue and gently lapped at the silken curls, diving closer to Mistress' clit. Sucking the little nub into his mouth, he curled his tongue over it, nibbling at her tiny clit ring.

A loud smack echoed in the stillness of the room. Russ jerked back.

"I didn't tell you to stop." Mistress curled her fist in his hair, and jerked him back to her pussy. Another smack sounded, followed by a faint whimper. Then another, this time Mistress jiggled against him as she rained another blow on Tina's cheek.

Mistress' legs opened wider, allowing Russ greater access. With a hurried movement, he unbuckled the sword and set it aside. Lifting his hands to her legs, he gently stroked her inner thighs.

"Mmmm, that's good." Mistress rocked against his face, her fist in his hair grinding him against her dripping cunt.

"Lick it all up, slut."

Thrusting his tongue deep, Russ applied every trick he'd learned. And he was rewarded when Mistress Diana's thighs tightened, wedging his head firmly in place. Her pussy clenched around his tongue as she climaxed. Her hand slowly relaxed, as did her thighs, allowing him to breathe again.

Moving back, he wrapped his belt around his waist and buckled it, resettling his costume. He was breathing heavy, and his cock strained for any feminine touch. But he waited to see what Mistress Diana was going to do next.

As if her orgasm had released the hold on the occupants of the room from a spell, they pared off into couples, threesomes, and more as Russ watched. Heading into alcoves, bedrooms upstairs, or just collapsing to the floor, the group descended in a mindless orgy of lust.

Standing with the grace of a queen, Mistress waved her hand at Tina and said, "Enjoy my little slut here for a while. She'll take care of you. When you're done, come find me." With that she turned and crossed the room, greeting each of her copulating guests as if they were sitting down to teatime.

Her ass rosy from her Mistress' spanking, Tina sat back on her heels and looked at him. This time, her eyes were lowered slightly.

"Where were we?" he said, trying to ignore his reaction to Mistress Diane. "Ah yes, you were about to tell me how things have been going for you."

"Russ, I'm sorry about the way things ended."

He reached down and cupped her chin in his palm. Forcing her to look at him, he allowed a smile to curl his lips.

"Don't worry about it. Ancient history right?" he thought his own words sounded hollow, but hoped she didn't notice. "How about a blow job, for old times sake."

"Russ, I've been thinking about you a lot. Then when I saw your name on Mistress' list...."

Russ reached down and fingered the chain dangling from her nipples. Tugging slightly, he got her attention.

"Let it go. Now be a good little slut, and suck me off." Despite his desire to believe her pleas, he knew how easy they dripped from her tongue.

Tina's eyes widened as he lifted his costume and slipped his cock free from his bikini-briefs.

Fisting his hand in her hair, he pulled her up to crotch level and waited. Forming an O with her mouth, Tina soon had his length deep-throated. It was one of the many things that he had missed about her over the years. But catching her sucking off his roommate had killed the thrill of her mouth for him.

Now, it was only a reminder of another fuck up on his part. For after she had been caught in the act, Tina had begged for a second chance and Russ had given her one. It had taken several months, but he had finally caught on that she was still cheating, and left her.

Thrusting hard into her mouth, he worked his cock in and out, using her as she had once used him-for a cheap thrill.

He should have learned from the lesson she'd taught him, but he'd hoped that with his wife, things would be different. He had hoped that by offering her some of what she craved, they could make it work. Instead, he had driven her away.

As he came, spurting a jet of come into her mouth, he pulled back. Another spurt hit her square in the face, with a third splattering her breasts. Watching his spunk mark her, he admitted to himself he needed to find a way out of the rut he had fallen in to. Mistress Diana's words came back to him-"when you're done, come find me."

Using a fistful of her hair, he wiped her spit and his come off of his cock and slipped it back into his briefs. Settling his costume back into place, he forced a smile.

"Give your Mistress my thanks." He watched Tina's eye widen.

"But I thought that maybe you and I could-"

"Not a chance." At his curt tone, Tina stalked off, crossing the room to her Mistress.

His fake scabbard slapped against his thigh, Russell tracked Tina's movements and caught Mistress Diana's eye. With a curt nod of his head, and a slight smile curving his lips, he acknowledged her. Even from across the room, he could see the majestic smile that curved her lips.

For a moment, he stood there and debated what to do. He had an idea of what Mistress wanted to talk to him about, but he wasn't quite sure how he felt about it. The two women he had loved most had fucked him over. But what Mistress was possibly offering wasn't love, but a way to change.

His steps lighter than when he arrived, Russell stood tall and crossed the room. With every step, his resolve firmed.

Fuck his ex-wife--she gave up a good thing.

People turned to watch his movements. He could feel dozens of eyes on him, but he kept going.

Fuck Tina--she deserved whatever she got, with the possible exception of Mistress Diana. She'd lucked out there.

He only hoped that he had guessed right and he was going to be offered the position of her pet. The idea of her bare ass-cheeks resting on his back kind of appealed to him.As did no-strings attached, no chance of getting emotionally hurt sex.

As he arrived in front of Mistress Diana, he dropped to one knee. He wasn't certain what she wanted, but he was hopeful.

"Tina, you're excused with my thanks." Mistress decreed. Bowing her head, Tina left the room. Russell could see tears shimmering in her eyes. He found himself feeling a bit of sympathy for her; she finally knew what it was like to be discarded. But knowing her, she wouldn't be leaving the party alone. Having been one of Mistress' pets, she would be a valued submissive.

"Follow me, my General, and we shall discuss my acquisition of a new pet." Turning on her heel, Mistress left the room. Standing proud, Russell followed.

He only hoped that in a year, when his time was up, he wouldn't feel that he had made another fucking mistake. Then again, if he walked away right now, he had a feeling that would be something he would regret for a long time.

Author's Note: This story came from the line "Regrets, I've had a few" that I read in someone's tag line in email a long while back. I can't remember whose email it was now. Anyway, I wanted to play around with this concept, and write a story about someone who had faced a few things in his life he regrets, and is given a chance to try for something new. He's been hurt so many times, he doesn't dare hope – and yet, bitter as he is, he knows it is too good of a chance to pass up; because if he does, that is one regret that he might not be able to accept.

SOME PERSONAL TIME

Despite her later day at work, Angela forgot to reset her alarm, and it awakened both her and her husband bright and early. Tristian and Angela lay awake, debating what to do to fill the hour or so before she had to get ready for work. While going back to sleep was an option, she really didn't want to do that, but getting out of bed didn't appeal either.

"I can call in sick and we can go out and do something," Angela offered for the third time. Squeezing her tight, Tristian declined her offer, for the third time.

"Are you sure?"

"Yes. You need to go to work." Tristian muttered, his hands molded to her hips, pulling her on top of him. "But first, I want to fuck you."

"Tristian!" she gasped, pretending shock at his coarseness. Carefully rolling over so that he was on top, Tristian pulled back a bit.

"I want to watch you," he whispered, then pressed his lips against her collarbone.

"Watch me what?" she asked, uncertain if he meant what she thought he did.

"I want to watch you masturbate. Get out your toys and please yourself, while I watch. Show me what you sneak up here when I'm busy. I can hear you, you know. But I leave you alone. Now I want to watch. I want to watch you shove a dildo into your pussy, your lips sucking it greedily into your wetness."

A blush warmed her cheeks at his words. She knew he knew about her toys, he had bought half of them for her after all. But she hadn't known she got vocal enough that he could hear her playing with them.

"I want to watch." Looking into his eyes, Angela saw the love and the lust for her. He really did want to watch her.

She knew about the porn movies on the computer that he sometimes watched at night. Sometimes, they even watched them together, though rarely. But never had he asked her to touch herself while he wasn't inside her.

Moving up to lean against the headboard, Tristian watched as Angela dug around in her dresser, pulling out her vibrators and other toys. They had experimented with nipple clamps and anal plugs from time to time, but mostly Angela played with them by herself.

Setting her toys next to him, Angela laid down beside him, her auburn hair brushing against his legs. "Where do you want me to start?"

"Where you normally do. Pretend I'm not even here." Closing her eyes, Angela tried. Flinging herself into her fantasy world, she imagined the things that got her hot. Moments later, her hands traced gentle lines upon her flesh, teasing her senses with light touches. Stroking up and down her chest and stomach, she let the backs of her knuckles graze her nipples on the upward stroke, then return again. Over and over she teased herself with light touches, enough to awake her passions, but not let them overwhelm her.

Lost in the world of her own making, Angela had almost forgotten Tristian's presence. Eyes closed, she reached out for her toys, grasping the long thin vibrator she preferred. Rubbing it against her engorged nether lips, she wet the tip with her juices, and then pressed it against her clit. Turning it on, she gasped as the buzzing toy vibrated against her bud of desire.

Her hands trembling, Angela played the toy upon her aching flesh, well practiced at the exact motions to set her body aflame. Done teasing, she thrust the toy within her pussy while reaching for her smaller vibrator. Pressing it against her clit, she worked one toy in and out of her pussy, while rubbing her throbbing clit with another.

Grinding her hips upward, she gasped as tiny spark of pleasure ignited deep within her. Her orgasm quickly built as Angela pumped the buzzing toy in and out of her body.

"Oh yeah," she gasped as she sped up her motions, her eyes flaring open, her gaze fixed on Tristian. She watched as beside her, Tristian began to leisurely stroke his cock, fisting the length of hard flesh she craved to feel filling her. The scent of her pussy was rich within the air, her moans softened by the buzzing of her toys.

"Oh fuck," Angela gasped, "mmm, oh yeah." Her moans growing breathless, she tightened her thighs, clenching her pussy tight until delicious shudders raced through her inner muscles.

A whimpered scream escaping her lips, Angela arched her hips, driving the vibrator deeply into her pussy as she climaxed.Moments later, her body relaxed, as her orgasm slowly threaded itself through her body, dissipating with every second that passed.

Releasing his stroking hold on his cock, Tristian reached down and carefully pulled the vibrators from Angela's limp hands and turned them off, before setting them aside. Kneeling between her legs, he grabbed her ankles, and gently lifted Angela's legs, laying them over his forearms. Lying down over her, he had her pinned beneath him.

"Tristian, what are you doing?" Squirming slightly, Angela ground her sensitive pussy against his hard cock, his pre-come mixing with her juices.

"Making love to my wife."

"Mmmmm," she murmured, arching slightly against him, trembling as his cock-head brushed her engorged clit. "Then fuck me already."

Groaning, Tristian laid his forehead against her face and thrust forward, his cock slipping past her pouting lips, still slick with her earlier passion.

Pumping hard, Tristian worked his cock in and out of Angela's pussy as she withered beneath him. "I love you," he whispered, his teeth nibbling at her neck. Placing her hands on his shoulders, Angela shifted her legs to rest in the crook of his elbows as he pounded away at her tender flesh.

"God, Tristian," she gasped as his cock pumped hard within her. Arching slightly, she tightened her legs as another orgasm flooded her body.

Letting her legs go free, Tristian grasped Angela's hips and held her still as he thrust faster into her quivering flesh. Clenching sporadically as every new thrust surged through her, Angela whispered words she had only imagined saying to him before.

Listening to the words spewing from her precious lips only seemed to excite Tristian further. Pumping hard and fast, he groaned aloud as his cock jerked and he came, filling her with his essence.

Collapsing atop her, he wrapped his arms around her, holding Angela close to him, almost as if he wanted to crawl inside of her.

"I love you baby,' he whispered, his voice thick with emotion.

"I love you too."

With a quick glance at the alarm clock, Angela groaned. "Damn."

"Huh? What?"

"It's almost time for me to get ready for work."

Tristian shifted to the side and collapsed on his back, then pulled her against his chest. "If you call in sick, we could stay in bed all day today, although maybe we could run out, just for a bit and go shopping."

He rolled with her as Angela reached for the phone. Nibbling her ear, he stroked his hands up and down her back and legs while she called her boss, and asked to take a personal day.

THE TENDER HAVEN OF HIS ARMS

"Man, look at the ass on this chick."

Heather's day was going downhill fast. Laid off at work, then her car had run out of gas on her way home, forcing her to walk a mile in heels to the nearest station – and there she found herself face-down on the floor, in the middle of a robbery.

Fear curled in her stomach as one of the men approached her.

"Shut the fuck up and get back over here," his accomplice snapped. "Let's get this done and out of here."

The man with an eye for Heather's ass crouched next to her. She could smell his reek of alcohol as he rubbed the barrel of his gun against her leg, and that was the last thing she felt before fear took her consciousness.

* * *

It was a few nerve-wracking hours before the police finally released Heather into her husband's waiting arms. Scott held her close to his chest and whispered his love into her hair, Heather's tears flowing as he cuddled her tight.

"Shhhh, it's gonna be all right. I'm here, love. Let's get you home and I'll take care of you," he said, scooping her up and carrying her to the car.

Heather was still shaking during the short drive home, and Scott carried her from the driveway to the house, then into the bathroom. Together they stepped fully clothed into the spray of the shower he had run, Heather wrapping her arms around his neck, burying her face into his chest and weeping tears she thought would never stop.

"I love you, Heather. It's going to be OK, honey. I've got you, I'm not going to let you go."

Sliding to the floor, Scott stretched out his legs and held his wife tight against his chest. They didn't move until the water began to run cool, and Heather's tears had stopped.

"Let's get you dry, baby," he whispered, having helped her out of the shower, and by now was peeling the wet clothes from her body.

Pliant, emotional, exhausted, she stood and allowed him to care for her. He toweled her dry, then removed his own clothes and toweled off. He then carried her into the bedroom, cuddling with her beneath the covers.

Heather was trembling again, and Scott pulled her more tightly to his body, whispering to her his words of love. Her trembling ceased, her breathing normal once more, Heather moved back and turned to face her husband, curling her body against his.

"I was so scared," she whispered.

"It's OK, love. You don't have to talk about it until you're ready."

"Scott, I love you. I was scared that I was going to die, but I was more scared that I was going to leave you."

"I know, baby. I know. But you're safe now. You're here, with me, and I've got you."

He rubbed her back and smoothed her hair from her face as he recalled his own fear, when the police called to tell him his wife had been witness to a robbery. They assured him she was fine, but he had needed to see this with his own eyes.

Heather leaned up and pressed her lips to Scott's, drawing him back to the present. His hands curled against her head, holding her lips to his in a kiss more of desperation than love. All the fear they both had felt flowed through their kiss.

Moving against him, Heather rubbed her breasts against his chest, her body restless.

"Make love to me," she whispered.

"Sweetheart," he whispered back, "you've had a shock today. Are you sure?"

Heather nibbled his neck.

"Yes, Scott, I want this. I need this."

His hands moved down her back and lightly caressed her hip and lower back, and Heather shivered as the soft touch set off a chain reaction in her body. Rolling her onto her back, he lowered himself over her and began caressing and nibbling at her feet; slowly, tenderly, he worked his way up to her thighs.

He moved past her pussy, for now, and gently pressed his lips to her eyelids. Then he nibbled at her breasts, licked and blew against her nipples, doing everything he knew she liked.

Scott slid his tongue over her stomach and gently parted her pussy lips, licking the sweet flesh inside. Gasping, Heather threaded her fingers through his hair and pressed up against him.

"Ohhh Scott," she whispered, breathless.

Scott smiled and continued to lick the lovely feast before him. Softly, Heather orgasmed, her pleasure displayed only in the twitching of her legs, a soft whimper and the flowing of her juices. Scott gave her tender flesh one final lick, then moved up her body to lay full length upon her.

She opened her eyes, wearing a tentative, satisfied smile. Scott pressed his mouth to hers, delighting as she licked her juices from his lips.

And then he gently slid his cock into her waiting warmth.

Heather moaned and lifted her hips.

"More, baby, more," she whispered.

Scott gently slid deeper, wanting to make this last for them both.

Time seemed to stand still as he slowly slid inside her pussy just a bit, then pulled back, before sliding in a little deeper. Heather's nails raked down his back in frustration, her entire body humming with desire.

Little orgasms, aftershocks, threaded through her body every few moments, but Scott maintained his tender assault, enjoying the restless movements of her body beneath his, the moans she whispered into his ears, the fiery trail of her nails down his back.

"Scott, please," she whimpered. Scott groaned, her words were sweet music to his ears.

Thrusting his hips, he pushed his throbbing cock into her wetness. Heather clenched him tightly as he continued to thrust again and again. Her whispered moans and breathless whimpers set the tempo of their bodies.

"Ohh yes, Scott, ohhhh."

She moaned as her body clenched around his and held him locked in her heat.

Scott merged his soul with hers and joined her in bliss.

After reason returned once more, their bodies having calmed, Scott rolled to Heather's side and pulled her against him. His hands again smoothed her hair from her face, and they whispered their I love you's as the crickets outside began the symphony of the night.

Cuddled against his chest, Heather savored the warmth and safety of his arms. Finally, exhausted and satisfied, sleep came to her and wrapped her in the tender mist of dreams.

Scott watched the lines of her face soften; the slow rise and fall of her chest as she took each breath. Closing his eyes, he thanked whatever deity was listening for protecting her and keeping her safe.

He lay awake for a while, absorbing the beauty of his wife before sleep claimed him, too.

TRUTH OR DARE

"So, how do you like the kiss?"

"You're kidding, right?"

"Nope. And I'd like an answer."

"Just what was the question?"

"How do you like the kiss?"

"What does that mean? The kiss?"

"You know, the kiss?"

"This Kiss? Like by Faith Hill? I like it fine."

"No, silly, THE KISS. How do you like it?"

"Look, I stand a better chance of answering you, if I knew what you meant."

"You are so dense, I am talking about the kiss. You know the kiss?"

"No, I'd don't. Sorry, I can't answer you, the question doesn't supply enough information."

"Fine, your turn."

* * *

"Truth or dare?" John asked, grinning from ear to ear. He loved getting Leah all flustered. She was so cute when she got irritated. He also had a pretty good idea what she had been getting at, but with her adorable way of mixing up a few words when speaking, he had been able to tease her instead of answering. Buying himself a little bit of time to see how far he wanted to take things.

"Hum, I'll go with dare this time."

"Ok."John drew that one word out, making Leah really consider changing her mind and going with truth.

"I dare you to show me what you meant with your last question."

"What?"

"You heard me. It doesn't break the rules. It's not immoral, it's not illegal, and it's not harmful. I want you to show me what you meant by 'how do you like the kiss?'"

"And just how am I supposed to do that?"

John grinned again. Leah sat there, blushing, waiting for him to answer her. "However you feel best."

Leah took a step closer, her eyes almost level with his.

"Ok, fine, smartass."

John grinned. He knew Leah was bluffing. She'd never make the first move. While bold in words, when it came down to it, she was very shy.

"Do you like it like this?" Her lips brushed against his, gently, fleetingly. In shock, John just stood there. Her lips pressed against his firmly for a few seconds. "Or like this?"

Leaning in again, she licked his bottom lip. Of their own volition, his lips parted. Her tongue slid past his lips and rubbed against his. She pulled back and smiled. "Or maybe like that."

John moved swiftly. His hands curved around the back of her neck and pulled her to him. Boldly, his tongue entered her mouth searching for hers. His crotch rubbed against the zipper of her jeans, causing them both to groan.

With a blush she pulled back. "Ah, like that. I could grow to like your kiss." John smiled, his whole face lighting up and kissed her again. Feeling faint at the sheer intensity of his kiss, Leah grabbed hold of the front of his shirt, fisting her hands in the soft cotton. Breathless, they both pulled away, still holding on to each other.

"THAT is how I like the kiss." He muttered, and then returned his lips to hers. Against his lips, John could feel Leah smile. Oh, his shy friend was coming out of her shell.

Author's Note: This little vignette is a nod to one of my favorite scenes, in one of my all-time favorite movie -- HATARI! with John Wayne. If you have seen the movie, you should be able to pin-point the scene I am mirroring. If you haven't seen the movie – well, why not? It has John Wayne, Red Buttons, lots of animals, a love story, some comedy, and a cheetah that likes to interrupt. Oh yeah – and a rocket! What more can you ask for?

VANILLA WISHES AND HONEYED DREAMS

Sitting at his computer, Darius had a fairly good view of Vanessa. Occasionally glancing at her, he watched her until she wandered out of his sight into the kitchen, returning a few minutes later with an ice cream sandwich.

Smiling impishly at him, she sat back down in her chair, legs slightly spread. Slouching down, he saw that at some point in time, she had removed her panties. Eyebrow raised, he focused his full attention on her, no longer attempting subtlety.

"What?" she asked, an innocent look on her face. Licking the side of the ice cream sandwich, she watched as his pants developed a slight tent.

"Nothing babe, just admiring the view."

Parting her legs further, Vanessa grinned and slid down in her seat, her smooth pussy fully bared under the hem of her t-shirt.

"Want a lick?" Darius' eyes flare with heat. Almost hypnotized, he stood and walked towards her, the sweet ambrosia of her pussy beckoning him. Kneeling before her, he leaned forward and nuzzled her, inhaling the musky scent of her desire.

Flicking his tongue against her lips, he heard her giggle. "What?" he asked, his tongue lapping at her musky essence.

"I, oh gees, I meant want a lick, oh, of the ice cream." Moving back, Darius grinned at her, "Yes, I do."

Giggling again, Vanessa lowered the frozen sandwich as Darius watched, held in slight shock at what she was doing. Gently parting her own lips, Vanessa rubbed the cold vanilla ice cream over her lips and clit, shivering and gasping as it trickled into her pussy.

"Then have a lick," she teased. Parting her legs further, Darius threw them over his shoulders and attended to his task. Licking the sweet vanilla treat from her lips and clit, he thrust the velvet heat of his tongue into her aching pussy.

Soon he had her trembling in his arms. Sliding her hands over her body, Vanessa used one to pinch her nipples, and the other to caress her throbbing clit.

"Oh god, Darius, yes," she whispered as her hips arched into his touch. Driving his tongue faster into her heat, he soon felt her tightening around him, her light moans filling the air. Her legs gripped his head, her hand going wild over her clit.

Liquid vanilla honey coated his tongue as she orgasmed, her body clenching as tight as possible then suddenly releasing. Collapsing back into the chair, Vanessa tried to calm her breathing as Darius kneeled before her, lapping at her juices as they trickled from her.

Hazing in the afterglow of her orgasm, she didn't at first notice that Darius had left. Opening her eyes after her breathing returned to normal, so looked around the room for him, and finally called out his name.

"In the bedroom."

With a sigh, Vanessa stood, her legs shaky from her exertions. Moving slowly down the hall, she could feel her pussy quivering as she knew the night was not yet done.

Leaning in the bedroom doorway, she gasped in surprise. Darius lay on the bed, stretched out in all his splendor, his cock in his hand as he stroked his hard flesh.

"I always wanted to watch you masturbate," Vanessa rasped out, her hand cupping her pussy as the need to touch herself renewed.

Smiling, Darius beckoned her to his side. Kneeling on the waterbed, the slight wave motion shifted her off balance and she landed face first in his crotch before pulling back.

Her eyes were less than an inch away from his hand as it moved up and down his hard cock, which had brought her so much pleasure on many occasions. Looking up at him, Vanessa saw his eyes fastened on her, watching her reaction.

Running her hands over her body, she played with her nipple and clit as she watched one of her fantasies come true.

"How did you know I wanted to watch you?" she asked softly, her breath whispering across his skin. Shuddering slightly, he worked his hand faster for a moment, before calming.

"You told me one day, gasping it out as you orgasmed. Now, baby, I have a question for you." He stopped stroking with a moan of frustration, then reached to his side and picked up his treat. Opening the wrapper for the ice cream, he rubbed the rapidly melting desert over his nipples, and down the trail of his chest to his groin.

"Do you want a lick?" he asked, a devilish smile on his face.

Leaning down, Vanessa licked at his nipples, then nibbled the hardened tips. Shifting under her, Darius debated momentarily the sanity of his game. Under normal circumstances the woman could drive him insane.

Licking her way down the vanilla-marked trail of his chest and stomach, Vanessa debated weather to tease him until he was delirious with lust, or to be nice and coax him slowly to orgasm.

Nibbling at his navel, she asked herself "When have I ever been accused of being nice?" Mentally smiling, she shifted her body so that her pussy and ass was nicely displayed for Darius' view, then sucked his cock into her mouth.

Working up and down, she alternated the depth and speed of her motions just enough to soon have him breathless with frustrated desire.

"You cock tease," he groaned. Fluttering her tongue over his cock head, Vanessa couldn't have agreed more. She was a tease.

Grabbing the almost melted ice cream, Darius smeared the remainder over her pussy and grasped her hips in his hands, pulling her down to his waiting mouth. Feasting on her sweet essence, he knew she was better than any desert.

Playing tit for tat, he drove Vanessa to the edge of orgasms abyss, and pulled back. Time and time again they teased each other, frustrating, then denying.

Her pussy quivering, her nipples aching, Vanessa knew Darius had to be in just as bad a shape, if not worse. Pulling back, she felt a moment of regret as his cock slipped past her lips.

"Fuck me," she whispered. Never had he moved so fast. Sitting up, he shifted to his knees and moved behind her, impaling her in one thrust on his cock. Closing her eyes, Vanessa saw stars as her pussy clenched him. Whimpering, she orgasmed at his second thrust. Pumping his hips, Darius pounded into her, the motions of the waterbed making a set rhythm hard.

Sliding onto her stomach, Vanessa twisted against the silk sheets as Darius thrust into her pussy, over and over, driving her to a crest, then as her body came down, pushing her back up. One orgasm blended into two, into three. In breathless whispers, she encouraged him on, feeling the sheer power of his body over hers, in hers.

Darius felt his orgasm rise. The sound of his balls slapping against Vanessa's ass was drowned out by his groan as he came, erupting like a volcano. Vanessa's pussy clenched his tightly, milking the hot jets of come from his cock, as she orgasmed again.

Collapsing against her back, Darius felt every tremor of her body as if it was his own. He rolled over and pulled her against his chest, both of them feeling too weak to do more that tremble and lightly caress each other.

After their bodies had stilled, and their breathing had calmed, Darius carefully picked Vanessa up and cared her to the bathroom, where they tenderly bathed the lingering vanilla traces from each other's bodies. Later, holding each other in bed, Vanessa closed her eyes, and whispered another of her fantasies in Darius' ear. Chuckling, he promised to soon fulfill it.

WITH A LOVING TOUCH

Tina lay in the lonely bed, not quite sure just what to do. Nothing like this had ever happened. She never in her wildest dream imagined that it would.

She could hear the shower running, and had to fight the urge to go to Erik and hold him. He didn't seem to want her to touch him when he had left the bed, and considering what had happened, she wanted to respect his wishes.

She sighed and flopped onto her back. Threads of desire stilled wrapped about her body, but she just knew if she started to satisfy herself, Erik would walk into the room. That would just shatter him, he couldn't get it up, so she had to masturbate. She sighed again.

"Maybe it's me," she thought, "Maybe after ten years of marriage, he just doesn't find me as attractive as he used to." With that thought driving her actions, she climbed out of the bed and headed towards the mirror. On the way, she passed the bathroom door, and had to fight the urge to go in and comfort Erik.

The full-length mirror on the back of the closet door revealed what it had revealed the night before and would the next night. A thirty- three year old woman who was still attractive. Tina's hands caressed her hips and stomach, her fingertips tracing barely noticeable childbirth stretch marks. Sure, she wasn't her high school weight of one hundred and thirty five pounds, but her body was still good looking. Maybe a couple pounds too many, but still attractive.

"Maybe Erik disagrees." Images of his students flashed in her mind. The tall willowy blondes and brunettes, the curvy redheads. "I am just no competition."

A new image joined hers in the mirror. Strong arms wrapped around her waist, and a dark head lay on her shoulder. Tina could feel Erik's heated breath against the side of her neck.

"Oh baby, I'm sorry." His voice sounded odd, choked, almost as if he had been crying. Tina delighted in his touch, grateful that he was seeking comfort from her, but still wondering if she was the cause of the problem. She turned in his arms and pressed herself against his body, not in a sexual way, but comforting, wrapping him in her warmth, her love.

"Let's go to bed, honey. You need your sleep." Erik nodded and together they climbed into bed, cuddled close and awaited sleep. Both lay awake for several hours, not speaking, just drawing comfort from one another. Wildly, thoughts raced in Erik head. He needed to make an appointment with the doctor, maybe see a sex therapist, and get medication, anything to correct the problem. Tina restlessly tossed and turned against him, the feel of his leg hair on her soft legs driving her wild. Needing to feel his fingers sliding over her breasts, his breath on her pussy, but not able to ask. Not willing to make an issue of her lingering desire.

Finally, after several hours of tossing and turning and shifting, she fell into an exhausted sleep.

* * *

The dream was so good. Erik's slender body was stretched out over her's, his lips nibbling at her neck. All five foot eight inches of his body pressed her down into the soft mattress, his heat replacing the blanket. Unhurried he worked his way down, to her breasts, the one part of her body that she loved now as much as in high school. Perfect in their smallness, despite their slight sag, they responded to his wet mouth. Almost like liquid heat, his lips wrapped about her nipple. Her back arched, driving her breast further into his mouth. Soon the other nipple hardened under his loving lips.

A fire of passion was slowly forming deep inside of her body, rekindled from the embers of earlier. Not wanting the dream to fade, she moved slowly, her hands going to caress her sides. They landed on skin, rough from labor outside. Her eyes flew open and encountered Erik's serious green ones.

Her lips parted in surprise. A moan escaped. Tina watched as her husband began to work his way down her body, licking, nibbling, and kissing his way to the very core of her.

She felt his moist breath against her lips, tingling, teasing them. His eager tongue searched out her clit, flicking against it, fulfilling her needs. Tina wanted to pull him up to her, kiss him, love him, but the earlier memory stopped her. She decided to relax and enjoy the precious gift Erik was giving her.

Carefully, but with loving knowledge of her body, Erik aroused her. His sole intention to please her, as he hadn't earlier. Wet and hot, his tongue entered her pussy, driving spikes of heat throughout her body. Tina withered under the sensual assault of his lips, his tongue.

Erik's callused hands caressed her body, moving over her breasts, down her thighs and back up again. His tongue continued to work her clit, flicking it. Tina arched up against him, her hands fisted in his hair, holding his head against her wetness.

Erik nuzzled as close as he could get, his stubble sliding over her sensitive inner thighs, thrilling her anew. Already an orgasm was beginning inside of her. Tina craved it, almost as she never had before. Craved the confirmation that Erik still wanted her, even as she was dying for him.

A million points of energy centered themselves deep inside of her core, curling tighter and tighter, then exploded. Tina's back arched off of the bed and she ground her pussy against Erik face, driving his tongue as hard against her clit as she could. Erik breathed deep of her essence, thrilled that she still reacted as strongly today as she had the night they first made love.

As her body calmed and the universe realigned itself, Erik slid up beside Tina, to cuddle her close. The last traces of orgasm slipped gently from her body and Tina opened her eyes. Love shone in Erik's eyes as he looked at her.

"Erik, I..." she began. Erik lips covered hers. She tasted her sweet dewy essence on his tongue as it danced with her. He pulled back, reluctant to end their kiss, but knowing he had to before he went crazy.

"I love you Tina. I love you more with every passing year. My heart swells with love for you, even if my body can't right now with desire." Tears filled Tina's eyes. She loved him so much, loved that they could talk and share their feelings. Loved that as time went by, they grew closer. Feeling silly for her doubts earlier she snuggled close to him, vowing she would do whatever it took to help him get better.

WITHIN A TANGLED WEB

Those that knew her called Ivy a black widow, and with good reason. Although she didn't kill her mates, she generally left them wanting her and begging for more. It wasn't that Ivy was cruel, and maliciously set out to ensnare men and leave them craving more when she tossed them aside. She just got bored - very easily. Once the conquest had become the conquered, the frantic passion she enjoyed and savored dulled to a mindless copulation, without any spark. It was the spark that drove her, the flavor of something new, the chase.

As she moved between the gyrating bodies at the nightclub, she couldn't help but reflect on her perfect catch - a young man named Daniel. By far, he had outlasted the others, spending over six months in her bed. And in the end, it wasn't his lack of spark that drove Ivy to spurn him; it was his talk of commitment - the ultimate no-no in Ivy's sexual rulebook.

The two men that followed him were but pale shadows in comparison, and she knew it. Even before she took them into her bed and drove them wild with passion, she knew they wouldn't last. And it drove her mad with frustration that Daniel had to ruin it all.

Already, she had seen several possible candidates for her next lover, but none quite appealed. The blond at the bar was the most promising, but he seemed too full of himself. Ivy had found that men like him weren't generally worth the effort it took to break them in.

Turning to walk the room again, she caught sight of a tall man leaning against the wall near the doorway, seemingly unsure of himself. Careful not to catch his attention just yet, she moved herself into position where she could observe him, unnoticed. She wanted to see how he interacted with others before making her move.

She wasn't sure how much time had passed, but it didn't matter. All night could go by, and she wouldn't care as long as she got what she needed.

Several women approached her dark haired lurker, and each time he would blush and awkwardly stammer his way through an introduction and each time the woman would leave, giggling.

Finally, she had seen enough.

Making certain she caught her prey's gaze, Ivy walked towards him. With each step she took, his outward signs of nervousness increased. A faint stain of a blush darkened his tan skin; his eyes widened, his Adam's apple bobbed repeatedly.

Allowing herself a moment of smug satisfaction, Ivy smiled. He was hers for the taking. Without even a word passing between them, she knew. All the subtle signals were there.

She stopped a foot away from him and licked her ruby lips. "I'm Ivy," she drawled.

"I'm um, Tobias. I, ah, I mean Toby. My name is Tobias, but um, my friends call me Toby." Shifting away, he broke eye contact. His shoulders slumped, and Ivy could tell he was waiting for her to walk away.

Shy. Nervous. Probably hadn't had much experience with women. Perfect. Mentally, Ivy rated Toby and found him to meet her criteria.

"Well, Toby, how about asking a lady to dance."

His head lifted at her words. His eyes were wide open, with a trapped look in their blue depths.

"You?" he croaked out, then cleared his throat.

Licking her lips again, Ivy made sure he was watching the slow movements of her tongue. She had been told her lips were her best feature, perfect for wrapping around a cock. Although she wouldn't say it out loud, she quite agreed.

"Yes, me."

"I, um, would you, uh, like to dance?"

Stepping closer, she traced a red tipped fingernail over his lips, watching them part slightly in hopeful anticipation. His eyes gave everything away; every thought, every emotion.

Catching her nail on his lower lip, she lightly pulled, then flicked it free. Continuing her path, she traced over his chin, down the column of his neck, to the vee of his shirt. Circling the button, she watched him watch her. His gaze glued on her fingers as she slipped the button through its hole, and pulled his shirt open a bit more.

When he just stood there, not stopping her. She opened another button, then another, until she had his shirt halfway open. Sliding her hand between the light material and his skin, she smoothed it over his firm pecs.

With her other hand, she reached around and cupped his ass, pulling him against her. "I'd like to dance Toby, but not now."

His eyes lost some of their glow and he started to pull away.

Timing her move, she pulled him back against her scantily clad body and ground her groin against his. "What I'd rather do is, fuck. So how about it Toby? Ask a lady to fuck?"

"I ..."

Ivy shifted her hand from his pecs to his shoulder, and up, curving it around his neck. Gently, she moved his head down, and lifted hers, until a breath of space separated them. Flicking her tongue, she traced the outline of his lips, her gaze locked on his.

"You can say it Toby. Say, 'would you like to fuck me, Ivy?'"

He swallowed heavily, uncertainty shinning in his eyes. Ivy could feel his shoulder muscles tighten under her hands, his body preparing for flight. She couldn't help wondering how many women had toyed with him.

"Would you, um, would you like to ... um, that is, would you like to have sex with me?"

Ivy exhaled softly, blowing her breath into his mouth. Slowly, with barely a hint of motion, she slipped the tip of her tongue into his mouth, sliding along the edge of his teeth, then pulled back.

"I don't want to have sex Toby, I want to fuck. Now ask me, ask me if I want to fuck you."

"I can't."

Her tongue tracing his lips, she moved her hand around and grasped his. Jerking lightly, she pressed it against her mound, curling his fingers in to press against her creaming sex.

"Say fuck Toby, and we will."

He swallowed heavily and then said in a hurry, "Would you like to fuck me, Ivy?"

"Mmmm, yes."

Still holding his hand in hers, she moved back and turned. Walking calmly and boldly, she crossed the dance floor, pulling Toby behind her. Several heads turned, watching them cross to the door.

She wormed them both through the throng of people waiting to get in, and around the side of the building.

"Where are we going?"

Ivy didn't say anything, she just kept walking. As she turned around the back corner of the building, she dropped his hand and kept going. After about ten steps, she stopped and looked over her shoulder. "Coming?"

His steps hesitant, Toby followed.

Halfway down the alley, Ivy stopped and leaned up against the brick building, bracing on one leg while the other was bent, her foot pressed against the wall. Her flared skirt bunched up at her hips, leaving the lower half of her body bare to the eye. Thigh high silk stockings were held in place by a black garter belt, her pussy and inner thighs framed perfectly by the straps.

Toby moved towards her, stopping a few inches away.

Crooking her finger at him, she coaxed him closer, until he settled into the cradle of her body. Slithering against him, she wrapped her arms around his neck and pulled him down for a kiss.

She ravished his mouth, biting at his lips before sweeping her tongue past them to mate with his. It was an open mouthed, no holding back, lust-filled kiss that was meant to leave no doubt in his mind as to how much she wanted him.

Her movements carnal, she pulled her foot from the wall and wrapped it around his waist, grinding her moist pussy against the front of his pants. Slipping a hand between their bodies, she slid his zipper down and freed his shaft.

Carefully she stroked her fingertips over his cock head, enough to tingle, but not sting. She watched as his cock lengthened, hardened, until it was perfection. The veins stood out, a pearly drop leaking from the tip.

She felt the first rush race through her veins, and her inner thighs grow damp. This was what she thrived on. The hunt was over; it was time to move in for the kill.

Gripping his cock in her fist, she stroked up and down the hard length, caressing even as she squeezed. With her other hand, she reached down and parted her moist pussy lips. "Fuck me, Toby."

"I ..."

Her hand tightened around his cock and she pressed the tip against her opening. "Now."

Tentatively, his hands moved to her hips and gripped lightly. Almost hesitantly, he slipped the head past her parted lips. Ivy tightened her leg around his waist.

With a firm grip on his shoulders, she pulled her other leg up and wrapped it around his waist, interlocking her ankles.

Her gaze locked on Toby's face, she demanded, "Fuck me, hard."

The barest hint of awakened confidence entered his gaze as he thrust hard and deep into her pussy. It felt so good, his velvety skin sliding against her slick muscles. Even as her lips curled in a smile, she knew it would come across as smug. She had gotten what she wanted.

Toby leaned against her, his chest crushing her between the solid muscular wall of his body and the cold, gritty brick of the club.

He shifted slightly, pushing a bit further into her aching pussy, then withdrew. After a few slow and steady thrusts, Ivy dug her nails into his shoulders. "Harder, damn it!"

His grip tightened on her hips, and he slammed forward, the grain of the wall digging into her back. His gaze focused on hers, he pulled back and thrust forward again, pulling her down hard against him.

Almost animalistic, he repeated his movements, as Ivy gripped his shoulders tight enough to draw blood. His grunts drowning out her gasps, Ivy allowed herself to be swept away by the sensations, the awakened cravings of her flesh.

Yet she couldn't help but compare him to Daniel. The way he moved, the gentleness at first, giving way to his deeper, baser nature. They were both very similar, even if the physical Toby was night to Daniel's day.

"More," she gasped, her body on fire with need.

His hips pumped hard and fast against her, grinding her up and down against the wall. Ivy could feel the thin layer of her silk shirt tearing.

Her pussy clutched with each thrust and withdrawal of his cock. She reveled in the tightness of his grip on her hips, even as she knew she would be sore and bruised in the morning. Ivy trembled as he almost viciously ground against her, his cock buried within her to the balls.

She could feel a bead of blood sliding down her finger, even as she dug her nails in deeper. Toby groaned and slammed against her, his come flooding her clenching pussy, setting off a chain reaction within her.

Tightening every muscle in her lower body, Ivy milked his cock for every last drop even as she rode the wave of pleasure racing through her body. Her head lay back against the brick wall, she shifted slightly as Tony collapsed against her, his legs trembling.

Her pussy mourned the loss of his cock, even as it trembled with the last ripples of orgasm.

Feeling strangely invigorated, especially given the brutal passion of their coupling, Ivy unwrapped her legs and pushed Toby back, forcing him to stand on his own. Starting at his feet, she slowly trailed her gaze up his body, admiring the way his cock glistened with their juices, the way his stomach muscles rippled with each breath he took.

Her gaze lifting to meet his, she opened her mouth slightly and licked her lips. Lifting a hand to his chest, she followed a trickle of sweat as it streaked down his body to pool in his groin hair. Teasing him, baiting her last hook before the snare, Ivy leaned in and licked at the next droplet, following it from his neck to the middle of his chest, before moving back up again to his ear.

Nibbling his lobe gently, she whispered, "I have a bottle of wine at my place, silk sheets, just perfect to fuck on, and a craving for more of your cock. How about it Toby, fuck a lady senseless?"

"Actually Ivy, I think I'll go home and take a shower." His eyes opened, a spark of confidence and satisfaction shinning that hadn't been there before. "Once I've been chased and caught, it kind of looses its thrill. But thanks for the offer."

Stunned, Ivy watched as he zipped up his pants and walked away, his cream still dripping down her inner thighs.

Author's Note: With this story, I wanted to turn the tables on a character, to explore that moment of realization when things become clear, and someone gets a taste of their own medicine.

A TOUCH OF SILK

Jordan groaned as her alarm went off, drawing her from her delightful dreams. Rolling over, she stared blurry eyed at the annoying machine. It's beady red dials showed the time as 9:00 am, but she knew, just knew it was lying. It couldn't already be 9:00. Slapping the infernal machine, she snuggled under the covers as the realization that it was Saturday dawned. She had nowhere she had to be at any particular time.

Several hours later, Jordan again returned to the land of the living as her phone rang.

"Hello," she mumbled, sleep causing her tongue to feel heavy.

"Hi baby," Stephan whispered in her ear, his faint French accent a tale tell sign as to his identity, regardless of how sleepy she still was.

"Mmmm, coming home soon?" Rolling over she looked at the clock and gasped when she saw it was almost eleven.

"Should be wrapped up here by Wednesday, Thursday at the latest. Miss me?"

"God yes," she replied as her body instinctively responded to his voice. Already she could feel herself growing wet and he wasn't even there. "I plan to keep you in bed for at least a week when you get home."

"Sounds delightful," Stephan responded, his voice husky with desire. "I miss your touch so much babe, your warmth drawing me deeper inside of you, your hard little nipples pressing against my chest."

Jordan groaned, her hand sliding between the elastic band of her silk boxers and her stomach.

"But you know what I miss most baby? I miss the taste of your sweet pussy as you arch against my tongue."

"Stephan," she gasped, "you're driving me insane. I want you so bad."

"I know baby. Are you hot for me?" he asked, already knowing the answer.

"Yes," she gasped. Her fingers lightly caressed her lips.

"Touch yourself for me baby. I want to listen to you come. I'm sitting here in my hotel room, wearing nothing but my boxers, stroking myself and imaging you on your knees, sucking my cock into the warm recesses of your mouth. I want to hear you as you touch yourself, I need to hear you."

Jordan moaned at the image of him stroking himself, his strong hands wrapped around the hard length of his cock. Her fingers parted her lips, and then dipped into her wet pussy, coating her fingertips with the sweet juices. Lightly, she began to caress her clit, moving in little circles. The silk of her boxers rubbed against her pussy lips, causing a delightful friction.

Over the phone line she could hear Stephan's voice whispering hoarsely all of the things he planned to do to her when he arrived home. How he planned to kick the door shut and lift her into his arms, feeling her long legs wrap around his waist. He wanted her to wear a skirt and no panties so he could impale her on his cock, and carry her to the bedroom, feeling her clench him tight with each bouncing step.

Flicking her clit with her right hand, Jordan's other hand pinched her nipples, drawing a pleasurable pain from the hardened buds. She relished the time alone with herself, as much as she enjoyed feeling Stephan sliding his cock into her waiting depths.

"Oh baby, listening to you gasp and moan has me so hot. Come for me Jordan, let me listen to you orgasm as I stroke myself."

Jordan moaned again at his words. Listening to him groan between words was almost her undoing. Rubbing faster, she felt the first sparks of orgasm racing through her body. Stephan groaned as his orgasm hit, the harsh sound music to Jordan's ears. With a whimper, she let herself go. Euphoria coursed through her body as her orgasm began. Her legs straightened and tightened, her clit throbbed under her fingertip.

"That's it baby, come for me. Oh god Jordan this is so erotic. Oh baby, yes, come for me." Stephan's harsh breathing sounded over the phone line.

Jordan trembled as her orgasm waned, lingering traces remaining in her clit and nipples. "Oh god Stephan, I need you so much. I need to feel you inside of me."

"I know baby. I'll be home soon."

"Call me tomorrow?"

"You know that I will. I love you Jordan." Jordan grinned as she whispered her love for him and hung up. Curling on her side, she started to lightly flick her clit again, while across the continent, her lover began stroking his rapidly hardening cock, images of Jordan filling his mind.

ENTANGLED

"Bye, Adam, see you Tuesday."

Adam's eyes followed the gentle sway of Marissa's hips as she headed outside, the closing swoosh of the automatic doors snapping the lustful thoughts from his head.

"Still need that ride home?"

Jerry's voice was filled with amusement. He knew just where Adam had been looking, his own eyes there as well.

"Sure, just let me finish up here so management will let me go."

"OK, meet me at my truck."

Jerry hurried out the doors, hoping to catch up to Marissa.

* * *

It was almost an hour before Adam came stomping out of work, his eyes cloudy with anger.

"Some days I hate working retail, and other days, I REALLY hate it."

Jerry nodded sympathetically and closed his door. Adam wanted so many times to get a better job, to tell his bosses here where to shove it. But one thing constantly held him back: if he quit his job, he wouldn't see Marissa almost every day, and that simply wasn't acceptable.

Adam climbed into the passenger side of Jerry's truck, wanting badly to sit and talk with Marissa. But she didn't have to work until Tuesday at 11 p.m., so that wouldn't happen for two more nights.

A crazy idea began to form in his head as Jerry turned the ignition.

"Weren't you the one who had to take Marissa home the other night when her car acted up?"

Jerry glanced at Adam, eyes smiling as he took in Adam's suddenly changing mood. Talking about Marissa always seemed to brighten him.

"Yeah, what of it?"

"How about swinging by there with me, and seeing if she's home?"

Jerry pulled out of the parking lot, away from Adam's apartment. Both men sat quietly during the 20-minute drive to Marissa's house, listening to the throb of Metallica. But Jerry's thoughts wouldn't allow him to focus on the music. He was worried about Marissa's reaction.

From past conversations, he knew she was hot for Adam, and if he ever got around to asking her, Adam might very well get lucky. But would she be upset if they just dropped in on her?

Jerry cut the engine as he pulled into her driveway.

"Well, she doesn't have company," he said, Marissa's blue Chevy alone in the drive. "Still want to go through with this?"

Adam's eyes were drawn to Marissa's front door.

He knew what he wanted, but if he asked, what would she say? She had been giving him really mixed signals lately -- flirting one minute, assuring him she only wanted his friendship the next.

"Well, we only live once," he said, finally.

Jerry looked at his friend, quizzically.

"What did you just say?"

Nothing, Jerry. I'm going to go see if she is busy. If not, I'll see if I can get Marissa to drive me home. Wait until I signal either way, OK?"

"Sure," Jerry replied.

Adam started up the driveway, his walk neither hesitant nor brimming with his usual cocky self-assurance. Jerry shook his head at the stupidity of youth.

Adam could feel his thoughts running wild. He knew what he wanted to do: lay Marissa down and make wild, passionate love to her, maybe to the throbbing beat of Metallica. Not knowing for certain how she felt about him was slowly driving him crazy, and he wasn't sure just how much more he could take before he had to make his move. He only hoped it didn't cost him her friendship.

Adam climbed the three stairs with light, quick footsteps. This close now, he didn't want to wait any longer to see her, talk to her. Her movements often were hypnotizing in their sensuality.

He raised his hand to knock on her door, but what he saw through its small window stopped him, his hand still in the air. His lungs rapidly emptied, and he felt dizzy.

The woman who had filled his dreams for more than three months was lying gloriously naked on her couch, her hands caressing her body.

Jerry sat at the end of the driveway, wondering just what the hell Adam was doing. Had he chickened out?

Adam turned and waved at him to wait, then turned back to the door. Jerry sat a few moments more, memories of conversation with Marissa running through his head. Then he remembered: often she liked to go home and masturbate, images of Adam still fresh in her mind.

Adam's hand fell to his side, and he restrained the impulse to try the door. He didn't want to interrupt Marissa at such a delicate time, but he also couldn't turn away.

He moved to the window for a better view. Marissa's pale skin shimmered with a light coat of perspiration, her hands caressing her entire body. Long threads of red hair fell over her breasts and shoulders as her head tossed, her beautiful brown eyes closed. One hand stopped at her breasts, pinching the nipples, soothing the tender skin, while the other slid down to her precious core.

Adam's eyes focused on the pale hand between her legs, caressing her clit, rubbing against the petals of her feminity. His cock filled with blood and hardened almost unbearably. He wanted it to be his hands rubbing her little clit instead of her fingers, his cock sliding between her tender lips.

* * *

Marissa's body hummed with desire. She was aware that something in her fantasy world was out of place, but she was a bit too wrapped up in her own touch to question what is was. Images of Adam filled her mind, the way his wavy hair looked on the rare times he shed his hat. The tenderness, she was sure he would be appalled to know, that showed in his eyes. Despite his gruff demeanor, she knew he would be a good, considerate lover. If only she could work up the nerve to ask him, rather than wait on him to ask her.

She imagined his tongue, wet and soft, caressing her clit.

"Oh, yes, Adam, mmmmm..."

Whispered moans followed her raspy words, harder and harder to hold back, the images of Adam's body filling Marissa's every thought. The dragon tattoo on his right arm, the Celtic symbols on his left. Even the two earrings in each ear turned her on, and just imagining the ring through his navel. Oh, God!

* * *

Adam watched as she flicked her clit faster now. He wondered what she was imagining, whether she dreamed of anyone ... maybe even him?

Her sweet breasts, so perfect in size, called to him, the smooth skin, the hard nipples he longed to suck deep into his mouth. A faint coat of wetness glossed her fingers as she pulled them from her pussy to rub over her breasts, and Adam's mouth watered at the sight. He wondered whether she would be as sweet as he imagined.

He inhaled deeply, almost smelling her scent, but again restrained himself from trying the door and going to her side. Her hips rocked faster on the couch as tiny spasms wracked her body. Her hands returned to her clit, fingering it faster, as her needs grew.

* * *

Marissa wanted so badly to orgasm, but even more she wanted to feel Adam deep inside while she did. Two fingers thrust deep, and in her frenzied state she almost had herself convinced they were his smoothcock. Over and over she thrust them in, as far as they would go, her other hand manipulating her clit. Finally, so sweetly, the orgasm she had been craving invaded her senses. Her hips arched off of the couch as sweet flames licked at her body, tingling every nerve.

* * *

Adam watched as her orgasm overtook her, watched as her movements grew frantic, driving her higher and higher off of the couch. He watched as she calmed, her breathing slowed and she seemed to drift off into a satisfied sleep.

He slowly turned on shaky legs and headed back to Jerry's truck, a silly grin on his face. Jerry watched his friend approach and wondered just how long it would take Adam to make his move, now that he had seen Marissa naked.

"Chicken out?" he asked as Adam climbed inside.

"Nah, she was sleeping."

Jerry's grin spread. He delighted in teasing Adam and Marissa, two marshmallows who acted tough.

"It took 10 minutes to figure out she was sleeping?"

"Just shut up and take me home, Jerry."

* * *

Marissa stirred when she heard the sound of a truck's engine revving. For a moment she imagined someone in her driveway, but shook it off, settling back down on the couch, the delightful post-orgasmic haze wrapped about her mind.

* * *

Jerry was barely into the parking lot when Adam unhooked his seat beat and opened the door.

"Thanks for the ride, Jerry," he said. "See you tonight."

Adam entered the lonely bedroom of his bachelor apartment, furnished only with a twin bed, a fish tank and a bookshelf. He sank onto the bed and stripped off his clothes, allowing himself to process what he had just seen.

Once before he had been as close to Marissa as today -- closer, in fact, but then, too, he had held back. At least on that occasion she had known he was there.

Just two weeks ago, Marissa had given him a ride home and he had shown her his sparsely furnished apartment, shared his thoughts, his prized possessions, and his dreams. She hadn't mocked him, unlike most women he knew. In fact, she actually listened, and she cared.

She had knelt on this very floor, not even a foot from where he lay, and talked with him. Her eyes had seemed to invite him to drown within them. But he had begun to feel himself falling, too fast, too deeply, and unaware how to respond, he had pulled away.

Knowing he was hurting Marissa, he spent the next two weeks distancing himself further.

Today just blew that idea out of the water. After seeing her naked, in the throes of self-gratification, there was no way he could pull back any more. But getting back to where they were would be a problem.

Her hips arched, her fingers rubbing fast and furious over her clit. Pale, coral nipples stood firm and tight, full lips parted in half moan, half whimper.

Adam shook his head, trying to drive the image away, but the scene was changing. Instead of lying on her couch, now she was stretched out across his bed, her red hair fanning out around her, so long and beautiful.

So often he had heard her say it was her best feature, but if only she knew how many good features she possessed. She could afford to lose a little weight, sure, but she was a very beautiful woman. Full, pouty lips that begged to be kissed. Eyes a man could gladly lose himself in. She had a way of looking at him that could make Adam feel like a god, or at least her willing slave.

Marissa held up her arms, reaching for Adam, and he lowered his weight onto her. Her nipples pressed against his chest and he groaned, loving the feel of her strong legs gripping his hips. Adam wanted to sink into her moist heat, to feel her muscles clench him tight. His cock hardened, straining for her touch.

He jolted upright, his hand wrapped around his cock, lightly stroking. Normally he could separate fact from fantasy, but he had been so wrapped up in this daydream that he had begun to caress himself.

He wasn't one to masturbate, but Adam had to admit that, with images of Marissa in his mind, this felt very good. Lying back again, he allowed fantasy to take over and his hands to fulfill his needs.

Visions of Marissa stretched out, her hands running over her body, fuelling his desire. Slowly at first, his hands caressed his cock. But as his fantasies evolved, Marissa's hands replaced his own.

Her fingertips traced tender lines over the head of his cock, spreading his pre-come. Feather soft, her lips kissed his entire body, her tongue flicking against the rings in his ear and navel. Moving just a bit faster, her hands worked over his cock, drawing low moans from between his clenched teeth.

He fought the rapidly spreading threads of desire, wanting to make this last, to draw out every sensation, to keep the fantasy alive. But Adam soon admitted defeat and continued this massage. As well as he could "see" Marissa before him, he knew this wasn't her touch, but his own.

Stroking up and down, squeezing tight, Adam worked his cock closer and closer to orgasm. Images of Marissa's head thrown back filled his mind as his balls tightened. Come began to dribble down his cock, coating his hands as he worked harder and faster toward his goal.

He wondered frantically what Marissa's lips would feel like closed over his cock, and that sent him over the edge. Liquid heat poured over his hands as he orgasmed; faster and harder he jerked his hands up and down, milking his hardness for all it was worth.

Adam sighed deeply, satisfied, and after some time he pulled himself to the bathroom to clean up.

The steady heat of the shower soothed him, bringing him down from his agitated state, and prepared him for sleep. He was alone in this room once more, the fish that swam lazily in the tank his only companions.

* * *

Several Days Later

Adam was watching Marissa eat, the almost tentative way she took small bites of her burger, her joyful look as the salty fries mixed with the sour ketchup. She really enjoyed her meal, even if it was from a lousy truck-stop.

She glanced up and her eyes met his, a smile curving her lips. Shannon finished the joke she was telling, and Marissa laughed along, not really feeling that she fit in, but rather that she there because Adam had insisted.

Her eyes met Adam's again and she winked. Adam sucked in a breath, images flowing through his mind. For the past week, at odd moments, visions of Marissa's naked body flashed through his thoughts. Adam sighed and tried to focus on Brian's voice.

Marissa's pulse began to race. Every time her eyes met Adam's she felt a connection. She had always felt so comfortable with him, bonded to him, but lately it had begun to feel deeper, more intense. Three weeks ago things had started to change, when she has gone to Adam's place as a friend hoping for more.

Though nothing sexual had come of that day, she still felt something had clicked -- a new closeness between them, a more emotional connection.

Marissa shook her head, clearing these thoughts and calling herself a fool. What would a guy like Adam, charismatic if admittedly not God's gift to women, want with someone like her? Feeling every one of her 160 pounds, Marissa looked again at her food and felt her appetite wane.

Adam watched her changing expression as she pushed her plate away and got up from the table. Brian stopped in mid-sentence, the table growing quiet as they watched Marissa pay her bill and step into the parking lot. Adam went after her.

"I wish those two would just screw and get it over with," Shannon muttered.

"Yep, Marissa is driving me insane," Brittany agreed.

Brian smiled and added his two cents' worth: "Maybe someone should clue them in as to how the other feels."

The women burst out laughing.

"Even if we did, you know as well as I do that neither would believe it," Brittany said. "They are too damn thickskulled to listen."

Shannon nodded. "Too self-conscious, too."

Adam hurried across the parking lot after Marissa. The clouds dispersed the moon's glow just right, and her face was suddenly bathed in silver light.

Adam drew in a quick breath. Eyes closed, arms out, head back, Marissa stood unmoving in the field behind the truck-stop. At that moment Adam wondered when she looked more beautiful: naked or bathed in moonlight.

"Maybe both," he thought. "Naked in the moonlight would be best."

"What do you want, Adam?" Marissa asked, her arms dropping, her eyes opening.

"How did you know it was me?"

Marissa smiled, her eyes twinkling.

"And just who else would it be?"

Adam approached hesitantly, waiting for her mood to change.

"You never know, it could have been Shannon, or a trucker coming to steal you away."

Marissa chuckled. Just being with Adam like this was already improving her mood.

"So what made you leave like that?" Adam asked.

Marissa's smile faded and her arms wrapped around her waist, as though she were protecting herself, or hiding.

"I'd rather not talk about it," she replied.

Adam stopped inches away. Looking into his blue eyes, Marissa felt her heart flutter.

"No problem."

For the first time since they met, Adam moved to touch her, wrapping her in his arms, soothing her. Uncertain how to respond, Marissa tentatively wrapped her arms around his waist, snuggling her body against his.

They were not unnoticed. Shannon was first to turn away, wanting to give her friends some privacy. Brittany averted her glance a moment later.

Almost transfixed, Brian continued to observe Adam's uncharacteristic behavior, unable to match this tender Adam with the hard ass he worked with. Shannon tapped his shoulder, and he swung around to face her. Taking the hint, Brian returned to his dinner.

"You know, you can always talk to me if you have something on your mind."

Marissa sighed and snuggled against Adam, feeling his arms tighten around her.

"I know. It's just ... " she began.

"It's OK. We'll talk later."

Marissa nodded against his shoulder, hoping he would forget all about it.

"Still taking me home after work?"

Again she nodded.

"Good."

Eight a.m. arrived quicker than anyone on third shift had expected, and there remained a lot of freight to be put out. It was 9:30 before they were done, and everyone was tired, some even in pain.

"Marissa, dial 181," Adam's voice rang out over the intercom.

She hurried to the break room phone to call him back.

"Ready to go yet?" she asked.

"Yep. Meet me in the break room."

"I'll be waiting."

Marissa smiled as she hung up the phone. Like every morning, he would want to a cigarette or two before heading out the door.

Adam slouched down in his chair, wondering how to execute his plan. Getting Marissa up to his apartment was the easy part: all he had to do was ask her if she wanted to see his new sword. She would be there in a heartbeat. The problem was how to tell her how he felt about her -- especially considering he was still unsure himself.

Together they left the break room.

"Come on lazy bones, let's get out of here."

Adam always did have a way with words.

Marissa turned the radio off in the car, as was her habit when she took Adam home. The stations just didn't play his type of music.

A familiar silence filled the car, and following tradition set over months, Marissa waited to see whether Adam wanted to talk, or just to think.

This morning he seemed to want some quiet time, and respecting that, Marissa did her best not to grumble at the other drivers. It was hard though -- some of them couldn't drive worth shit.

When they got to the last block before his lonely apartment, Adam finally spoke.

"Want to come up and see my new sword?"

"Yes," she whispered.

Adam watched Marissa's face as she admired his ever-growing collection, their love of swords just one of the many things they had in common. She remounted the blade on the wall and headed for the living room, feeling a hint of sexual energy as she brushed past Adam in the doorway.

She waited, awkwardly, to see if Adam wanted her to stay, or if he was so tired that he simply wanted to doze. Normally when he invited her up, they watched TV for an hour or so and then she left, leaving him to sit in his lonely apartment, until finally sleep called him, too strong to be denied.

Adam seemed lost in thought.

"So what do you want to do today, babe?" she asked him.

His eyes met hers. Typical male that he was, he shrugged, then grinned. Huffy with faked indignation, Marissa play-slapped at his shoulder.

"Well, I would like to hear that CD you have been telling me about," he replied. "It sounds interesting."

Marissa smiled, getting the hint. He wanted her to stay awhile.

Thrilled, she headed out the door, met by a light drizzle. The quick trip to the car and back was enough to coat her in a thin layer of moisture and bring a delicious chill to her skin when she re-entered Adam's air-conditioned apartment.

His eyes were drawn to her hardened nipples as he removed the CD from her trembling hand.

"Don't you know it's not polite to point?" he said, brazenly.

She blushed as Adam slid the CD into the stereo, deep, beautiful voices soon filling the room. The passionate Latin chant seemed to enter their bodies, soothing and arousing.

Marissa removed her wet shoes, shivering as she felt the cool floor beneath her bare feet, and was surprised, even shocked, when Adam returned to carefully gather and towel her hair dry.

Slowly they sank onto the couch as Adam draped the towel around her shoulders, then pulled her against him. Still uncertain, Marissa went with the flow and fulfilled one of her fantasies: snuggling in his arms, listening to the sound of the rain beating against the windows, absorbed by the melodic voices of the monks.

Whispering breath gently flowed against Marissa's neck. Adam leaned down and tenderly began to nuzzle against the smooth white flesh. She tipped her head to the side, waiting to see what he might do next. So badly she wanted to respond, but he finally was making her secret dream come true, and she didn't want to do anything to discourage him.

Adam allowed himself what felt right, and gradually Marissa began to show her response, too overcome by her desires.

His lips had kissed the side of her neck, hesitantly at first, their wet heat shooting straight through her body. Marissa's lips parted and a tiny moan escaped, barely heard by either. Slightly shaking, Adam's hand began to slide from her hair to her shoulder, caressing down her arm, to her breast. The nipple hardened beneath her shirt, begging for the attention his work-calloused hand might provide.

Marissa's head tipped back, her eyes closed, and she gave herself to his touch, glad that finally, if only for one night, she would be his.

Almost lovingly, Adam lifted her T-shirt inch by inch, baring her smooth stomach to his view. Leaning down, he had begun to nibble and kiss his way up her soft belly from her navel to the bottom edge of her breasts. Black lace tickled his nose, and he pulled back. Marissa's eyes opened and her passion-glazed look met his.

Adam met Marissa halfway and their lips met briefly for the first time, then returned again for a deeper exploration. His hands slid over her stomach; Marissa's eyes closed and she fully relaxed.

Every fiber in her demanded release. She knew this would follow, in good time. Adam's time. He never did anything before he was ready.

Her hands moved to his cotton-clad shoulders. Adam's lips left her ribs and he moved his body over hers, pressing her against the couch. The armrest bit into her shoulders, but she barely noticed. It felt too good to have him atop her, his weight slight but noticeable.

Their lips met again and hers parted, gladly granting his tongue entry. Marissa's hips began to gently grind against his pelvis, teasing them both. His hardness became pronounced and she felt faint. This was not just a dream anymore.

Adam's hands continued their journey, traveling over her ribs and around to her ass. His pelvis mimicked her movements, grinding against her. His lips moved from hers and began to kiss her neck again. With a shiver, Marissa tipped her head to the side.

"Oh Jesus, Adam," she mumbled, delighting in his movements.

She moved her hands to the bottom of his shirt and started sliding it up his torso, baring his smooth back and chest.

Adam pulled back long enough to remove it, then settled back onto her warmth. The edges of her bra tickled his chest and soon it was gone, baring her breasts to his desire-clouded eyes.

With a smile, he dipped his head and began sucking one of the hardened peaks into his mouth. Marissa moaned and arched against him, their hips rocking together.

"Let's go to the bedroom," she gasped, needing more room.

Adam swallowed a sigh and stood. Marissa followed, her mind numbed with desire. Standing inches from him, she grasped the belt loops of his jeans and pulled him with her. Together they headed for the bed, and to a new level of their friendship.

Her knees hit the edge of the bed and Adam's hands grasped her hips to keep her from falling.

"Easy now," he soothed, his nimble fingers undoing her jeans. With a self-conscious sigh, she allowed him to remove her jeans and panties, then flopped back onto the bed, reaching up for his hands.

Kneeling between her legs, he slid down on top of her, falling the last few inches. Momentarily breathless, Marisa lay there as he again caressed her stomach with his lips. But this time, he moved down instead of up.

She murmured a weak protest, but he was determined to please her. Marissa closed her eyes and gave herself to these delightful sensations. Gently, his tongue licked at her folds, parting them slowly with his fingertips.

His nose pushed against her tender clit, and she gasped as new nerve-endings came alive. With an almost evil look, he set about tormenting her, arousing her, then backing off. Over and over his tongue brought her to the edge, then he backed off.

Her hands fisted in his hair, trying to hold him still, but he had his way nonetheless.

Marissa's frustration mounted until Adam finally gave in, and continued beyond the point of no return. Her body arched off of the bed, orgasm shaking her.

Adam stood and quickly shed his jeans and boxers, then joined her again on the bed, this time sliding all the way up her body. His hand smoothed her hair out of her face as she tried to regain her breath. He leaned down and kissed her, letting Marissa taste herself on his lips, the sweetness of her body. Marissa moaned, her hips arching against his.

He pushed Marissa up onto her knees.

"Your turn," he whispered, then began caressing her breasts from a new angle. She carefully settled herself over him, then gasped as he slid in deep.

"Oh my God," she whimpered.

Adam lifted lightly against her, Marissa moaning again. She began to move against him, jerkily at first, until his hands settled on her hips, guiding her. She leaned back slightly, adjusting her body, and settled into a smooth rhythm. Her mind was clouded with exquisite sensations, as she finally felt the fullness of her lover, her love, inside her.

"So this is what heaven is like," Adam thought as new feelings awakened in his body. He began to sense things with Marissa, which he had never felt before. Comforted, yet sexy. Aroused, yet peaceful. Her muscles clenched him tight and he had to grit his teeth to keep from ending it too soon.

A tightness settled into Marissa's pussy, a warning of what was to come. All of her nerve-endings seemed to be screaming for release, begging for an end to this sweet torture. Marissa settled into a fast rhythm, clenching Adam's cock deep inside her. Their breathing became moans and pants of desire.

Both wanted it to last forever, but neither could hold out much longer. Adam just wanted to make it long enough to drive Marissa over the edge. His hips started lifting in synch with her motions, pushing her closer and closer. With a gasp, she orgasmed, her sweet fluids coating Adam 's cock, her muscles gripping him tight.

She collapsed against her chest, his arms wrapped around her, and he thrust twice more, and then gave in. Muffling his moans against her neck, Adam felt a sweet release of tension flow through his body. Nerves seemed to explode, but all was right with the world.

Marissa shifted to Adam's side and tried to move away slightly, knowing he would want time to himself, but his arms tightened and he held her close. She sighed happily and snuggled against him, glad he wanted her close, glad that he felt something for her.

Adam knew Marissa well enough to guess her thoughts. Letting someone in was hard for him, but for her, he was going to try. REALLY try to let her know what he was thinking, feeling, wanting.

"She's worth it," he thought.

"Marissa?"

"Um?" she mumbled, waiting for him to ask her to get dressed.

"Would you, um, well, would you like to, er, stay tonight with me?"

Her head jerked up, needing to meet his eyes to see if he was teasing.

"Yes, I'd like that, a lot, but only if you're sure."

How like her to consider him first.

"I wouldn't have asked if I didn't mean it."

She leaned down and kissed his shoulder then settled against him again.

"Then I'll stay."

* * *

Adam held Marissa close, content to lay and watch her sleep. A feeling of deep contentment washed over him, and he knew in his heart that he was falling for her.

What was once friendship had, over time, blossomed into the beauty of love.

His head fought it, not wanting to open up and leave himself vulnerable, but his heart felt it nonetheless.

He knew Marissa would never hurt him; she had already proven that. She was content to wait and accept whatever he could give, but he knew it wasn't enough. She deserved more. She deserved all of the pretty words, that until now, he couldn't give.

Marissa's breathing eased. Her eyes fluttered open, closed, then opened again, her gaze meeting Adam's. She saw her own thoughts in his eyes.

"Marissa?"

"Uh-huh?" she replied, almost afraid of what he would say, afraid he would pull back, to protect himself.

"I love you," he whispered.

She smiled, wondering whether she had only heard the whispers of her heart, rather than the words he spoke.

"What did you say?" she asked, needing to hear it again, to know the truth of it.

"I ... I love you."

Adam leaned down and kissed her, his lips reinforcing the point. The kiss was tender, not one of lust, but of something deeper.

"Oh, Adam," she murmured against his lips. "I love you, too.

He pulled back and sat up. Marissa tumbled onto her back and looked at him in shock.

"Say it again. I need to hear it, say it again."

"Adam, I love you. I have for a while. I though you knew. That's why I pulled away for a while. Why I was distant. I was giving myself time, time to learn to deal with it, to not ask anything in return."

"Did I do that to you?" he asked, knowing the answer.

"Yes," she replied, almost destroying his composure. Adam pulled her close, holding her, wishing he could take away the pain his selfishness must have caused her.

Marissa kissed his chest, letting him know she forgave him. She forgave him everything.

"Adam, it's OK, my love. It's OK."

For the first time in years, Adam allowed himself to cry. Marissa held him, thinking him more of a man than ever. He felt her soothing touch on his back as she rubbed his shoulders, heard her whispers in his hair and knew it was all right. He allowed the tears to flow, crying for the boy he had been, for the love he had almost lost, and for the gift of her love that she had given him.

Finally the tears dried. He felt tired, but free. The past couldn't harm him any longer, it wouldn't rule his actions, it wouldn't demand his heart and soul. The future loomed bright, and though it might be filled with hardship, with loss and with heartache, he knew Marissa would be there, making it bearable. Making it ... beautiful.

"Is there anything else you want to tell me?" she teased him, lightening the mood. "Some little detail I might need to know?"

"Yes, there is, actually," he replied without the lightness of banter.

Marissa would love him no matter what, but she braced herself nonetheless. "A few weeks ago, after work, I had Jerry bring me by your house. I wanted to pour all of my problems on your shoulders, like always, and have you make me forget about them. I wanted to talk with you, to yell with you, to sit beside you and watch TV as we both escaped into a movie and left our problems behind.

"When I got there, I went to your door and saw that you were, um, busy. I know I should have turned away, I should have knocked. I should have done something, but what I did..."

"You stayed and watched, didn't you?" Marissa said calmly, feeling the blood rush to her cheeks.

Adam sighed. As images filled his mind of her hand running over her smooth curves, he could feel his body responding.

"Yes, and it was the most erotic experience of my life. Every day since then, I have gone to sleep with images in my mind of you caressing yourself."

After sharing her body with him, learning all of his sensitive spots, Marissa still was shy. Then another voice filled her mind, telling her that sometimes she was too cautious, that sometimes she needed to just throw caution to the wind, and act.

Knowing this inner voice was right, Marissa slowly moved out of Adam's arms until she was sitting beside him. She smiled, not quite knowing what she would say, but knowing she had to say it.

"Adam, darling ... would you like to watch again? Maybe a little more closely this time?"

Adam smiled, enjoying the confidence in her voice, her more direct gaze.

"Yes. Oh, God, yes I would."

And so she showed him, and he enjoyed watching.

REFLECTIONS IN TIME

"Greeeggg!" Alyson giggled. "Now stop that. Would you ... please ... stop." Alyson doubled over in laughter, wiggling to get away from Greg's hands. Very sensitive, her ribs were a perfect spot to tickle.

Greg tipped her over, slightly baring her midriff. Her wiggles continued, as did his tickling. In an effort to stop her movement, Greg settled his body over hers, pinning her down in a perfect tickling position. Holding her hands over her head with one hand, his other hand was free to torment her tender flesh, and her giggling resumed.

But Alyson's giggles soon were gasps. Greg immediately stopped tickling, allowing her to draw in a few deep breaths. She shifted her hips and Greg became instantly aware of just how he was positioned. Alyson's breasts rose against his chest with each breath she took. Greg lifted his chest slightly, and looked down at their bodies. Her shirt had ridden up enough to show the briefest hint of her lacy bra. Alyson lay totally still beneath him, her arms over her head even though he had already let her wrists go.

Strange feelings swelled inside Alyson's body. She wasn't quite sure just what she was feeling, but it felt good and kind of scary at the same time.

Greg turned his gaze back to Alyson's eyes, and saw her thoughts reflected in the brown depths. Hesitantly, he leaned down, his lips barely brushed against hers. Time seemed to stand still for them both.

* * *

"Alyson. Hello, Earth to Alyson. Alyson!" The brunette's head lifted, memories pushed to the back of her mind.

"Did you hear what I said?" Alyson nodded, too choked up to speak.

"I still can't believe it. After four years, Greg is coming home."

Beth prattled on, unaware that Alyson had ceased to listen again, too lost in her own memories of Greg.

* * *

Twenty, maybe thirty minutes after their first kiss, the dam burst. Emotions held in check far too long swept them both away. Alyson lay naked on the carpet with Greg, his youthful, hard body covering hers. His lips pressed against hers, muffling her gasp of pain as he joined them. He stilled, feeling her muscles clench around him, the sensation so wonderful, and the desire to move strong. But Greg held back, giving Alyson time to adjust. He knew that he was her first, as he had dreamed of being as he lay in bed at night.

Smiling at him through her tears, she bravely lifted her hips, encouraging him to move. Greg laid still, his teeth gritted, resisting the temptation. Carefully he slid a hand between her legs and found his goal, the little nub of flesh that was the center of her sexuality.

Seconds turned to minutes as Greg waited. Finally, tentatively, Alyson started to move against him, lifting her hips in pleasure. Greg waited, his nerve endings in agony, until he knew she was close, then he started to move, driving them both over the edge quickly.

* * *

Alyson watched her stepmother flit about the house, straightening couch cushions, checking on the dinner and a million other little things. One would think that the president was coming to visit rather than a son coming home.

With a sigh, she turned back to the window, watching for his headlights, waiting for the signal that her love was home.

* * *

Neither in the room heard the door open. Nothing could have prepared them for what would follow.

"What the HELL?!" Alyson startled, looking into her father's angry eyes.

Greg pulled away from her, grabbed his shirt and covered her, then moved to pull his pants on.

"Dad, I can explain," Alyson started, but her father cut her off.

"Not a word, not one damn word. Get up, and go to your room NOW! I will deal with you later." His gaze swung to Greg, who was zipping his jeans up.

"As for you, you little ..." His voice trailed off as his new wife touched his shoulder. Barely restrained, he stormed out of the room, leaving his wife to deal with her son. Alyson had already left, tears in her eyes. The most breathtaking moment of her life was tarnished with anger.

* * *

Greg pulled into the driveway with a sigh. He cut off the engine and leaned back against the headrest. Closing his eyes, he allowed memories to swarm his mind.

Over the last four years he had stayed in constant contact with his mother, but despite her pleadings he hadn't returned home to make amends with his stepfather. In his mind, there was nothing to apologize for. He and Alyson were both eighteen when they made love. Sure, they hadn't picked the best location, but still. With a sigh, Greg finally admitted the truth to himself. He did owe his stepfather, and Alyson, an apology. He should have known better and stopped things before they got out of control. Alyson had been sheltered all of her life, first with nannies and later with an all-girls' high school. She hadn't much experience with men, or boys for that matter. Greg doubted she had ever been kissed before that night.

Sitting up, he opened the car door and smiled as the cool Nebraska air greeted him. Over the last few years, he had missed the cold of winter almost as much as his family as he found himself stationed in one hot climate after another. The military was good to him, giving him a roof over his head and three square meals a day, not to mention an education, but it sure didn't locate its people in the best of spots.

Smiling at the reindeer and other yard decorations, he headed up the walkway and stopped once he reached the porch. Looking at the window, he saw a familiar face. Alyson hadn't changed much over the last four years. At least he didn't think so, judging from her sleeping face.

Greg knew that he had. The military had seen to it. The sudden loss of his family and support system has seen to it. And so had giving in to his hormonal urges.

He knocked twice, and then waited. His mother, a smile already bathing her face, soon opened the door. The years had added a few more lines around her eyes and mouth and a lot of gray hair, but her smile still lifted Greg's heart.

"Mama," he whispered, felling like a little boy again as she enfolded him against her loving body.

"My baby," she whispered against his hair. Unlike most boys, Greg had always allowed his mother to call him baby, provided they were alone. Stepping back, he grasped her hands in his and took a good look at her.

"Your stepfather has forgiven you, Greg. He asked me to call you home.

The stroke scared him, and I think he realized it was time to let the past rest."

Grinning, Greg followed her inside, glad that he wouldn't have to fight to stay with his mother for Christmas. Her letter asking him come home had been a surprise, and he hadn't been quite sure what to expect.

A squeal alerted Greg only a moment before a blonde launched herself into his arms. Wrapping around him like a cat does legs, she giggled as she ruffled his hair and commented on his tanned skin.

"Hi, Beth," Greg replied, already knowing that she wouldn't pause long enough for him to get more that a word or two in here and there. Some things even four years couldn't change.

Alyson had been awakened by Beth's squeal and now she stood in the shadows, watching as her stepmother and her sister greeted Greg. After four years, he still caused her heart to race. Though his hair was shorter, his body tighter, and his face more chiseled, she still would have known him anywhere.

Alyson's father approached the boy he had last spoken to in anger to find a man had replaced him.

"It's good to have you home, son," he muttered as he enfolded Greg in his arms for a brief hug. Pulling away he cleared his throat. "Your mother has missed you. Maybe with Christmas upon us, we can forget, or at least forgive, the past."

With a nod Greg acknowledged his words.

With the beat of her heart hammering in her ears, Alyson swallowed her courage and approached the group around Greg. Nudging Beth aside, Alyson stepped into Greg's view.

For a moment, they were transported back in time when they had seen each other last. Greg's mother shooed everyone from the room, leaving Alyson and Greg alone. Blushing, Alyson looked at the floor in front of her, instead of meeting his eyes. Despite the years, she felt like he could see into her soul.

"I missed you," she whispered, cringing inside at how that sounded. Their first words in four years and she already sounded like a lovesick schoolgirl.

Greg lifted a hand to her chin and tipped her face up, forcing her eyes to meet his.

"Alyson, there is something I need to say. I, um, I'm not very good at this, never really had to say it before, but, ah hell. I'm sorry Alyson. I took advantage of your innocence and your loving nature."

Alyson stared at him in shock and disbelief. After four years of waiting for him to come home, hoping that he still loved her, she couldn't believe what she was hearing.

The slap sounded loud in the stillness of the room. In shock, Alyson covered her mouth with her hands, and ran from the room. Moments later, the sound of her bedroom door slamming could be heard through the house.

* * *

Adam debated letting Greg know he had seen and heard everything and finally gave up. It was time that the past was fully revealed and laid to rest.

"She loves you, son," he stated, and waited for Greg to respond. Instead

Greg just stood there, rubbing his cheek where Alyson's hand had landed. When he saw that Greg wasn't going to comment, Adam continued, "Four years ago she loved you, and she still does today. Lord knows I tried to get her to date other men. Some of the local boys have been after her since you left, but she doesn't see any of them. The only male friends she has are either firmly and happily attached or gay.

"I made a mistake four years ago, throwing you out. And my daughter has paid for it every day. I judged you harshly in anger. It was hell for me, walking in to find my baby girl having sex with a man, any man, on my living room floor. But as the days went by, I came to realize that she wasn't my baby any more, but a woman full grown, with a mind of her own.

"Now I know that you are trying to heal the wound you though that you caused, but the truth is, I caused it. And now, I am trying to heal it. If you care for her, if you still love her, as I know now that you did, then go to her.

"Your mom, Beth and I are going to run out for a bit to do some last minute shopping. You'll have the house to yourself for a bit. Regardless of what happens while we are gone, when we come back, I want my daughter and you to get along, for no one else, but your mother if need be. She has been so happy that you are coming home.

"Well, I've spoken my piece and I going to go round up the women now. You do what you feel is right, son. Just remember, a woman's heart is a fragile thing, but a woman's love is resilient. They can forgive most anything, given enough reason and want to."

Adam left the room, having spoken his mind, and within minutes was ushering his wife and younger daughter out the door, despite their protests that they couldn't leave Greg. Finally, in desperation, he admitted that they were going shopping for Greg and having him along wouldn't work, and that he had asked Alyson to keep him company. Beth grinned, and headed out to the car. Greg's mother lingered a moment longer, her eyes looking over the lonely form of her son. Her heart ached for him, her maternal instinct urged her to fix his problems for him, but her head told her that he and

Alyson needed to work it out. Turning, she grasped Adam's arm and led him out the door.

The hall clock ticked the seconds as Greg stood still in the hallway, debating what to say to Alyson. Finally he gave up planning and headed up the stairs to her room. Knocking softly, he listened to her sobbing, feeling like his heart was about to break.

"Go away."

Opening the door a crack, he peeked inside and looked for Alyson. Her tiny form lay sprawled out on the bed, her face buried in the pillows.

Stepping into the room, he closed the door behind him.

"I said go away," she muttered, her voice muffled by the pillow.

Greg knelt beside her bed and lifted his hand to her hair, smoothing the soft brunette strands from her face.

"I love you," he whispered. "I have for more years than I can remember. I think I have loved you from the first moment I saw you across the playground right before Tommy Britain pushed you and I came to your rescue. I think I fell for sure when you kicked me as payment for coming to your rescue."

"We were six," Alyson retorted, lifting her head from the pillow, fear that he was playing with her clouding her eyes.

"I know. I remember even then loving your feistiness, even as I rubbed my sore leg. And over the months as our parents got to know each other, trying to figure out how to keep us from fighting, I think I knew then that you were the girl for me. It just took my head a few more years than my heart to understand that."

Leaning down, he pressed his lips to hers. As hers parted in response, a feeling of euphoria clouded his mind. "This is where I was meant to be," he thought, "here in her arms."

Pulling away, Alyson looked into his eyes and saw the love reflected in their depths. "We can't Greg, our family, my father…" she began.

"Everyone is gone. Your father took them shopping and he gave me his blessing."

Alyson giggled.

"What?" Greg asked as his hands trailed up and down her arms.

"If he took Beth shopping he must be ok with us. She always spends more that he wants her to, and takes forever to do so. He HATES shopping with her." Greg grinned in memory of several shopping trips he had been struck going on with Beth.

"I remember."

Leaning back down, he kissed her again, then stood. "I guess we should head downstairs," he started, only to find himself pulled down on top of Alyson. Grinning up at him, she wrapped her arms around his neck.

"I have waited four years for you to say the three little words I have longed to hear most and then to make love to me again. So far half of that wish has come true." With a tender smile, Greg leaned down and kissed her again, determined to make the second part of her wish more than she dreamed possible.

Slowly, he undressed her and himself, determined to kiss and caress every inch of her body. By the time he worked his way down to her stomach, Alyson was gasping and squirming beneath him.

"Greg," she panted, "make love to me."

Blowing softly against her nether lips, he grinned. "I thought that is what I have been doing."

In frustration, Alyson tried to fist her hands in his hair, but it was cut too short. Moaning, she moved her hands to his shoulders, and left little crescent shaped marks with her nails as he flicked her pussy lips with his warm tongue. Arching against him, she moaned again at the new and exhilarating sensation. It was better than she had been told it was by her friends. Within moments, a remembered feeling began spreading throughout her body.

"Greg," she gasped. Replacing his tongue with his fingertips, Greg moved up her body and pressed his lips to hers. Reaching down, he grasped his cock in his hand and slowly guided it into her warmth. Thrusting slightly, he almost passed out as she opened to accept an inch of him, then tightened. Thrusting again, he slid in deeper, then again and again until they were fully joined. Holding himself above her with one hand, he used his other to gently rub her throbbing clit as he thrust his cock inside her. Alyson wrapped her legs around his waist and did her best to move with him.

Soon they found the rhythm older than time and began reaching for the heavens. Alyson gasped, her body tightening around him as pleasure radiated from her pussy throughout her entire body. Within moments, Greg gave in the clenching of her muscles and joined her in ecstasy's arms.

Time passed as the two lovers lay partially joined on the bed, holding and kissing each other, sharing the highlights of the past four years. Alyson told of her degrees in science and education and of her acceptance of the offer at the high school to teach next fall. Greg shared stories of the exotic lands he had seen, the different cultures and languages.

As afternoon threaded into evening, they shared together and grew close once again, until finally they had to get up and dress, knowing that their family would be home soon.

When Adam opened the door an hour later, he smiled at the picture before him. Alyson lay cuddled in Greg's arms, sound asleep. Greg looked up at his stepfather and smiled. As he watched him struggle to carry what were no doubt Beth's purchases into the house, he had to bite back a grin. Some things never changed. Holding Alyson close, he repeated to himself in his mind, "Some things never change, and I am so fortunate that they don't."

RENEWAL

To say we had hit a rut in our lives was an understatement. Jared worked all of the time, and after five years together, frankly, I was lonely. Sure, we went out to dinner occasionally, took our twin hellions out to a pizza place or the ever present McDonald's, but it just wasn't enough any more.

When Jared suggested a weekend away, I was shocked. I had no idea he knew that I was feeling unhappy. Our sex life had taken a turn after the girls. Instead of being playful, and taking all night just kissing and making slow sweet love, now it was hurry up so that we could get some sleep. Or as happened so often, hang on a sec while I see what the girls are crying over.

For a month, I wondered just where we were planning to go, but Jared insisted on being close mouthed. He wouldn't tell me anything. The week before we were scheduled to leave, Jared called from work.

"Hi honey. You doing ok?" he asked, his tone showing how tired he was.

"Yeah. Just getting the girls their lunch."

"Mm. After lunch my mom is swinging by to pick them up for a few hours. Why don't you go shopping for our trip."

"If you'll tell me where we are going, I'll know what to buy."

"Hum … let me see. No. Still not telling. Just buy yourself something nice and make sure there isn't too much to it." He laughed that sexy laugh I remembered from so long ago. It sent shivers of sexual awareness down my spine. If only his mom were taking the kids for the night instead of just a few hours.

"Ok. I'll wing it then. Aree you going to be home by dinner time?"

"Yeah. Hopefully, if I can ever get this paperwork done."

"Ok love. See you then. Bye."

"I love you Lynn."

"I know, love you too."

Jared's mom arrived just as the girls were finished eating, promising to keep them entertained until five, and I hurried out the house for the mall. Not knowing where we were going, I wandered into several stores, but saw nothing that appealed to me. Finally, I wound up in Victoria's Secret. What used to be a part of my normal shopping, over the past few years, I hadn't even glanced at Victoria's as I headed through the mall, on the sporadic occasions that I was able to get out alone.

Entering the store, I marveled at the changes. Sheer and sexy as hell. The lingerie was mostly the same, but with a more outlandish quality and presentation. Crotchless panties took up an entire rack next to panty and bra sets.

"Can I help you?" I startled at someone's voice. While I had been standing there gawking, a saleslady had come up beside me.

"Um, I'm not sure. I want something for a weekend away, but I have no idea where we are going. I'm just hoping ..." my voice trailed off as embarrassment set in. Here I was telling a stranger that I wanted to get laid.

"Well, do you see anything that catches your eye?" Frankly I wasn't sure. Before the girls I would have said yes, but I guess I wasn't sure what "I" liked anymore. My body had undergone so many changes, I felt almost different about myself.

"I don't know."

"Hum. With your coloring I would go with something green to play on the red to your hair and your deep green eyes. Do you have a fabric you like?"

"Yes," I smiled, "I like silk. It feels so comfortable and sexy." I stopped and blushed again.

Within an hour with the helpful saleslady by my side, I had spent several hundred dollars on sexy nightgowns, scandalous panties, lotions and bath accessories that could last for a month. After having looked at myself in the mirror, trying on the new clothes in the dressing room, I was starting to feel better about myself.

I returned home and put my purchases in the top of the closet and enjoyed a nice long bath while waiting for the girls to get home.

* * *

A week later, the day had finally arrived. Jared stayed up late the night before packing our bags. I watched as he packed jeans and t-shirts, day dresses and necessities. I pulled out my Victoria's bag from the closet and added it to the suitcase very much wondering just where we were headed. Still he wouldn't tell me.

Tossing and turning half of the night, I finally drifted off to sleep.

Morning arrived and with the kids taken care of, and lunch eaten, we headed off to wherever we were going. I sat beside Jared and tried to act as if I wasn't curious as hell, but after I re-read the same page of my book seven times, I gave up and just enjoyed the scenery. The trees had all lost their leaves, but there was something about the mountains rising from the morning fog that lent a further air of mystery to our outing.

After about three hours on the road, we turned off of the highway and headed down a nice country lane.

Ahead of us where two stone columns with an arch over them, roses and leaves intertwining. I thought, beaming slightly, that has possibilities.

About a half mile later, a charming house rose out of the landscape. I gasped as the house came into view. It was beautiful. Quaint and yet endearing, a perfect bed and breakfast.

We pulled into a lot to the side of the house and getting out of the car, I looked around me in wonder. Stunning. Fountains and sculpted trees filled the landscaped lawn around us. Jared clasped my hand within his and led me to the front door. Upon entering, I gasped again. Hardwood floors, a beautiful carved staircase, and a stone fireplace, it was a decorators dream. I loved it, just as much as I was jealous of the decorator who did what I felt I could never do.

"Mr. And Mrs. Paterson?" a shy voice asked. From far away I heard Jared answer. I was too busy looking about me to pay much attention. I was going to love this place I kept thinking. Turning, out of the blue I grasped Jared's face in my hands and kissed him, shocking us both.

Desire curled in my belly, but embarrassment flared wildly across my face. In shock I pulled back and looked at the person Jared had been talking to.

"I'm sorry ..."

"It's ok," she smiled, "we are glad that you like it. Mr. Paterson has been calling about once a week or so for the last month making sure everything was just so."

I smiled at Jared and he smiled back, love shining in his eyes. "I love you so much Jared." The lady, whom Jared later informed me was the owner, turned and began to climb the staircase, while her husband introduced himself and grabbed our bags. Jared grasped my hand again, and led me to the staircase, where halfway up, the owner had turned and was waiting on us.

"I think you will like your room. Jared told me of your love of silk, so you are booked for the Silk and Satin room for the weekend, but should you want to move to another room, we still have several open."

"Thank you." I murmured as we arrived at our room. With a flick of her wrist she opened the door and stepped back.

"Should you need anything, just ask." Then she left, but I barely registered it. I was too busy staring at our room. Beautiful black satin covered the chairs. A cherry wood table and chairs set sat in the corner by the windows. "Jared, I love it." I whispered.

"I'm glad. Now I think we should get out of the way. I remember our bags aren't exactly light." Blushing again, I stepped into the room, so the owner's husband could set out bags down and leave. As the main door clicked shut, I moved across the room and headed to a door to the side. Opening it, I discovered the bathroom, with a tub built for two. Reentering the bedroom, I saw Jared still standing in the middle of the room, a familiar smile on his face.

I walked swiftly across the room and launched myself into his arms.

Our lips met and for a few moments, and I forgot all else, save the love I felt for my wonderful husband. His shirt was almost unbuttoned before I recovered myself enough to form a thought. "Do we have to be anywhere at any specific time?" Jared smiled and whispered "no" before his lips returned to mine.

Soon his shirt hit the floor and Jared swept me into his arms and laid me on the bed. I wanted him, and kept trying to unzip his pants, but Jared kept pushing my hands away. "Not yet love. There's no rush." I liked that.

"Why don't you show me what you bought?" Pulling back, I cocked my eyebrow at him. HE really was in no rush, even though I could feel the evidence of his desire pressing against my hip.

"Would you like that?"

Nibbling my neck, he whispered, "Oh yeah. A lot."

Pulling away I headed for my suitcase and grabbed my Victoria's Secret bag. Grinning I wandered into the bathroom and quickly shed my clothes and started the shower. The warm water cascading over my skin almost seduced me into staying under the spray much longer than I should. After all, Jared was waiting on me, and we had the whole night ahead of us.

Choosing which outfit to wear first was a difficult chore. I liked them all, and I knew Jared would too. Finally, I settled on a green silk nightgown and matching lace silk robe. Stepping out into the bedroom, I saw Jared had been busy. Candles flickered all over the room. Soft sweet classical music played from a CD player next to the bed.

Jared was reclining on the bed, wearing a pair of jeans and a smile, but he sat up when I came into the room. He whistled softly and motioned for me to turn around.

Feeling younger than my thirty years, I giggled and twirled for him. It almost felt like our honeymoon again.

"Come here love."

I moved to his side, and leaned down to kiss him. His hands grasped my hips, but I pulled away.

"Uh uh lover. Not yet." I moved to the music back away from him and did several bumps and grinds. Swishing my hips I re-entered the bathroom and closed the door. My next choice was even harder. I wanted something sexy, but I knew it wouldn't stay on long anyways. I was so aroused; I wouldn't be able to resist him next time.

A sexy jade teddy, a pair of jade silk panties, garter belt and hose and three-inch slip on heels were my decision. A simple lace scarf completed the look. Stepping into the bedroom again, I noticed the bulge in Jared's boxers as I danced towards him.

"Miss me darling?"

"Mmmm."

I started to glide towards him, slowly, teasing him with every step. Halfway to the bed, I stopped and turned. Sliding the scarf down my body, I turned towards him and lightly caressed up my own arm. Jared growled, but remained motionless.

Swaying my hips, I headed towards him again, licking my lips, and running my hands over my stomach. His hands balled into fists at his side, but he stayed put, enjoying my show. Stopping at the side of the bed, I lifted a foot and placed it beside his hip. With a flick, I unsnapped the garter and rolled the hose down. Removing it slowly I pulled the hose off, tossing it at him then repeated this with my other leg.

Jared's eyes glazed when he caught a look at my panties. They were crotchless.I got as far as removing my other stocking before Jared sat up with a sudden move and wrapped his arms around my hips.

Pulling me over him, he buried his face into my silk covered breasts and inhaled deeply. With his teeth, he gently pulled the material aside and nuzzled my exposed nipple. He rolled us over and carefully spread my hair out into a red wave on the black sheets, then began nuzzling my neck again. I purred, it felt so good. Slipping his hands between us, he soon had me undressed, but to my frustration, he insisted on keeping his boxers on.

Soon my naked flesh met the coolness of the silk sheets beneath me and I shivered with desire.

"Hang on just a second," Jared whispered and climbed off the bed. I twisted on the sheets, enjoying the feel of the silk against my warm flesh, as I watching him head to his bag and remove something. Climbing back on the bed, he whispered, "now close your eyes for me." Curious, I closed my eyes and waited. First he grasped one hand and pulled it above me and I felt silk slide against my skin. I started to open my eyes, but Jared noticed. "Not yet." I closed them again and waited, as I felt silk slide against my other wrist, then tighten.

"Jared what …"

Silk slid against my check and over my eyes. Lifting my head slightly, he slid the blindfold behind my eyes. By the time my shocked mind opened my eyes, it was to late. All I could see was darkness.

"Remember how we used to play? How we used to delight in pleasing each other, tormenting with frustration so that it was all that much more incredible?"

Carefully I nodded, catching on to his game.

"Good."

Tenderly Jared began kissing my neck again, working his way to my lips. Thrusting his tongue in my mouth, I arched against him.

Chuckling, he moved down on the bed and began to lavish my breasts with his attention. First licking, then blowing on them, then finally nibbling lightly on the nipples. I was going crazy with his light touch. Flicking his tongue one last time against my left nipple, he moved down my stomach to my navel. Dipping his tongue in, he twirled it then pulled it back into his mouth. I felt him chuckle again, as he moved lower. I held my breath, waiting for his touch. I could feel his breath against my lips and clit, but nothing more. Then lightly, he flicked his tongue against my nipple and I moaned.

"Shhhhh, it's all right love. I promise, I'll get to that." I felt the bed shift again, then his teeth against my inner thigh as he nibbled the tender flesh. Arching against him, I whimpered, but he continued his assault on the tender flesh.

Nibbling his way back up my thigh, he lightly flicked his tongue against my lips then slid it between them. I gasped and arched against him. Without my hands free, I couldn't gasp his hair and hold him again me, and he knew it. I knew he was grinning in delight at my frustration as he lightly flicked his tongue, and then thrust it inside of me. He was driving me crazy. Moaning, I moved restlessly against the silk, trying to drive his tongue against my sensitive flesh.

He chuckled again, my beloved cad, then settled down to his task, flicking his tongue against my clit, pressing just hard enough to send slivers down my spine.

Within minutes, I felt a curling inside my pussy. A twinge that warned me of what was to come. Gasping and moaning, I felt the bud of my sexuality tighten, then flare as an orgasm ripped through my body.

The sound of a zipper barely registered on my passion-clouded mind, then Jared's weight settled over me. His lips met mine and I tasted my sweet juices on his lips and tongue as he slid between my legs and thrust his cock deep inside of me. I bend my knees and wrapped my legs around his hips. Arching against him, I matched the slow rhythm, as he thrust inside of me, then pulled back, almost leaving me, then thrusting in again.

My breasts rubbed against the light covering or hair on his chest with each arch of my back. It felt wonderful. Soon, I was building to another orgasm, and I felt myself flying. Jared's hands grasped my hips and pulled me to him harder and faster with each thrust. Again I crested my mountain, this time his harsh breath echoed his pleasure in my ear.

Deep inside of me, I felt his cock twitch, then the warm liquid of his passion. Spent, he collapse don top of me, and I twisted my hands, trying to get them free of my silken bonds to hold him close. Shifting slightly, he arched up and untied my hands then removed my blindfold.

I slid my hands around his back and pulled him down on top of me again, delighting in the familiarity of his weight. Closing my eyes, I had started to drift off to sleep, when Jared shifted to my side.

"Just a little nap now love, I have more plans for you." Smiling, I snuggled against his chest and let sleep take me into its arms.

* * *

I'm not sure how long Jared was awake, but I woke up orgasming. My clit tingled and my pussy clenched about his tongue. I laid there for a few moments, enjoying the haze of sleep and desire, before opening my eyes. What a beautiful sight it was, Jared lying between my parted legs, licking at my juices.

"Mmmmm," I murmured and lifted my hips against him, ready for more. A few slicks of his tongue, and I was reaching for the stars once more. As the haze of passion left my mind, I opened my eyes and looked at Jared once more. His head was laid on my thigh and he was smiling at me.

He lifted his head and smiled. "Did you know it's snowing outside?" I ran my hands slowly through his hair, enjoying a few moments of cuddle being I dragged myself out of bed and to the window. Sure enough, the land outside was nothing short of beautiful. I always loved it when it snowed, and I could stay inside, where it was nice and warm and watch it snow.

"Let's go outside for a walk before breakfast." Jared said, as he was getting dressed. I grumbled a little, but it was too beautiful to resist, and we didn't have to worry about the girls getting sick, or one of them falling and hurting themselves. It was just the snow and us.

Leisurely, we dressed in jeans, and long sleeve shirts, our coats and gloves, sharing kisses as each article of clothing was added, then headed out the door.

Outside Jared and I started to walk about the grounds, holding hands and talking. At one point his show lace came untied and he stopped to tie it, as I continued on a few steps.

Suddenly a snowball hit me in the back. I turned to see who threw it, and saw only Jared, with a devilish grin on his face. He bent down and scooped up more snow and threw it at me again. Laughing in mock out rage, I screamed, "I'll get you my pretty."

"Ha." He laughed at me, he actually laughed at me. Grinning I knelt down and packed a snowball then threw it at him. Bull's eye, right in the chest. Laughing we darted about the snow and had our snowball fight. Who knows how much time passed, before tired, we collapsed on the snow in laughter. Clapping was the only sound we heard. Turning, we saw some of the staff had gathered outside to watch us, and some were even involved in their own snowball fights.

Smiling at Jared, I held my hand out to him and he helped me up. Arm in arm we headed back to the inn. The owner's husband stopped us, his blue eyes twinkling with merriment. "Maybe you two should head to your room and thaw out. I'll have some hot cocoa sent up for you in about a half hour." Smiling, he bent down and packed a snowball. Heading inside, we never saw his target but we heard someone's outraged scream, followed by more laughter.

Inside the doorway, we stopped to remove out shoes and padded barefoot up the stairs to our room. Pausing inside the doorway, I kissed Jared and thanked him for a fun time.

"It gets more so, my love. Just wait."

Stripping off my wet clothes I headed into the bathroom for a nice hot shower. Under the spray, I felt my body relax and my cares drift away. A cool breeze tickled my body, then warmth settled against my back. Jared's hands wrapped around my waist and he pulled me back against his body. I purred as my back rubbed against the light sprinkling of hair on his chest.

Reaching over me, he grabbed the soap and the washcloth and began lathering my body. I placed my hands against the side of the shower and relaxed, enjoying his gentle touch. Once he got every single inch of my body lathered, he began rinsing me off.

After all the soap was gone, his hands began their path over my body again, but this time with a subtle change, they were no longer cleaning, they were caressing.

Turning in his arms, I began running my hands over his chest, caressing his nipples and ruffling the fine hair on his chest.

"Make love to me Jared."

His lips caressed mine as water cascaded over my head. Pushing me back against the wall, he grasped my butt and lifted me against him. I grabbed his shoulders, and pulled myself up against him and wrapped my legs around his waist. Carefully, he lowered me onto his cock and pressed his chest against mine.

The tiles of the shower felt cold against my back, by I didn't care. The feelings in other areas of my body were too intense. Our tongues mated as he slide me up and down on his cock.

The friction of his chest against my sensitive breasts caused me to gasp. After my body adjusted to the coolness against my back, it felt incredible, the cool tile contrasting with the warmth of his skin.

Jared's cock pulsed inside of me, and I clenched around him. Arching against him, I rocked my hips as much as possible and enjoyed his moans of pleasure. Gasping, I arched again and felt shivers of pleasure race though it. If felt so good to have him inside of me, so damn good.

Grinning, he bounced me on his cock, sliding in and out, as fast as he could. Moaning, I road the wave of passion, and finally crested. A scream welled in my throat at the intensity. Jared groaned in my ear as I clenched him tightly, waves of orgasm causing me to clench and release, over and over.

With a grunt and a final thrust, he joined me in orgasm. His knees weakened and he slide to his knees, my legs and arms still wrapped around him. Leaning his head against the tile next to me, he struggled to breath normally.

"Lynn..." he gasped.

"I know baby. Fuck that was intense." I set one foot down and gained my balance, then set my other foot down and stood. Grinning at him, I stepped around him and grabbed a towel then set to work drying him off. Once his breath returned to normal, he stood and held out his hand for the towel. Slowly, he dried me off then wrapped the towel around my hair.

A knock sounded at our door, and I grinned at Jared. "That will be out hot cocoa. Right on time." Jared wrapped the other towel around his waist and headed for the door.

"Are you really going to answer the door like that?"

I blushed at Jared's response. "Lynn honey, they knew what we were doing in here. Why do you think that he said the cocoa would be here in a half hour."

Opening the door, he shared a grin with a slightly wet man. "Looks like you lost your snowball fight."

"Nah. Just round one. How about you?"

Jared chuckled, "I'd call ours a draw." Jared grasped the mugs and closed the door with his foot. Turning, he found me snuggled under the comforter on the bed.

Carefully climbing into bed with me, he handed me my mug and snuggled against me, my head pillowed against his chest. IN silence, we enjoyed the warmth of each other and our drinks.

"Warm now love?" After setting my mug on the table next to the bed, I turned in his arms.

"Not quite, but I know a good way I could get warm. Hot even."

Tickling and caressing, we enjoyed the same playfulness we shared during the snowball fight, but with a hotter edge to it.

As each hour passed, we renewed our love for each, and our pleasure in each other's bodies. Lying in bed that night, after a long dinner and an even longer time making love, we vowed not to let our lives interfere with our private time together anymore. It was too precious to us.

AUTUMN BREEZE

Lying in bed one night, I grew restless. The room was to hot, too stuffy. I climbed out of bed and opened the window, enjoying the feel of the cool night air against my body. I lay back down and tried to sleep. My eyes drifted closed and soon I was in a light doze.

My name being whispered woke me. I looked about the room, my eyes quickly adjusting to the dark, but I didn't see anyone or anything. I lay back down; sure I had just dreamed it.

A cool breeze drifted crept through the window and again ... "*Victoria*" seemed to be whispered.

I sat up with a start, not this time it couldn't have been a dream. Again a breeze floated through the room, this time it ruffled my hair, and seemed to caress my cheek.

"*Relax.*" I knew I heard that, but not where it was coming from. Knowing I had to be crazy, I laid back down. Another breeze, this time the sheet rippled. I kicked the sheet off and snuggled down on the bed. The coolness of the night had caused my nipples top harden and my pussy to grow very moist. I barely resisted the urge to touch myself as I waited for what would happen next. I was sure that at any moment, men with a little white coat would run in and cart me off to the funny farm.

"*Relax Victoria. Enjoy.*" Another breeze, this time caressing my breasts. For a moment it almost felt like a strong hand, then just a cold draft of wind. I followed its path and began to gently caress my breasts, teasing the nipples, but not devoting myself strictly to them.

One hand stayed on my breasts, the other moved all over my aroused body, stopping to touch and tease my sensitive points. Over and over light breezes drifted in through the open window, caressing me.

I could feel my body tingling and finally I gave in to the temptation to caress my moist pussy. The lips felt so smooth and tender under my fingertips. I couldn't resist moaning.

"*Relax*." The voice seemed to deepen, still soothing, but now called to me on a different level. The chill in the air continued, arousing me further, cool air on hot flesh. My fingers pinched a nipple between them as my other hand caressed my pussy. Gently I slid two fingers in deep as my thumb rubbed over my clit. Another breeze entered the room, but this time it didn't dissipate. It almost seemed like the breeze was a lover's breath, gently caressing my heated flesh and I slowly brought myself closer to an orgasm.

Over and over I brushed my thumb against my clit and slowly I slid two fingers in and out of my wet pussy. I could feel my muscles begin to clench and release as I thrust over and over, deep inside myself. The breeze swirled over me, cooling my nipple, tightening it into to a hard little bud.

Faster and faster I flicked my clit, feeling it tingle under my thumb, until finally I felt my orgasm begin. Little waves raced throughout my body, cresting in my nipples and deep within my pussy. I arched my back, and felt the tingling increase. My inner muscles clenched on my finger, drawing them in tight, prolonging the orgasm.

As I lay there, breathing heavily, I felt the breeze draw along side me. Almost feeling arms wrap around me I lay still, enjoying the moment.

The words "*I love you, my sweet*," were whispered before the breeze left. A strong aroma of cologne remained, oddly, the same brand as my lost love wore.

BE CAREFUL WHAT
YOU WISH FOR

Chris sat at the dining room table and waited for his cake to be brought out. His best friend Steve had decided that he had to have a birthday party to celebrate his quarter of a century birthday. All of his friends and their wives, significant others or just a one time date were there. He was the only single man there. The lights were dimmed and out came the cake carried by Steve's wife Carrie. Gently she set the cake down in front of Chris, and as she pulled away, Chris got a great view of her breasts. Earlier when she had first arrived, she had asked to kiss the birthday boy and he had almost spilled himself right then and there. He had been so long without any physical contact with a woman he was going insane. At twenty-five and with his good looks he should have been able to find a woman, but he just had one small problem. He doesn't understand women, not at all. Their actions astound him; the hidden meanings to their words confuse him.

Closing his eyes tight, Chris wished that for just twenty-four hours he could be a woman, to know what they feel and think - to have multiply orgasms, and wear a sexy dress. As the candles went out, so did the lights. Everyone laughed. As Steve went to find the breaker box, Chris felt a hand on his crotch, caressing him through the fabric of his jean shorts. The lights came back on with a sudden brightness that everyone in the room was momentarily blinded allowing the hand to leave his crotch without anyone seeing it had been there.

Around eleven the party wound down, after all, many of the people there had kids to go home to. Steve and Carrie stayed to help him clean up, and when they were done they left, with Carrie giving Chris another birthday kiss. By midnight he was sound asleep in his bed, alone, like every other night.

* * *

The next morning when he awoke, Chris stretched his arms over his head and felt a pull in his chest. Thinking that maybe he had slept wrong the night before, and his arms were sore, he shrugged it off and went to the bathroom to shower. Off came his clothes and he glanced in the mirror. He stopped cold. Staring back at him were his blue eyes set in a beautiful face. Long black hair covered his head and fell down to his mid back. A pair of pert breasts set high up on his rib cage. Chris was about the completely loose his cool when he remembered that he had wished for this for twenty-four hours. Assuming it happened at midnight, he only had seventeen hours left to enjoy it.

Chris jumped into the shower and quickly washed. When he/she went to get dressed the fun began. Chris decided to wear a pair of boxers, a long jersey style button up silk shirt and a pair of jeans. Everything fit except the jeans. She kept trying on clothed until she found a pair of jeans that fit, then with her wallet in her pocket and keys in her hand, Chris went shopping.

Chris was amazed at how different sales people were to women than to men. For men, they left them alone unless they saw they looked clueless, but for women they hung around like vultures sure that their next meal would come from her. Chris had picked this store because she knew Steve's wife Carrie worked here. Chris asked for Carrie and within a few minutes the petite blonde was headed her way. The only two things Chris had retained from her male state were her coloring and her height. Her sexual orientation had changes along with her reproductive parts. She now found herself looking at men as well as women. She hoped that would change when she went back to being a man.

Carrie wore a silk suit, and her hair was braided. Still, she looked beautiful, maybe even more so today than last night when she wore jeans and a T-shirt.

Chris had a bit of inside knowledge about Carrie. She was bisexual, and her and Steve were looking for woman that they both found attractive to have a threesome with. Without her ego in the way, Chris knew she was just that woman. She picked out a dress that buttoned down the back and asked Carrie to help her button it up. Having done this before for other customers, Carrie didn't even hesitate. Inside the small dressing room, Carrie watched as Chris disrobed. She pulled the dress off of the hanger and had it ready to help Chris into.

Off came the jeans and shirt, leaving her wearing a pair of black silk boxers on her six-foot frame. Slightly curved hips, small but firm breasts and long, slim legs. Carrie couldn't take her eyes off of Chris' breasts. Hesitantly Chris caressed the side of Carrie's face. Carrie leaned in and took on of the hard peaks into her moist lips. Chris moaned as new sensations raced about her body. Normally her nipples were sensitive and ticklish, now they felt like they were wired to her crotch.

Carrie leaned back and looked at the smile on Chris' beautiful face. It looked familiar, yet different. She mental shrugged it off.

"Mmm, I liked that. Why don't you tell your boss you're sick and take me home and make love to me?"

"I don't even know your name, and besides, I'm married and he would feel left out."

"I'm Chris … Christina. And I want you so bad I don't care who watches."

"I'm Carrie, but Chris, you don't understand ..." Chris began kissing the side of the blondes neck, weakening her knees and her resolve. "... he would want to, well, to join in."

"Mmmm, a threesome? Is he cute?" Already knowing the answer, Chris believed Carrie when she breathlessly said yes. Chris' teeth were lightly nibbling at Carrie's ear so she whispered into her ear again that they should go to her place.

Carrie pulled back and began to compose herself. Chris was told to make her purchases and meet her in the food-court in front of the Chinese restaurant. Chris had withdrawn some money from the ATM, not wanting the hassle of a check or a credit card, because both required a driver's license, and hers still called her a man. She bought her dress, shoes and under things and went into a nearby restroom to change while she waited on Carrie. She had seen the lust in her eyes; she knew Carrie would show up. Right now she was probably on her cell phone telling Steve she was bringing someone home with her.

Chris watched the people go by, she saw men strain to look at her legs and breasts without their woman noticing. She saw some woman cast their eyes her way. After a while, she grew bored with the looks and a few minutes after that she grew frustrated. She began to feel like freak on display.

Carrie walked up behind her and placed her hands on Chris' shoulder and leaned down to whisper in her ear.

"Steve is expecting us in a few minutes. It is only a five minute drive to my house. Are you sure you want to do this?" Carrie's breath in her ear aroused Chris' again, she could feel her nipples harden and a wetness between her legs.

"Mmm, yes I'm sure." Chris stood and took Carrie's hand. Together they exited the mall and Carrie led the way to her car. Chris sat in the passengers' seat and watched Carrie's hands as she drove, how they slid over the steering wheel. Chris could almost feel those hands gliding over her body followed by those pouty lips. They pulled into the driveway and Carrie cut the engine.

"Here we are. Still want to go in?" Chris stepped out of the car and stood waiting on Carrie to gather her purse and get out of the car. Chris felt eyes watching her and smiled. She turned to walk to the front door and her smile grew as the curtains quickly shifted back into place. She knew Steve had an impatient nature.

The two ladies arrived at the front door and Steve opened it. His could feel his cock rising at the site before him, his petite blonde wife standing next to a tall black haired woman. Being six two, it was hard for Steve to find a woman his height, and even though he loved his wife, he often wished she were taller.

Steve kissed Carrie as she walked through the door and then stood back, allowing Chris to enter unhindered. She pretended to look about her, studying the room, when in actuality she knew all about the house, she had helped to build it, when she was a man. Steve watched the young woman, feeling a nagging sense that he should know her. There was just something so familiar about her. As Carrie introduced them he shrugged it off.

The three of them sat down in the living room and just spent an hour talking. Chris had to make up a life story since she couldn't very well tell facts about her real life, Steve had been there for most of it. As they talked Carrie's hands ran little lines up and down Chris' leg, slowly going just a bit higher each time. Steve began to watch the motions with more concentration, as they grew higher.

Chris could feel herself growing aroused; it was a familiar, yet totally new sensation. Her nipples hardened as Carrie's hand began to trace over the crotch of her panties. Then the hand was removed. Warm, full lips met hers and hesitantly she responded. Now was the time to decide if she could go through with this. Steve helped his wife to remove her shirt and skirt as she kissed Chris. His big hands caressed Carrie's breasts then Chris' through her dress. Off came Carrie's bra, then her panties. Gently Carrie undid the buttons down the back of Chris' dress as she kissed her. Their tongues rubbed against one another. Desire set off small sparks deep inside Chris' pussy. Sensations never before felt dizzied her senses. She felt herself falling, then realized that she was, Carrie had pushed her back against the cushions of the couch. Somehow her dress had been removed and Carrie's lips were about to touch her nipples. Wet lips met hard nipples and Chris shuddered. Her panties grew soaked as she arched her back into Carrie's touch.

Steve sat watching them, his clothing removed and his large hands stroking his cock. He had never seen anything more erotic than this wife and this beautiful stranger. Moans escaped Chris' mouth as Carrie kissed her soft body. No part of her was left untouched, un-kissed. Gently, almost lovingly Carrie caressed her, bringing her to new peaks of arousal. Their lips met briefly then, Carrie would return to kissing her breasts or her stomach or her legs. Steve could no longer stand just watching, so he moved to the ladies and began to gently caress Carrie. His hands moved over her body, touching the places he knew she liked to be touched. Chris and Carrie moved to the floor so that they could all have better access to each other. Chris stroked Steve's cock as he gently fingered Carrie. Carrie's hips rocked on his fingers, driving them deeper inside of her. Chris whispered to Carrie that she wanted to feel Steve inside her. Carrie nodded the pulled away form Steve.

She moved so that she sat by Chris' head facing Steve. Steve took a moment to roll on a condom that he moved slowly inside of Chris. It felt wonderful having someone inside of her. She was so tight around Steve's cock, so tight despite her height. Chris didn't know what to think of the sensations she was feeling. It was so different from what she was used to, but still so similar. Carrie straddled her head and lowered her pussy to Chris' lips.

Carrie's sweet pussy rode her face and she worked her tongue against her. She wanted to use all of her new found knowledge of the female erogenous zones to please this beautiful woman. Steve thrust gently, aware that Chris was a virgin; he kept his pace slow and easy as he caressed her hard clit. In and out he thrust his cock, feeling her muscle tighten around him, trying to hold him deep inside her.

Carrie caressed her own breasts as she kissed Steve. She paced herself with him, but still she came first. She shook slightly then slid to lie beside Chris. As her orgasm ended, she kissed Chris, tasting herself on her lips. Steve sped up slightly, sensing that Chris was close. She tightened her legs about his waist as she came. He kept thrusting, over and over, driving her higher and higher. Carrie gently caressed Chris' face, watching as her husband pleased this beautiful woman. Her blue eyes grew slightly glazed as her second orgasm hit. Steve gave a few last thrusts, then came as well, his body collapsing half on top of her , half supported on his shaking arms.

Chris pulled him down to her, wanting to feel his full weight, needing to feel it. After giving her time to calm down, Carrie moved Steve from on top of Chris and leaned down and gently began to lick her pussy. Steve removed his condom while he watched Carrie lick and kiss Chris' pussy. He smiled and leaned down to kiss Chris. Her lips parted and he slid his tongue inside her mouth as Carrie was sliding her tongue deep inside of

Chris' pussy. Chris felt her body shudder as once again she built up towards an orgasm. Gently Steve kissed her as Carrie tongued her pussy. As she climaxed, Steve held her shuddering body close to him. They continued to kiss as Carrie watched. Chris was in a state of high emotional turmoil. She liked Steve, he was a good friend, but now she was seeing a side of him he reserved for females. It was arousing, but she didn't know how it would affect her actions with him when she was once again a man.

Afternoon turned to night as still the three attractive people made love, teaching Chris all that a woman could like and feel. As the hour grew late, she said good-bye, with an open invite to return. She knew she couldn't though.

* * *

The next morning Chris woke with a hard-on. It felt uncomfortable, like his underwear were binding him, but that shouldn't be. He always slept in boxers. As he headed to the bathroom, he shook his head at his dream. Imagine that, thinking he had been turned into a woman and made love with Steve and his wife. Though he would have a little bit of knowledge of the female mind from his dream. It was very intense.

As he went to remove his underwear so he could take a shower, his hands encountered silk and lace. His mind refused to acknowledge what in his heart he knew - it wasn't a dream.

BY THE LIGHT OF THE MOON

Looking out over the ocean, Nina gave in to the temptation of a late night swim. Pulling her sweatshirt off over her head, she kicked her feet free from her slip-ons and shimmied out of her sweatpants. The cool night air whispered across her skin, raising goose bumps. She glanced at the sky, admiring the fullness of the moon, before surrendering to the pull of the waves.

For several moments she waded in the water, waiting for her body to adjust to the cooler temperature; her nipples were hard, but her body slightly warmer. She started out her swim, pacing herself. Nina kept her eyes on the shoreline, careful not to swim out too far. She'd heard the stories of night swimmers pulled to far from shore and had drowned. In barely enough water to swim in, she felt safe. At any time, she could stand up and it might reach her waist, maybe.

When her body began to tingle, and she knew it was time to head back. After months of living near the ocean, of swimming daily, she knew her limits, even if she delighted in pushing them a little farther each day.

After always having decisions made for her, she exhilarated in her freedom. If only she could be so free sexual, she thought, she would be content. But after years of being held up next to other women and always found lacking, her self-confidence was in shreds. The only time she felt beautiful was at night, in the ocean. The waves were her like a lover, unseen hands caressing her flesh, hardening her nipples with their icy touch and pulsating between her legs.

Shivering as the wind brushed across her skin, Nina admitted defeat and waded from the water. Heading quickly to her towel, she picked it up and wrapped it around her and leaned down to grab her clothes, only to stop short. They were missing. Her clothes were gone. Slipping her flip-flops on, she looked around. Pulse racing, she scanned the shoreline, looking for any signs of someone else's presence. There was only a set of footprints leading from her clothes to the path leading to her cottage and the other guest cottage on this side of the island.

Certain she was alone, she relaxed slightly. As the adrenalin rush receded, Nina became aware of the goose-pimples covering her arms.

Teeth chattering, she hurried to her cottage, completely aware of how little the beach towel covered. By the time she reached her door, she was trembling, with the cool night air and fear of being caught. Someone, her neighbor it seemed, knew her secret.

Part of the reason she'd chosen the island for her retreat, was no one had booked the cottage next door for another month. Needing to be alone, with just her laptop and her thoughts, she hadn't bargained on a clothes-stealing neighbor.

By the time she opened her bedroom door and toweled off, she was ticked off, bordering on pissed. *'How dare he ... she ... oh hell, they or it ... take off with her clothes,'* she fumed. Grabbing a pair of panties and a bra, she sat down on her bed in a huff. She was tempted to go next door and give her neighbor a piece of her mind.

Snapping the bra, she yanked it down over her ample breasts and stepped into her panties, pulled them up and adjusted them. A few steps brought her back to the closet, where she found a black t-shirt and jeans, and donned them. She knew if she were going to go next door and demand her clothes back, she'd have to hurry and do it before the nerve left her.

A knock at her front door startled her. Jumping, she yelped and was instantly irritated with herself.

Stomping to the door, she pulled it open only to stop short. The most attractive man she'd ever seen, stood across the threshold. Long black hair curled about his neck, a rakish lock drifted over his light blue eyes. He was tall; easily a foot taller than her five and a half feet. He was nothing short of perfection, except for two things.

His skin had a faint bluish tinge and he was wearing her sweat suit. Her comfortable, curling up with a book, favorite, after work outfit. The thief!

"How dare you!" she began, only to have him lift a hand and press his fingers against her lips. Very long, webbed fingers.

Nina stood still, in shock. His skin was covered in scales, but that couldn't be. It must be a trick of the moonlight.

"My name Ti'doth. I sorry I take you things. Air uncomfortable against me. You forgive?"

Nodding her head, Nina slowly pulled away so that his fingers were no longer resting against her lips. His hand dropped and she took another step back.

"I'm Nina. So, um, you're my new neighbor?" Licking her dry lips, she gasped as he stepped closer, his eyes following the subtle movements of her tongue.

"I live there." A graceful arm rose, his fingers pointing towards the ocean. "You sad when you visit. You glide through waters, should be healed. But you sad."

Dropping his hand, he lifted his other towards her hair and stroked the soft golden locks. "Why sad?"

Against her better judgment, Nina gazed into his eyes and, in that moment, she knew peace. His eyes, so clear and crystal blue, were like looking into a wave as it crested. Yet there was a harmony within, an inner pace that bled through.

Licking her lips again, she swallowed. "It's hard to explain. I just never fit in. I was always a dreamer in a world of realists and everyone expected me to change. Add to that my weight, and my looks, and I just ..." With a sigh her voice trailed off. She couldn't figure out how to explain it.

Blinking slowly, Ti'doth made soft humming sounds. Nina watched as his eyelids closed from the sides, covering his eyes; then another set of lids slid down much as a human's would. In that instant, reality lost its meaning, as she that he wasn't human.

Oddly, she wasn't afraid. . He fascinated her. With his webbed hands, his soft blue scales – which she now admitted were real and not a trick of the light – and his gentle manner. He was so unlike anyone she had ever met. His movements were slow and beautifully graceful.

When he opened his eyes again, Nina was shocked to see that they'd darkened to a deep blue.

"You no sad with me Nee-nahh?" Her lips curved into a soft smile as he elongated her name.

"No Ti'doth, I'm not sad with you. I feel something else, I'm not sure how to describe it, but I'm not sad."

"Good. You are beautiful female. You no should be sad." Gently his hand glided through her hair, tightening just enough to coax her forward.

"You scent, as you glide through waters, it called to me. You so beautiful, so perfect."

Leaning down, he touched his nose to her hair and breathed deeply. Nina closed her eyes, suddenly feeling faint. She could feel the energy rippling between them, a hidden wave of need and emotion. For the first time in a long time, she needed to be touched. It was a heady experience, to feel beautiful.

"You taste flowed through me as you move through waters. It flooded me, filled me. So light, so sweet. Knew then, must meet. Must heal, must claim. Mine Nee-nahh. Mine."

He pressed his cool lips against her forehead, then slowly traced a path down her cheek to her mouth. As they moved, they slowly warmed, so that when his lips met hers, the heat of a fire touched her. Soft humming sounds filled the room as his mouth opened over hers. Muted, they rumbled from his chest as their kiss deepened.

Gently, he placed his hands on her hips and pulled her against him. Her breasts strained against her bra, begging for contact with bare skin.

Everything felt surreal to Nina, but she didn't care. Even if she woke in the morning to find it was all a dream, all that mattered was the now. And the now felt so right.

Ti'doth's hands moved from his hips to her back, holding her and molding her against his body. Gently, he thrust his tongue into her mouth, drawing her soft moans into himself.

Pulling back, he whispered, "You want me?"

Nina quivered her body answered begged, nerve ending screaming for more. "Yes, Ti'doth. I want this, I want you."

"Good."

As if she weighed nothing, he bent and picked her up, lifting her into his arms, holding her against his chest.

"Where?"

Her hand trembled, and she pointed the way, while exploring the soft hollows of his collarbone with her tongue, his soft scaly skin. She couldn't believe how soft and smooth he was. Tiny lines of flesh peeked from between his scales, like pores on human flesh. Not stopping to debate the possible consequences, Nina allowed her heart to lead her. Most of her life was a regret anyway.

Once he'd entered, Ti'doth crossed the room and set her upon her bed. Stepping back, he pulled her sweatshirt over his head, baring his toned flesh. Light robin's egg blue scales covered his chest, darkening as they wrapped around to his back.

"You want?"

Not trusting her voice, Nina nodded. Oh how she wanted.

"Nee-nahh mine."

Grasping the waist of the pants, he pulled them down, baring his body to her view. Hesitantly, she allowed her eyes to trace his legs, the corded muscles of his thighs and finally glanced at his cock. Or at least where his cock should have been. In its place was a small raised ring of flesh.

"Um, Ti'doth ..." she started then gasped as she watched the ring of flesh started to grow until his cock was fully exposed. It was beautiful, covered in pearly blue scales. There were no veins visible, but the curvature was odd. Towards the middle, his cock was wider, then tapered off again towards his body.

With inhuman fluid movements, he climbed onto the bed and gently pushed her back against the silk sheets.

"You scent, so good; you perfect."

Moving his hands over her clothing, he started to lift her shirt over her stomach.

"Ti'doth wait. I, um, we need to turn the lights off."

"No." Softly spoken, the single word held a wealth of meaning.

"I don't, I um, I'm not happy with my body. True I have lost weight since I started swimming daily, but I still have so much left to loose and I would rather turn off the lights. I don't ..."

"No. You beautiful as you glide through waters. You beautiful now, in you place to rest. You mine. You, perfect Nee-nahh. No hide."

Placing his lips against hers, he gently pulled her black t-shirt up and over her stomach and her breasts, then slowly pulled way, coaxing her into a sitting position with his lips.

Pulling back, he tugged the t-shirt free from her body and leaned back down, joining their lips again. The soft humming started again, slightly louder this time.

Desperate to please him, as much as he was pleasing her, Nina slid her hands over Ti'doth's shoulders, holding him against her flesh, his scales tickling her nipples.

Caressing gently, she guided him over her, remembering her jeans as he settled into the curve of her body.

"Damn," she muttered, wiggling beneath him.

A sound, suspiciously like a chuckle, crossed his lips as Ti'doth pulled back and sat on his heels. Up close and gloriously naked, he was enough to make Nina's head spin and her pulse race.

"You take off." He stated, pointing at her jeans. Nina sat up. She was terribly self-conscious of how her weight settled around her waist and how her breasts slightly sagged.

Tugging the button free, she slid the zipper down and debated how best to wiggle from her jeans without loosing the mood. Lying back, she lifted her hips and slid the jeans past her butt, then gasped as strong hands closed over the waist of her pants, pulling them down her body.

Tossing them aside, Ti'doth moved his hands back up her legs slowly, his lips dancing kisses upon her flesh.

"So smooth," he whispered.

Stopping to nip at her inner knee, he started humming again. As his lips moved up her leg to her wet pussy, he nuzzled her glistening pearl, drawing a gasp, then a moan. Nina arched her hips, and spread her thighs, offering him her flesh to feast upon. He nuzzled and licked at her tender, quivering pussy while his hands played upon her ample breasts, kneading and teasing her nipples.

Nina stopped thinking of what she looked like and gave herself up to the incredible sensations flowing through her. She was aware of things as never before. The soft rise and fall of Ti'doth's chest against her legs, his fingers and tongue, everything rolled together.

Craving more, she reached down to his shoulders and pulled him against her, his body rose over hers, then softly crashing down. When he'd settled himself between her thighs, Nina arched against him, offering all she had to give.

As Ti'doth slid his cock into her welcoming warmth, the sound of the rushing tide filled her ears.Over and over, he thrust into her then retreated, a gently moving tide to her beach.

With each rush, he drove further forward, claiming more ground, until finally they were flawlessly joined. With every retreat the slightly rough scales adorning his groin caressed her soft pearl, sending sparks of pleasure through her. Thrusting forward again, he reclaimed her flesh. Again, and again, they rubbed their bodied together, seeking to please each other.

Panting, she arched against her lover as her body demanded satisfaction. Now, it screamed. Clenching him with each down stroke, Nina barely noticed his humming deepening and her own gasps and moans filling the room. With her entire being, she focused on one thing – their mutual pleasure.

Thrust, retreat,
Clench, release.

Over and over, their bodies mated, as their pleasure built, until finally, with a soft scream, Nina climaxed. Ti'doth's next thrust drove her higher, then higher again, as the warm rush of his pleasure filled her. Gasping, she wrapped her arms around his neck and held him against her, until her trembling subsided.

Lethargic, her body completely relaxed against the bed. Her mind however, started to whisper things she didn't want to think about.

Feeling him pull back, she met his gaze. As she watched, his eyes closed then opened again. Still marveling over his double eyelids, Nina missed his softly spoken words.

"I'm sorry? I didn't hear what you said," she whispered, uncertain, now that their passion had crested.

"Nee-nahh mine. Tomorrow, we work on together. Tonight, we love."

"Does that mean you want a tomorrow?" She had to know. Regardless of their differences, he made her feel so beautiful with just a gaze. She couldn't know for certain, but she had a feeling here was the man she could love and who would love her.

He lifted his hand and brushed the hair from her sweat-dampened forehead. He placed a soft kiss there, before rolling to the side and pulling her against him.

"Mine."Cuddled against his cooling body, Nina smiled and accepted his one word answer for its hidden meaning. It was definitely a good thing that she enjoyed long silences and wasn't used to a lot of conversation. But on the other hand, the things he made her feel, the emotions he packed into what words he did speak, more than made up for any losses.

GOING DOWN?

The elevator smoothly slid down, the floor dial showing 10, 9, 8, 7 until suddenly, all hell broke loose. The elevator heaved, the lights flickered twice, and then everything went dark. Quinn had no sooner reached for the phone, than the elevator heaved again. The metal walls echoed the harsh screech of the brakes as they struggled to catch and hold.

Quinn closed his eyes and struggled to calm his racing pulse. As the elevator lurched to a stop, the tiny blond he was sharing the ride down with plastered herself against his side. Whimpers filled the metal cubicle, soft and husky.

"Shhhh," he soothed, responding to her fear as best he could, attempting to comfort her while controlling his sudden and intense hunger. Just another few minutes and he would have been safe in his hotel room. If need be, he could have paid a willing woman to service his duel needs. Gently, he stroked her hair as she trembled against him.

"Is it going to fall?" He could hear her pulse throbbing, her heart pounding in fear.

"I doubt it. It just seems to have lost power, for some reason. We're stuck for a while, but we're safe." If anything, the blonde's trembling increased. "We're going to be ok." Quinn stated, hoping his voice sounded reassuring. "They'll come get us out soon, I'm sure."

As gently as he could, Quinn pried the blonde's fingers from his arm, and set her back a few steps.

"I don't worry so much about falling as I do about getting stuck here. I hate small spaces." She stated, her voice breaking. "I can't breathe."

"Ok. Most importantly, just try not to panic. Sit down. That should help some." He could see her lean back against the wall and slid down, curling her legs under her. Quinn knew that even though he could see her, she couldn't see him. He worried that she would soon begin to panic in earnest, which would make the scent of her blood that much more seductive.

Squatting down in front of her, he made sure his leg brushed against hers, that she knew he was close. "What's your name?"

"I'm Sharron. And you?"

"Quinn."

"Quinn. That's nice. Quinn, I have to get out of here. I can't do this, I can't pretend everything's ok." He could hear the panic threading through her voice.

"Shhhh," he whispered, leaning forward. Settling his knees on the floor, he shifted, his hands framing her hips. "It's going to be ok. Nothing bad is going to happen."

"I died; I mean I almost died in a cave-in once. It was hell. Trapped inside, waiting for someone to notice that I was missing. I can't go through that again." Quinn could hear the panic rising in her voice, her pulse racing, her breath coming in shortened and louder gasps. "I have to get out of here."

"Don't worry Sharron. We're in this together." He almost groaned at the thought. Together, limbs entwined, bodies joined, her blood pumping into his mouth, the sweet scent of sex in the air.

Softly, he brushed his lips across hers. Almost at once sparks of red flashed behind his eyes. The sweet taste of her lips acted as an aphrodisiac, tempting him to drown within her.

"What, what are you doing?" Her breath whispered across his face.

"Taking your mind off of your fear. Want me to stop?" Without giving her a chance to reply, he leaned down, and settled his chest against hers. Pressing his lips against hers, he thrust his tongue past her parted lips, claiming her mouth. Her hands lifted, and gripped his shirt. Quinn waited for her to push him away, but after several breathless moments, she gripped tight and pulled him closer.

There was a subtle desperation to her kiss. Her pulse slowed, but the damage had been done. Quinn craved, more than the feel of her body against his.

Lifting a hand, he gripped the back of her neck and tipped her head, sealing his lips firmly to hers. The metallic scent of her blood filled his senses.

Restlessly, she moved against him, molding herself to his body. What he had intended to be an innocent kiss soon evolved into a mind blowing, need filled moment between them. As he pulled away, Sharron leaned back against the wall, gasping for breath.

The steady throb of her heart almost robbed him of reason.

He leaned down and pressed his forehead against her neck. Breathing deeply, he inhaled the sweet essence of her; the metallic tinge of her blood pulsing through her veins, her light floral perfume, and the hint of sexual arousal. He knew she was creaming her panties, her body preparing itself for a lover. He wanted, needed, to be that lover.

He could feel his gums tearing, as his fangs dropped into place. As much as he didn't like it, sweet Sharron was about to be dinner. Pulling back, Quinn pressed a series of kisses against her neck, then opened his mouth, sucking gently. He was just about to sink his teeth into her jugular vein when the elevator jerked.

With a screeching groan, the elevator lumbered up a floor, then another, coming to rest soundly on the tenth floor. He pursed his lips and sucked, coaxing his fangs back into hiding.

The door opened to several worried gazes. Sharron stumbled from the elevator, drawing in several deep breaths. Watching her in the light, Quinn couldn't resist grinning at her antics. Here was a woman who enjoyed life, grabbing it with both hands and holding on tight.

"Miss? Miss are you ok?" A jumble of voices all called out at once.

"I'm the manager and we'd like to ..."

"Sir, if you'll both step further away please." Given the smeared grease on his cheek and the overalls with the name sewn on, he had to be the maintenance guy. It took all of Quinn's considerable willpower not to pick up the scrawny geek by his collar and slam him against the wall, although he wasn't sure if it was because the elevator broke in the first place, or because he fixed it so fast.

Each gaze turned towards him made Quinn more and more uncomfortable. His gums quickly healed themselves, leaving on a faint taste of blood.

Sharron turned to look back at him, her hand held out. Gently gripping her hand in his, Quinn allowed the petite pixie to pull him from the elevator and into her arms.

"Thank you," she whispered, and then wrapped her arms around his neck, plastered herself against his body and kissed him. Holding her close, Quinn held her against his chest and moved out of the crowd.

"Really sir, we need you to..."

Past startled spectators, he stalked down the hall to his room. The door opened with a swipe of his key card.

"Miss? Sir? We'd like to offer you a discount - -" . Quinn slammed the door shut in the manager's face.

He could smell the increase of her arousal, now that she felt herself safe. She reeked of need, of fear and of something infinitely more appealing. She smelled of lavender and sex, musky and light.

They fell into the room, groping at each other, pulling off her clothes and tossing them aside. Although he worried she would regret her actions in the morning, Quinn was too far-gone to stop himself. He needed her, needed what she could give him, and he was willing to take what she offered.

The pounding at the door grew distracting, so Quinn focused on the manager, guiding the man to tell everyone to leave them alone and return to their business. Quinn only hoped Sharron didn't notice the sudden lack of noise. As they tumbled to the floor, he knew she hadn't. She was too busy rubbing her naked body against his.

Her hands tugged his shirt from his trousers and jerked it open, ripping the buttons off and sending them in a cascade around them.

Her teeth nibbled at his lip, driving him wild as she pulled him down on top of her. Her hands worked quickly on his zipper, sliding it down and pulling his throbbing cock from its confines.

Quinn fisted one hand in her hair and pulled her head back as she arched against him, sheathing him within her heat. She was almost animalistic as she dug her nails into shoulders, her teeth sinking into his shoulder as she ground up against him. The stinging crescent of her teeth drove him wild, even as he jerked in shock at the familiar feeling of fangs slicing his skin open.

He could feel his heart racing, and hear hers beating a similar tempo. His blood flowed through his veins, a trickle sliding into her mouth.

"Sharron," he whispered, even as he could feel his fangs dropping, the scent of her blood a drug to his addicted senses.

Leaning down, he carefully sank his teeth into her jugular as his hands gripped her hips tighter, pulling her against his thrusts. The sweet, metallic twang of her life's essence flooded over his tongue as her pussy clenched his cock, gripping with her orgasm.

The emotional charge of her climax raced into Quinn, giving him a buzz he hadn't felt in years. He suspected the high would ripple through her as well.

Even as he knew it would leave bruises, he gripped her hips tighter, pistoning his cock in and out of her creamy core, as he drank her blood and she reciprocated by drinking his. Quinn could feel the tightness of his balls, and jerking his teeth free he quickly sealed the wound moments before his climax raced through him.

Sharron slipped her fangs free and cried out softly as she joined him in orgasm, her muscles milking his cock. He collapsed against her, his forehead resting against her racing pulse. Tiny beads of blood trailed down his chest from the tiny punctures in his neck.

Panting softly, she shifted beneath him. "I don't normally do that."

Lifting his head, Quinn smiled in what he hoped was reassurance. "Mmmm, neither do I. But damn that felt good."

"I can't believe you're also a ..." Her voice trailed off. Instead of the normal worries that would have assaulted a human female, he had an idea of what would plague Sharron.

He could see reasoning and a hint of caution return to her gaze. Sharron was gaining control of her emotions again, and as much as he had enjoyed the heat of the moment, he knew he had to let her go. Vampires didn't tend to co-exist well together unless one had made the other.

Rolling to lay on his side, he watched as she carefully climbed to her feet, her body wobbling slightly.

Carefully, he tucked his now limp cock back into his pants and zipped them up.

"Let me take you to dinner, out dancing, to a movie. Something. Anything. You choose."

Unashamed of his partial nudity, he stood and moved to stand behind her as she jerked on her pants. Gently, he cupped her hips, molding her back against him. "Say yes. I promise, no strings."

"I don't know Quinn. You know that we're too territorial to mingle well. And I don't know you well enough." A faint blush stained her fair skin, all the way down to the creamy curve of her breasts.

"You know me, the taste of my blood, the feel of my body. Say yes."

Sharron turned in his arms and gazed into his eyes. Quinn met her look and kept his eyes steady and dropped his mental shields slightly, letting her find whatever answers she was looking for. He could feel the riot of emotions flooding through the slender woman; fear, lust, worry, and a hint of hope.

"I, um, I guess we could have dinner. But no promises beyond that. Just dinner. And I need to rest first."

Nodding his head, Quinn smiled. "Just dinner."

"Then yes."

Pulling away, she hurriedly tossed on her shirt and holding her shoes in her hands headed for the door.

"I'll meet you in the lobby at six tonight for dinner. No strings."

Still savoring the sweet rush of her blood flooding his mouth, Quinn watched Sharron step through the door and pull it closed behind her.

HOWL OF THE FULL MOON

The first emotion I had felt when I saw him was not lust, but fear. Stark, cold, going to die fear. Moments before I had seen him, I had heard him growling in the enveloping darkness. Fool that I was, I had taken an unfamiliar trail, too close to night. Not seeing the gopher hole in front of me, I fell, spraining my ankle. Slowly I had tried to crawl my way back the quarter mile along the trail, but all too soon, night had fallen. My car, my sense of safety seemed so far away.

The strange sounds had began soon after, most easily identifiable and non-threatening: an owl hooting, a cricket chirping. Then something began moving in the underbrush less than fifty feet away, off to my left. The moon shined bright enough for me to make out a vague shape in the brush. Crystal blue eyes peered out at me, then the hair-raising growl. I just knew I was done for.

Off to my left came an answering growl. I was caught between two animals, with no way of escape. Then I saw him, covered in black fur, his eyes bright and almost kind; a wolf. The brush to my left shook and a skinny gray wolf emerged. His teeth were bared and his eyes gleamed with hunger.

The black wolf moved around me, settling between the gray wolf and me. I though that he might be guarding his prey, but didn't wolf packs share, with the dominant killing it and eating first? A shiver ran up my spine and my thoughts came to an abrupt halt as my mind screamed "I am the prey."

The gray wolf lunged and the power struggle began. Fangs bared, skin ripped, in moments, but within moments the battle was over. The wolf, badly injured, limped off. The black one sat on its haunches and watched it leave, then turned back towards me. I closed my eyes and cringed, waiting for the end, praying that it would be quick. I had no way to defend myself, and I couldn't outrun it, not on a sprained ankle.

Its nose rubbed up against my leg. In shock I opened my eyes. I had expected it to attack, instead it sat there, looking at me, its head cocked to the side. I wasn't quite sure what to make of it. Its intelligent blue eyes gazed back at me. The wolf pressed a paw to my chest. Unresisting, I lay back, knowing there was nothing I could to do stop my fate. Its black fur tickled my arm as it lay down beside me, its head resting on my chest. Pinned there, my thoughts whirled wildly. It could have been hours later, or only minutes, when sleep claimed my tired body. Oddly I felt safe, lying there cuddled with a black wolf.

* * *

My eyes opened, then closed immediately, the brightness of the morning sun blinding me. I blinked, trying to adjust to the sunlight. I was stiff and sore, my ankle throbbed relentlessly. The events of the night before flooded my mind and I flopped trying to roll over on to my side, to search for the strange wolf, but something held me pinned. My eyes began to function again and I looked down. A strong arm sprinkled with black hair was wrapped around my waist. I struggled to get away as a man's face merged with my line of sight, his light blue eyes looking at me quizzically.

"What the hell?" I was able to squeak out as I attempted to scramble away again. I squirmed and wiggled, every movement sending pain shooting through my lower leg and ankle.

"Shhhhh," he soothed. "You'll hurt yourself further. Shhhh, settle down." A strange calm descended throughout my body, almost of safety and I stopped struggling. My eyes met his again and I knew. I just knew – Strange as it sounded to my mind – that he was my protector from the night before. Somehow, someway he was the wolf.

He pulled back slightly; giving me some room to breath. His chest, like his arm, was covered with sprinkles of black hair. "His chest?" my mind finally caught up, "his chest is bare. Oh my goodness, so is the rest of him." My eyes shot back up to his, my face flaming red. He just grinned and watched me.

That's when the lust kicked in. His self-assured yet sheepish grin did me in. Not only had he saved me somehow, but he had stayed the night with me, watching over me, knowing that in the morning he would "change" and be left out in the middle of nowhere with no clothes.

I licked my lips, then smiled. It was a half smile, but it was the best I could do at the time.

"Thank you. For whatever reason, however you did it, thank you." He returned my smile, this time with less self-consciousness and more tenderness.

"You're welcome." I hadn't noticed it before, but his voice suited him, deep, almost gritty, but perfect. The oddness of the moment struck me and I collapsed against him, hysterical laughter wracking my body. His arms enfolded me and he just held me close. I laughed so hard, there in a stranger's arms, who appeared to double as a wolf sometimes. A naked stranger, I fully clothed, and I wanted him. I didn't know his name, or anything about him, but I wanted him badly. Hysteria turned to amusement and he continued to hold me close, running his hands up and down my back.

Finally I settled down, an occasional giggle escaping me. "What's your name?" I managed to get out, my voice sounding almost breathless from laughing so hard.

"David. And you are?" I smiled again, so formal he was, but so gentle, his hands stroking me.

"I'm Laura. Laura Ashburn." I giggled again. My eyes met his and I stopped giggling. I think I even stopped breathing, his look was so intense. I could see his desire, his tenderness, his hunger, and his every thought in his eyes. Slowly, his head tipped to mine and our lips met. Gently, his tongue traced my full lips, wetting them as I had before. A slight growl rumbled up from his chest. An answering moan passed my lips. I could feel his dominance, but only his tenderness showed.

His hands left my back and began caressing my hips, my ass. No longer feeling my ankle throb I turned more fully against him, molding my body to his. His lips left mine, made their way down my neck, nibbling and sucking their way to the collar of my shirt. Impatient, needing to feel my skin against his, I pulled back slightly and awkwardly began to undo the buttons on my shirt. He sat up pulling me with him, making the task easier.

I moved back against him, delighting in the first touch of his skin against mine. Our lips met again and again as our passions climbed. I no longer wanted him inside of me, I needed it. I needed to feel him claim me, to make me his.

Gently he removed my shoes, careful not to hurt my ankle. My senses were too clouded with desire. I no longer felt any pain. My socks and jeans followed, and soon my panties and bra.

We lay there, flesh against flesh, kissing and caressing each other for hours, learning each others' bodies. Finally he moved over me and down my body. His lips worshipped me as they lightly skimmed my flesh. Lower and lower, he worked his way down to the core of my sexuality. I held my breath as he laid his head on my inner thigh and breathed deeply, not learning, but memorizing my scent. He glanced up at me, the heat in his eyes caused shivers to course through me. Gently, his tongue licked at my lips, parting them slightly, then delving deeper. I moaned and fisted my hands in his hair, holding his head against me.

He carried me close to the edge, only to back away, then again. I was wild with passion, wanting to be filled with his heat. Again he carried me to the very edge, this time, lifting me over. I arched my back and moaned, my body tightening.

I lay there, my body humming with pleasure, he moved over me. Growling low in his chest, he gently claimed me. I lifted against him, driving him deeper inside of me. Our lips locked together, the velvet of his tongue caressed my mouth. I could taste myself on his tongue, the sweet nectar of my sex. He pulled back, his intense gaze held mine. I couldn't look away, or close my eyes as my body approached orgasm. I didn't want to look away; I wanted the further connection to him.

He thrust inside of me again and again, one of his hands holding my hip, pulling me up to his downward thrust. I ran my hands over his back and my breasts, not caring where his body ended and mine began. I gasped and moaned with every movement of his body. Tighter and tighter the feeling inside of me grew. Then, it exploded.

I arched against him, as an exclamation of ecstasy escaped my throat. Shudders of orgasm wracked my body, as he held me against him, his body frozen in mid thrust. I could feel his liquid heat flowing inside me, his growl in my ear as his body joined mine in orgasm.

I collapsed back to the ground, his weight following me. Wrapping my arms around him, I pulled him close, hoping that this wasn't the end.

* * *

Almost a year later, on the night of a full moon, I wandered out into our yard. A familiar howl sliced the stillness of the night, a wolf calling for his mate. Holding our child close, I tipped back my head and answered his call, the sound not quite the same, but the point made. David would soon be home. After all, wolves love and mate for life.

ON ANGEL WINGS

The dream began as it always had. Miranda floating in nothingness, held tenderly in Darius' arms. His feathery wings wrapped around them, protecting her, as his arms held her to him. Normally the dream was peaceful, serene, soothing.

This time it was different. This time comfort, the gentle caresses, the protective strength surrounding her, turned to desire. The arms that held her - aroused her. His wings shielded them, and for the first time, their nudity was more than just skin; it was the brushing of their flesh, the whispery breaths, the feel of a breast against an arm, a hand cradling a cheek.

Before then, she had been aware of their natural state, but it hadn't evoked any sensations besides comfort. Now it was on a whole new level, the awareness of Darius' hard, muscular form against her back took evoked things it never had before. She was aware of his muscular chest as it rose and fell against her with each breath he took. His nipples hardened and blazed sensitive trails across her back as she shifted on his lap. The hot length of his hardness slid between the smooth cheeks of her buttocks.

Miranda's breath caught. Her desire rose, she wanted him, but how could that be possible.

He was her guardian angel, but she wanted him to be so much more as she felt his flesh against hers. "Darius," she sighed and let her mind take the step - my lover.

His lips touched her neck, and as if time had no meaning, he slowly kissed his way to her shoulder. She tipped my head to the side, eager to feel the heat of his moist lips on her body.

Her hands trembling, she kneaded his thighs, enjoying the feel of his fingertips playing over her breasts, her stomach, curling in the small patch of her pubic hair. Sucking her lip between her teeth, she desperately tried to muffle her moans, not wanting to break the spell his touch was weaving.

Oh God, how she wanted him. Needed to feel his hands gliding over her- and they did. His touch was so gentle and tender, but so powerful. Her touch with reality shifted, until she was lost with the maelstrom of sensation, a willing prisoner to his sensual touch. All other thoughts had flown, as if by some magic he spread around them. All that mattered in that blink of eternity was his touch, the connection between them.

When he slowly moved his lips down her back she shivered as gooseflesh puckered her skin. Twisting further in his lap, she turned to face him, and wrapped her legs about his waist. The smooth flesh tickled at her inner thighs, a delicious contrast. Warm, glistening with a light coat of sweat, he was perfection to her.

Cuddling close, she closed her eyes and lost herself within the sensual storm of his touch. Slipping her hands over his broad shoulders, she marveled at the way his muscles flexed under the velvety-soft skin. His inner thighs felt so hard against hers, the muscles tensed. She embraced him tighter, shivering as his breath whispered across her shoulder.

With the most tender of nips, Darius nibbled her ear lobe as he shifted against her, his cock brushing her nether lips.

The gentle touch of his fingertips dancing about her back, made her skin sensitive to his slightest movement. Impassioned, she leaned back and caressed her breasts, cupping them in her hands, offering them to him. Darius' hands settled over her buttocks, caressing each cheek. His lips again settled on her neck, and kissed their way down to her breasts. Clasping hardened nipples between moist lips one at a time, she heard his sigh of contentment as he suckled. She arched her back, needing more of his touch.

The tip of his hardness split her lower lips and rubbed against her clit as it slid inside of her. She welcomed it - no, she craved it.

Needing more, almost frantic to become one with him, she began to rock on his lap. He gripped her hips, guiding her towards pleasure, towards heaven in his arms. Yet, all she could think of was - faster, harder, more.

Despite her frantic movements, he teased her and held back, pacing her, drawing out the enjoyment of every second - drawing it out into eternity of erotic sensation. She caressed her body, enticing him and herself, feeling the softness of her breasts, the firm toned strength of her stomach and the smooth skin of her legs.

The sensations were beyond anything she'd ever experienced before. They were more intense and passionate, more tender and caring. She'd opened herself to someone, in ways never before possible

She caressed his back, careful not to hurt his wings. A feather drifted against the backs of her hands - a wisp of silk.

Together they soared higher and higher. Her pulse raced and her body tightened, in anticipation of his next touch.

Gently, he lifted her up and when she thought she'd die of need, he let her drop again, thrusting deep within her. Her pussy clenched and tugged at him, drawing out his pleasure as well as her own. Desperately she tried to hold him within her, to delay their parting. A feeling of completeness enveloped her.

No longer able to contain them, her moans broke free as she drove herself against him, searching for fulfillment.

Finally, it happened - she lost herself to the orgasm. Her nails scraped down his back, in the valley between his wings, as she ground against him. Blood raced through her veins, her pulse throbbed - a tempo matched evenly by his heart. She could see sparks of energy flowing between them, arching, connecting them. In that moment, she became fully one with her lover, and she knew a part of him would always remain within her.

Her thighs tightened around him, holding him a slave to her need until she collapsed against him, her body delicious sated.

Moments - hours - later, she felt him pulse deep inside of, filling her with his essence. She clasped him closer, savoring the feel of his arms around her trembling body. His arms felt so calming, wrapped around her. Tears of happiness fell from her eyes, wetting both of them. She felt so at peace, yet strangely full of energy and restless.

In her dream she feel asleep in Darius' arms, the image of child of their union floating in her mind.

* * *

As dawn lightened the morning sky, Miranda was slowly pulled from sleep.She hesitated to awaken, wanting to prolong the contact with her dream lover just a little bit longer. The after effects of the sensuous dream still lingered. Her neck tingled with stubble burn, her nipples were tight, hard little pebbles. Between her legs, she felt a stickiness that only a night of passion could produce.

Shifting, she rolled her face against her pillow. Something tickled her nose. When she opened her eyes, she found a single, long white feather, perfect in every last detail. Tears in her eyes, she rubbed a hand against her belly and felt a soft tingling, an arch of energy flowing from within.

She had wondered for a while now, given the details of her dreams; the long conversations as Darius discussed what their future together would be like. Now that she knew it was all real, plenty of decisions would need to be made, but nothing was too urgent.

With a quick glance at her clock, her decision was made. She didn't need to be up for another hour. Closing her eyes again, she drifted back into a light doze, soon to be wrapped in comforting arms as the child forming within her began to develop.

ON THE PROWL

Disgusted at the way her day turned out, Breanna set a bag of take out the floor, tossed her purse on the coffee table and flopped onto the couch. Behind her, the bedroom door creaked open and a large black cat strolled out. "Hi baby," she purred as the sleek jaguar stalked its way towards her and jumped up onto the couch. "How was your day?"

"Rrrraaaaarrrr."

Breanna sighed as the jaguar nudged against her, finally curling up with his head in her lap. Lazily, her hands stroked down the silky fir, feeling her agitation drift away. There was something comforting about running her fingers through the smooth black fir.

"I missed you too baby. Work was miserable today. Everyone kept misplacing files and needed me to run off last minute reports before meetings." Her slender fingers curled around his ear, scratching his tickle spot. "I simply couldn't keep up. I wanted so badly to come home early and curl up with you, but I couldn't. That made me even more depressed."

The jaguar nuzzled her again, his trim head butting against the underside of her breast. A long warm tongue snaked out, licking at her hand, then retreated.

"Awww. Feeling neglected?" Intelligent eyes met hers, and whiskers twitched slightly before the black animal shifted again, pressing his head against her side a bit firmer.

"Rrrraaaaarrrwwwhhhh."

Laughing softly, Breanna shifted from under the creatures weight and stood. "Let's get you something to eat baby, and then I'm going to take a shower. "

Moving to the doorway, Breanna grabbed the bag of take out from the entryway and walked into the kitchen. Sitting a plate on the counter, she pulled the containers of food from the bag: a nice warm medium rare steak - still juicy, a bowl of corn and another of mashed potatoes, followed by two rolls, which completed the meal. Placing the plate on the floor, she moved to the refrigerator and pulled out a bottle of water and poured it into a matching bowl. Sitting it beside the plate, she waited until the jaguar had started eating and then walked down the hall to her bedroom.

Quickly undressing, she headed into the bathroom and soon had the room filled with steam from a hot shower. Standing under the spray, she arched her back into the water, letting the heated water pound over her tired and aching muscles. The faint scent of lavender wafted to her nose as she squeezed her liquid soap into a washcloth. Taking her time, she enjoyed a leisurely lather and soft scrubbing , before finally shutting off the water . Moments later, she had toweled herself dry and padded barefoot and nude into her bedroom.

Already lying stretched out on the comforter, the black cat surveyed her every movement, a confident lord of his domain.

"Finished with dinner already?" she asked as she opened her closet door and removed her favorite robe of virgin silk. She didn't expect an answer, but asked anyway. She knew the blue background of her robe perfectly accented her eyes and the jaguar stitched into the back was an exact replica of her feline friend.

When she slipped her arms through the sleeves, she couldn't contain her shiver as the cool material brushed against her sensitive skin. The ritual was the same every night, but she never tired of the sensual feel of the blue silk.

Turning to her silent companion, she smiled. "Ready for bed?" A few quick steps, and she was across the room. She climbed up onto the bed and curled under the covers. The jaguar shifted beside her, so that his head lay upon her arm. Stroking her fingers over the smooth fur, Breanna's eyes closed and she relaxed. Taking deep, even breaths, she waited for her lover to emerge.

All day long, he was trapped inside the feline form, but as the sun set, he would become human again. It never failed to amaze her how one moment her hands would feel soft fur, the next smooth skin.

Trailing her fingers down his back, she simply enjoyed the feel of his soft fur under her fingertips. Lifting her hand, she brought it back up to his shoulder blade, only to touch smooth, hairless skin.

Upon opening her eyes, she met and held Zander's amber ones. Although his form was once again human, his eyes still held the oval pupil of his jaguar form.

"I missed you," she whispered, this time hearing his deep voice repeating her sentiments. She raised her slender hand to his face, tracing the lines of his cheeks, the firmness of his nose, finally teasing the edge of his ears. She could spend hours gazing into his eyes, tracing the smooth lines of his body, savoring the elegant beauty of her lover. She wasn't quite certain how he came to be a jaguar by day and human by nightfall. The subject was one he refused to talk about much. She'd decided long ago she wasn't about to waste what little time she had with her lover on something that obviously angered him. He would tell her when he was ready. Until then, she would simply enjoy his company.

"Make love to me," she requested, her thighs parting in anticipation. Her hands moved to his shoulders, ready to guide him into position.

But this time, he pulled back. "Roll over," he growled, a faint air of authority in his voice. Her body trembling with need and excitement, she complied. His warm, strong hands moved to her legs, guiding her to draw them up against her, stomach and to rise up to her knees.

The solid heat of his flesh settled against her back, as he moved behind her. The faint dusting of hair on his legs tickled hers; his warm thighs settled between her parted legs.

Sighing softly, Breanna reached between her legs and grasped his cock, guiding him into position. His cock-head nudged against her pussy lips, then his hips arched, driving him deep within her. Another thrust, and he sank in to the hilt.

Eagerly, Breanna arched back against him, her slick core gripping him tight. She never wanted the moment to end, but at the same time she craved the intense pleasures to come. It was a quandary she found herself in nightly, but every moment always felt fresh and new.

She trembled as Zander shifted again, and fully mounted her. Her knees slid further to the side and her breasts pressed into the silken sheets.

Her tender nipples stood tight and proud, ready to be caressed, and she knew before the night was through that they would be. But this mating, their first of the night, was to be as it had always been, rough and quick. Passionate and driven, Zander needed to reaffirm his mortality and sexuality and she was more than willing to let him.

Moving her fingers to her clit, she manipulated the tiny nub of flesh as her lover pounded into her. Over and over, he thrust against her. Her knees slipped further, apart until her body sagged against the mattress, her lover's weigh sensually holding her down.

"More," she gasped, and Zander was quick to respond - thrust, withdrawal; clench, release. Their bodies meshed, two halves of the same whole; complete only when mated together.

Pinching her clit between her forefinger and thumb, a chain reaction flowed within her sweat-soaked body. Her nipples throbbed, her pussy quivered and tightened, until finally a molten wave of passion erupted, flooding throughout her body. Every nerve flared to life, and with a soft scream, Breanna reached for the stars from within the haven of Zander's arms.

His hands moved to her hips, holding her in a tight grip. Come morning she would have faint bruises, sensual marks of his possession, but she didn't care.

His teeth nipped at her neck as he continued to assault her willing flesh, until with a muted roar, he climaxed, his teeth sinking tenderly into the slim tendon of her shoulder.Careful only to nip and not injure her, Zander's bite only served to drive her once more into a cloud of orgasmic euphoria.

Clenching his cock tight, she milked the passion from him, until he collapsed against her.

Her body mourned the loss of his weight as he rolled to her side. Snuggling against him, Breanna dozed slightly, her body lethargic and her restless mind calmed. She knew that he would soon awaken her again, claiming her body with leisurely licks and slow, tender lovemaking. But until then, she enjoyed being held close, strong arms wrapped around her waist, tender hands caressing her back. A soft purring rumbled against her ear as she drifted into sleep.

PEEPING GHOST

A creaking sound shattered the night stillness. Jade rolled over and shook Marcus' shoulder.

"Honey, I think there is someone in the house."

"Hum?" Marcus asked, sleep still clouding his mind. Jade shook him harder, trying to jolt him awake.

"Honey, I'm too tired. Maybe in the morning." He mumbled.

"Marcus, stop thinking with your family jewels for a minute and wake up. There is someone in the house!" She whispered, her voice rising as hysteria began to set in. Marcus finally got the hint and woke up. Another creak echoed throughout the still house. This time it was coming towards the stairs.

Carefully he got out of bed and walked across the floor to the door. Beside the door was a chair, and on the chair were his pants. He and Jade had been a bit wild the night before, throwing off clothes as they came in the house.

Marcus pulled his pants on and opened the door slowly. 'I don't know what we were thinking to stay in this old house,' he thought, 'Just because Jade's mother wanted us to stay in the house where Jade lived as a girl is a silly reason to stay in a run down old house.'

Quietly he walked down the hall, and crept down the stairs. 'I don't know what I am supposed to do if someone is in the house. It's not like I'm armed or anything.' Wild thoughts flew about in his head, but the need to protect Jade demanded he find out if someone was in the house.

A half-hour later, fully awake, and rather disgruntled, Marcus went back upstairs to the bedroom.

"There is no one here love, just the old house settling I guess," he called out as he opened the door. His eyes were immediately drawn to Jade's creamy white shoulders and the sweet lives of her throat and face. She sat propped up against the headboard, reclining on all of the pillows.

The soft gray color of the sheets accented her dark blonde hair. Feeling himself getting aroused, Marcus smiled at his wife. The sheet dropped, now just covering her lower body. Her beautiful breasts beckoned invitingly, their peaks hard and proud.

Marcus' hands went to the button of his pants. With a flick of his fingers, it was freed. He was sliding his zipper down when Jade spoke.

"Did I ever tell you there is a ghost living here?" Marcus's hands stilled. His zipper was undone and his pants hung partway down his hips. Jade smiled at his look of confusion and continued.

"It is said a young doctor bought this house for his bride. On their wedding night an emergency called him away moments before he could take her virginity. While he was away, a jilted suitor of hers broke in and killed her. It's said that she watches while people make love in this house. For some reason, I just find that wildly erotic, knowing that maybe someone is watching us make love."

Jade lifted the sheet and Marcus removed his pants. This time they lay on the floor beside the bed. He had grow slightly chilled wandering around the hose in nothing but his pants, and the contact of his chilled flesh to Jade's warmth caused her to squirm. Marcus bit back a groan and covered Jade's lips with his. As always, their passions were well matched. Even after almost twenty years of marriage and two children Marcus still felt like a randy youth with Jade.

Marcus' lips left Jade's and he began to slowly kiss his way down her chest, stopping to suck and nibble on her nipples. Moans of appreciation greeted his ears. With a devilish smile that took him years to perfect, Marcus moved down further in the bed. Jade's hands began to fist in the sheets in anticipation of what he would do. The first contact of his tongue to her pussy lips was light, a butterfly landing on them. But soon the contact was harder, more forceful and much more satisfying.

Jade's hands pulled at the sheet and her back arched, trying to drive her pussy against her husband's face. Marcus thrust his tongue deep inside Jade's pussy, enjoying her sweet taste. Her legs began to tremble and her moans grew louder. Her muscles clenched and Marcus knew she was close. Seconds later she arched off of the bed, a keening moan trapped in her throat as her orgasm hit.

Marcus lay there, with his head between her legs until she calmed, then he slowly slid up her body so that he could again kiss her. Jade tasted her sweetness on his lips. Gently he rolled onto his back and pulled Jade up so that she straddled him. They both loved the way she clasped him in her hands and slowly slid his cock inside her. Already she could feel her energy returning, and the need to seek out another orgasm.

Marcus gently grasped Jade's hips in his hands and slowly worked her up and down on his cock. Her hands stroked over her stomach and breasts, caressing sensitive spots, stopping to pinch her nipples lightly, drawing forth a moan. One hand stayed on her breasts as the other slid down her stomach and began to caress her clit.

Marcus kept up a steady pace, pull down and thrust up, then relax. Over and over her thrust up against Jade, felling her fingers brush against his cock as she fingered her sensitive clit. Jade's back arched. A faint sheen of sweat coated their bodies as they worked together to satisfy each other.

Jade's fingers went wild on her clit and Marcus picked up the pace, thrusting harder and faster. Moments later, his effort ere rewarded. Jade began to moan and shiver. Her back arced again and her pussy muscles clenched and relaxed, over and over. Marcus worked to keep a steady rhythm going, drawing out Jade's orgasm.

He bit back a moan as he watched her, her eyes open wide and slightly glazed, her mouth forming and O of delight. She collapsed on his chest as he thrust up against her one last time. Jade smiled as she caressed his chest and felt his hardness deep within her. She loved him so much, and she loved knowing he still found her attractive.

* * *

Standing in the corner of the room, unnoticed by the smiling couple on the bed, Celeste grinned. Though sad she hadn't gotten to experience this pleasure in life, she very much enjoyed watching. Her ghostly hands stroked her breasts and clit as she watched Jade kneel on the bed and Marcus come up behind her. Gently she ran two fingers in circles over her hard little bud as Jade leaned forward and Marcus thrust against her.

Celeste loved to watch this position. She slid to the floor and used the shadows of the room to hide her presence. Marcus was thrusting fast and steady, his hands gripping Jade's firm breasts. All to soon the couple reached their peaks of orgasm together. Watching them collapse together, Celeste sped up her motions. Tiny tingles raced about her body. Her back arched and her hips thrust against her fingers. Celeste's pussy lips tingled as wave after wave of orgasm crested.

* * *

Jade and Marcus had shifted so that Marcus lay on his back with Jade cuddled to his side. As they drifted off to sleep Marcus though he felt a kiss on his cheek, but Jade was against his side, it couldn't have been from her. He opened sleep heavy eyes and saw for just a moment a tall, slender brunette, but after he blinked, she was gone.

TO DANCE WITH THE NIGHT

He stood outside the window, just watching her. She was so seductive as she swayed to the throbbing music. Her body twisted and her hands caressed every inch possible as she danced and pleasured herself. Pierre felt the throb of the music coarse through his body. His heart pumped faster and he grew more aware of her. Her scent, her heartbeat, her desire. At that moment, he wanted nothing more than to open the window and join her in her erotic play. Her shoulder length brown hair swirled about her, alternately hiding and accenting face. Her breasts were fully visible to his eyes, the nipples hard.

His hands reached out and slid the window up almost without him being aware of it. The music's base shattered the stillness of the night, though it was not loud enough to wake the neighbors. Pierre stepped through the window and the resetting of shadows alerted her to his presence. Her brown eyes swung to him, but instead of screaming, she continued dancing, her gaze locked on his. He made no move to control her mind, only to let her know he meant her no harm.

The song "Free Your Mind" by En Vogue ended, and a new one started, this one softer and more seductive. The next song on the tape was "Freak Me" by Silk. Her hands ran over her breasts and down to her stomach, then back up. Pierre felt a stirring his cock as well as in his mouth. A faint taste of blood filled his mouth as his fangs slid down into position.

Slowly he walked towards her, and hearing her pulse quicken, knowing it was from lust, anticipation and a small measure of fear, he smiled to reassure her. He stopped halfway across the room, leaving the rest of the distance between them for her to cross. Pierre's hazel-brown eyes drifted over her petite frame, looking at all of her, not just her breasts and hands, but also the delicate lines of her throat, the way her hips gently bolled out form her slender waist and the poutiness of her full lips. Lips that just begged to be kissed.

Pierre gently peeked into her mind, just enough to find her name. "Maria" he whispered, his voice soft and seductive.

Maria's eyes widened as she found herself stepping closer to him, stopping not more than six inches away. Her body continued to sway and thrust to the song's beat. Pierre raised a hand, and gently slid his knuckles down Maria's cheek. Her throat, feeling her pulse throb. On down her shoulder and stomach, finally stopping to cup her hip in his hand and pull her towards him. Sliding a leg between her, he rubbed Pierre rubbed his body against Maria, his clothing brushing against her sensitive skin. Pierre's hands caressed her body as Silk sang on, turning her heated arousal to a fevered pitch.

Their lips met, softly at first, each learning the others touch, then met again, harder this time. Their tongues began to gently learn each others lips and rubbed together. As her body swayed against his, Maria began to moan in Pierre's mouth.

The song wound down and the sweet seductive voices of Boyz II Men sang "I'll Make Love To You", a sensuously slow song. Moving slower now, Pierre gently stepped Maria backwards until she lay across the bed, her hands caressing her breasts and stomach as Pierre kneeled between her beautiful spread legs.

Feather soft his lips kissed her right knee and worked up to her hip.His hands ran up the backs of her legs to her butt and pulled her closer to him so that her butt rested right on the edge of the bed. Maria's hips began undulating on the bed, her hands moving in wider circles, steadily drawing closer to her pussy.

Pierre smiled at her, his eyes twinkling with a devilish glint, then he leaned down again. The tip of his tongue lightly flicked against her pussy lips and Maria almost lurched off of the bed. Maria's body began to tingle, her arousal was so intense. Pierre spread her lips gently and thrust his tongue in as deep as it would go, tasting her sweetness, hearing her moans. Her clit grew hard under his fingertips,. As he played with her body, finally giving her what she craved.

Over and over, he thrust his tongue inside, flicked over her clit or gently nibbled her lips, tasting her sweetness, feeling her body quivering. Maria began moaning with need, her body arching into his mouth, hoping to draw pleasure from even the lightest touches. Her hands gently played with her breasts, thriving on the sensations touching her sensitive nipple caused.

Slowly, expertly Pierre kept up his tender torture, driving her to the brink of orgasm, but never over. Finally, frantic with arousal, Maria fisted her hands in his hair, not allowing him to draw back. His eyes closed as he focused on her, pleasing her, loving her.

Maria's senses began to spin out of control. Tingles raced about her body. Her pussy flooded with her sweet juice as finally she orgasmed. Her entire body seemed to tighten as her moans turned into gasping moans. Then, her body relaxed, completely satisfied.

Pierre allowed himself a few moments to enjoy her sweet taste before kissing his way to her inner thigh. Gently, he pierced the skin and drank her warm blood. His thumb moved to her clit, and gently he massaged it, again arousing her.

As he drank her faintly metallic tasting blood, it mingled with her juices to form a truly heavenly taste to him. Gently he caressed her clit and as he removed his fangs, he once again brought her to orgasm.

* * *

Sunlight flooded the room, the sticky heat of the day finally pulled Maria from sleeps embrace. Memories of last night returned, and she almost had herself convinced it was but a dream until she moved. Still sensitive, her clit craved touches and her inner thigh felt mildly tender.

With the knowledge that it wasn't a dream came the certainty that her night lover would be back, that he craved her taste as much as she craved his touch.

* * *

As Pierre slept in his dark room, his mind stayed active. He could still faintly hear Maria's moans echoing in his ears, and taste her sweetness upon his lips.

He smiled in his sleep as he thought of her beautiful breasts. Maybe, just maybe, tonight, I will kiss and feed from them instead. He knew Maria might just like that as much as he would.

ABOUT THE AUTHOR

Born to ride on the back of dragons, to journey among the stars in a ship traveling faster than light, or to dance the night away in the arms of a mysterious vampire, Michelle Houston willingly shares the worlds in her mind in an effort to bring them to life.

Writing everything from short and sweet stories, to hot and spicy tales of kink, from contemporary tales of romance to erotic romances featuring Greek gods, vampires and were-creatures, she has crossed sexualities and has gone wherever her mental muse has guided her, a journey she has never regretted.

Beyond that, she has a love of the natural world around us (except for insects, spiders, snakes, scorpions, and jellyfish, and she reserves the right to add more at any time).

In other words, she is an ordinary woman with an imagination that is only held in bounds by how fast she can type.

You can find out more about Michelle Houston on her website at: www.michellehouston.com

www.ingramcontent.com/pod-product-compliance
Lightning Source LLC
Chambersburg PA
CBHW070857180626
46817CB00003B/803